Fixing Kate

Also by Amanda Murphy

The Art of Lost Luggage

Fixing Kate

AMANDA MURPHY

POOLBEG

Published 2003
by Poolbeg Press Ltd.
123 Grange Hill, Baldoyle,
Dublin 13, Ireland
Email: poolbeg@poolbeg.com

©Amanda Murphy 2003

The moral right of the author has been asserted.

Copyright for typesetting, layout, design
© Poolbeg Group Services Ltd.

1 3 5 7 9 10 8 6 4 2

A catalogue record for this book is available from the British Library.

ISBN 1-84223-112-X

Typeset by Patricia Hope in Goudy 11/14.5
Printed by
Litografia Rosés S.A., Spain

www.poolbeg.com

About the Author

Amanda Murphy still lives in the utterly glam City of Salford. She watches DVDs when she should be writing and has decided that she likes nothing better than staying in her pyjamas all day. Consequently, she writes very late at night and gets awfully moody in the mornings. Lately she's been living on bacon sandwiches and fizzy water, but that probably won't last much longer once her mother reads this.

Even though she's had yet another birthday – they just keep coming! – she won't even consider the possibility of owning a cat, especially since her last remaining houseplant threw itself off the mantelpiece in a desperate suicide attempt.

She still writes "A Whole 'Nother Story" for BBC Radio 4, which is about to enter its third series.

She has a bit of a limp, but her knee is holding up for now. She can be reached by email on:

Amanda@amandamurphy.co.uk

Acknowledgements

Debt of thanks to:

My adorable friends: Lucy Porter, Tracy Wilkinson, Simon Bestwick, Shaun Dooley, Saltz, Lydie Mark and Terry Brandy.

The people I treasure: Ros and Helenka at Edwards Fuglewicz and Gaye Shortland.

The people I admire: Billy Franks and Billy Bragg, two writers of the best lyrics in modern music.

The people I just couldn't live without: Carl Cooper, James Dowdall, Melissa Hind, Dave Murphy, Heather Murphy, my nieces and nephews, Sarah Hodgson, Lise McLean, Annette Ractliffe and my mother, Josephine Clairmont.

To Michael Murphy
The one member of the family who is so often forgotten –
But not this time, Mikey.

Prologue

It's funny how little things come back to you suddenly. One whiff of a certain smell and you're whisked off to your primary-school playground or you're lying on a beach in Florida again. Strangely enough, for me it's minestrone soup. I'm sitting here in this café waiting for my teacake to be toasted and the woman at the next table is slurping minestrone soup. Now, I don't know if it's the slurping or the minestrone, but I'm instantly back . . .

Listen to me rabbiting on and I haven't even introduced myself. I'm Katherine Townsend. By chapter three, we'll probably be best mates and you can call me Kate, but let's just stick to Katherine for now. Just because I'm going to be telling you intimate details of my life, there's no reason to get too familiar too soon, eh?

Let me start at the beginning and stop me if I go off on the wrong track. I tend to do it every now and again. Sometimes I end up somewhere worthwhile, but most of the time it's just boring, so do remind me.

Anyway, as I said, I'm Katherine Townsend and I'm thirty-one years old. This is a bit of a convoluted tale and you'll probably not believe any of it. I'm writing this because after all that's happened in the past twelve months, I'm at a bit of a crossroads in my life and the only way I can decide where I go from here is to go back and look again at everything that's happened.

There's that saying, the old Chinese curse: 'May you live in interesting times'. I could never understand why this should be a curse, but after what I've been through I know what they meant. If you live a nine-to-five existence just getting on with your life, with no 'interesting' developments, at least you know what's going to happen. You have the safety of the routine. My times lately have been way and above the mere interesting. For as long as I can remember, I've been affected by this curse. Sometimes, I don't even have to screw things up, they just do it on their own. When I was a teenager I used to think that every night fate would look at the following day and think about what it could do to make it different. Inexplicable things have happened since as far back as I can remember and I've long since given up asking the question why? I now ask myself, what the hell am I meant to learn from this latest disaster?

* * *

So here it is, my experience. I seem to remember it in small segments, rather like episodes in the ongoing sitcom that is Katherine Townsend. The starting facts are these: I'm an information technology consultant. I'm not sure if that should be 'I was' – I'll let you make your own mind up at the end. I specialise in computer solutions for my client companies.

It sounds boring (it usually is), but the best thing is that I work for an American corporation and most of my clients are in and around Europe, so it has the benefit of seeming glamorous, even though that may not always be the case.

I suppose now's as good a time as any to introduce you to the other people in my life. Jane, my best friend, is a psychic. Looks-wise, she is the living embodiment of the basic Irish stereotype. Long curly-red hair, which when she can be bothered to sort it out, reminds me of a beautiful corkscrew perm, but mostly it looks like a ginger explosion down her back. Most days she just sticks it up in a ponytail. Jane gets a profusion of freckles whenever the sun comes out. She is less than thrilled about this particular 'Nature's wonder' and spends every evening in the summer dabbing vinegar on her face (apparently it bleaches them, but I think it just makes her smell funny). She has lovely green eyes that make you start humming the tune to 'When Irish eyes are smiling'. All of this is only unusual when you consider the following fact: her entire family (at least three generations back) are from Eastern Europe. Her father is Polish and her mother came from what was, back then, Czechoslovakia. They think she must be a throwback, but they can't quite work out when or who she was thrown-back to.

Jane specialises in tarot card readings. One would think that having her around would be a definite plus, bearing in mind what I've just said about my life, but you will see that that's not necessarily true. Just think of her as Jane, the spiritualist with verve and panache. Her claim to fame in our group is that she's the only one to hold down a decent husband. Although you'd never guess it to look at her, deep down, she's blissfully happy and says that the proof of the existence of Fate is the fact that she's married to an accountant. His name is Craig and he will pop up later, so remember: Jane is married to Craig.

Then there's Louise. She's a fabulous lawyer, who works in Manchester doing something suitably impressive. Admittedly, as one of her best friends, I should really know, but as yet I've managed to avoid any real explanation. Louise is a particularly elegant and serious woman, up until the fifth glass of wine, at which point she has to be physically restrained from whipping off her clothes and dancing on the table. She's deliberately blonde in an attempt to disguise the fact that she's unfeasibly intelligent. She has these eyes that I swear can look into your very soul. Don't ask me why, but she's a bit of a snake buff and has a python called George. George is kept in a glass case, in pride of place, beside her bed. In our group, Louise is the antidote to Sandi.

Sandi is the biggest flirt on the planet. She's never been below a size 16 in her life, but always manages to have a string of men lusting after her. She's five foot six and is like a human tornado whirling in and out of rooms, leaving a trail of destruction behind her. During the holidays between the second and third year of university, Sandi went backpacking alone around the United States and returned having acquired a large sum of money and a husband in Las Vegas. The marriage lasted until she found her husband dressed in her favourite Donna Karan clothes and stretching her Jimmy Choo pumps. I secretly believe that the only reason she freaked was that he looked better in the outfit than she ever did. I'd love to tell you what hair or eye colour Sandi has, but what with hair dye and coloured contact lenses, I don't know what she'll look like until she appears in front of me, even then I can't quite believe it half the time.

The final member of our coven is Gen; her real name is Imogen, but anyone calling her that is likely to be beheaded in a matter of seconds. She's five foot nothing and is forced to shop in the children's section of shops. She complains about this on a semi-regular basis, so no doubt you'll hear more of this. Her father is Icelandic and in the right light (and after a few beers) she can be easily mistaken for Björk. She's the real organiser in our group and if it wasn't for her skills, we would all have lost contact years ago. She tends not to say that much, but whenever she does make an input, the effect is always profound.

So there you are, the coven of witches. We'd met on the first day of university. We'd all been assigned to Pentagon 12 in Martin Luther King house. Each pentagon had, surprisingly, five bedrooms, a kitchen, two bathrooms (very useful) and a living area. And even though it's been nearly twelve years, we managed to live together in various houses since then – right up until Jane got married two years ago when we felt it was time to separate and make our own ways in the world.

The bitchy members of Pentagon 11 gave us our name. Basically, none of us were good at cooking. At that point in my life I hadn't even discovered the magical Delia; Sandi was always one for takeaways; Jane was too scatty to remember that she'd already added the salt, so everything she cooked had a briny undertone; and Louise was always studying too hard to be bothered. So it fell to Gen to provide us all with sustenance. Unfortunately, the only thing she knew how to cook was a strange Icelandic fish soup, which she made in a huge saucepan. On the second night of term, Pentagon 11 decided to introduce themselves to us. They strolled into the kitchen, just as we were all crowded around the saucepan, listening to Gen explaining the Icelandic names for all the ingredients. Pentagon 11 saw the five of us staring intently at a cauldron-like vessel, while Gen spoke 'in tongues' – hence the witches' coven.

Oh, and while I remember, you have to be aware that my mother is a nutter, so don't be surprised at anything she says, OK?

So that's all you need to know from the beginning – anything else, I'll tell you as we go along. One thing I can say is if you're looking for answers, you won't find them here, that's for sure. If at any time you start thinking that this doesn't sound much like a story, just remember – to completely misquote Groucho Marx – 'That's no story, that's my life!'

Anyway, we start back in October 1999.

Chapter One

Not Dead Yet

Now, I'm not the sort of person who panics easily and I'm definitely not a hypochondriac in any way, but on that morning, I was convinced that I was dying.

It was a Thursday. I remember it because I'd been to Germany earlier in the week and the night before, I'd been really close to missing all my onward connections. So, I'd spent most of Wednesday evening running through airports, dragging my hefty handbag, briefcase and computer bag with me, every step of the way. I remember getting on both connecting flights just as the doors were closing. I was the kind of knackered that makes you swear to join a gym at the earliest opportunity.

Anyway, so there I was, Thursday morning, my alarm had gone off and I was preparing to exit my comfort zone. All of a sudden I felt the most outrageous pain in my chest, followed by awful twinges up and down my arms. My brain was confirming the existence of the pains and was hastily making a diagnosis. Chest pain + twinges up arms = heart attack. It then sent panic messages straight to the aforementioned heart, which then started pounding even harder, causing an increase in the agony. I gingerly reached out for the phone on my nightstand and dialled.

"Medical centre."

"Help, I'm having a heart attack."

"What sort of heart attack?"

"The kind with chest pains, which usually leads to the stopping of the heart. Is there another kind?"

"No Madam, I meant what kind of pain is it?"

"The heart attack kind."

"Well, I think we can safely say that you're not actually having one. Would you like to make an appointment?"

I was incredulous. A doctor's receptionist being patronising was relatively common, but making a completely arbitrary diagnosis was another matter. The pain hit me again.

"And you're basing this diagnosis, a highly unqualified one may I add, on the basis of . . . ?"

"The fact that you're not dead yet."

"Oh." She had a point; I had to admit.

"So, should I make you an appointment? I might be able to squeeze you in, this afternoon."

"Don't bother."

"Now, now, let's not be too hasty. You are still having chest pains, I take it."

Oddly, they'd subsided slightly, but I managed to groan: "Yes."

"Maybe, you should come in, just to be safe. We don't want to be sorry, now do we?"

"Heaven forbid," I grumbled. Now she was showing

empathy with my situation. Ring up with a heart attack and she couldn't give a damn. Refuse to make an appointment and she was nearly having kittens!

"How about four thirty this afternoon. Doctor has a gap I can squeeze you into."

"Fine." I gave her my details and hung up. Why do those sort of women always refer to their doctors as 'Doctor' in the same reverential manner most people reserve for God? She probably says things like 'Baby, needs his sleep, doesn't he' or she and her husband probably refer to themselves as 'Mother' and 'Father' in that really strange, 'Would you like a cup of tea, Mother?' 'No, Father, I'm fine' way. And they probably drive their children mad with it. But I digress.

So in the end, it turned out to be a strained muscle in the chest wall. Yeah, yeah, go on laugh as much as you like. At least the doctor didn't laugh at me. She managed to say, with a completely straight face, that that sort of muscle strain could be extremely painful and that people often fear the worst when they experience it. She assured me that it was perfectly normal and that it was probably caused by my 'running around with all that heavy luggage the day before' and that the arm pain was due to the muscles having had a 'jolly good workout'. She then suggested I think about packing a bit more sparingly in the future, prescribed two paracetamol, a 'couple of days resting up' and then went on, to my great shock, to suggest that I might like to think about 'frequenting some kind of health establishment' – apparently they could do wonders with muscle toning.

She didn't actually say, 'listen Porky, take yourself off to the gym and work off those tractor tyres, you flabby article,' but the implication was there.

I went over to Jane's afterwards and she had a bit of a giggle.

"Death was definitely not on your cards last time I looked. Do you want me to do them again, just to check?" she said jokily.

I decided against it on the basis that if I was going to peg out over breakfast, I'd rather not know about it. But I went home and made out a will, just to be on the safe side.

It's a very strange business making out a will at thirty. This was last October, so it was before my bank balance had discarded its sad, but showy red, in favour of a more healthy classic black. Even a bank account has to have a little black number to go out in every now and again. It is disheartening to realise, whilst listing your possessions, that you don't actually have much to leave. My entire life boiled down to four bequests: a ridiculously large and extremely expensive collection of Chanel make-up, a shoe collection of Imelda proportions, a more than adequate jazz CD collection and a small semi-detached house close to Manchester city centre and handy for the motorways. In any case, I bequeathed them with all the due care and attention required for such a solemn proposition.

I counted myself very lucky after my 'heart scare' as I'd taken to calling it, in an attempt to salvage a smidgen of dignity. Then, secure in the knowledge that if nothing else, my shoe collection would be well cared for, I headed off to procure some of that bed rest that the doctor ordered.

* * *

The noise woke me up the next day, not when it was making itself known, but just as it ceased to exist. So it was more like a lack of noise that woke me. I never did find out what it was . . . or wasn't, if you know what I mean. I gingerly held out my arm to test for residual chest pain and discovered that it had improved dramatically overnight. The sun was flooding in at my window and I felt energised. It's amazing how a bright sunny morning can lift even the gloomiest person's day. I wandered downstairs with the intention of pottering around a bit. I'd never pottered before, but I'd heard this woman talking on the tram about how she enjoys pottering around her garden and it sounded like a nice relaxing thing to do before I actually got down to finding something to occupy me for the day. I couldn't tell you exactly what activities would be included in this pottering, but I thought that wandering aimlessly in the garden planning what flowers needed planting, sounded like a good start.

I made coffee and disappeared outside. This was when I must have missed the phone call. I was happily engaged trying to distinguish the actual plants from the weeds.

It had been a slow month overall. As the European HQ allocated my consulting jobs to me, I always complained about the lack of control that I had over my own time. But, I'd had no real work to do for a while, apart from the quickie in Germany, and was beginning to get bored. They had been making noises about how expensive I was for them, because I was a full-time employee and therefore received my salary regardless of how much work they found me. There was one woman in the accounts department who was a particularly nasty character. Her name was Pirkka, some sort of strange Scandinavian name I think. Anyway, she was so frosty that at some point, Santa Claus must have considered relocating his grotto up her arse. And talk about a face like a bulldog chewing a wasp. She was more like the mutant-lovechild of Anne Widdecombe and Michael Foot with her social conscience bearing more resemblance to Hitler with leanings towards Stalin when no one was looking. She was in charge of the holiday allocation and wielded the resultant power like a light-sabre with all the delicacy of Darth Vader having an epileptic fit. Well, she started a really evil discussion amongst the office staff about how unfair it was that I was paid a salary without actually having to do any work. So it wasn't much of a surprise when I found out that the boss wanted to have a 'chat' with me. I'd been waiting for him to ring and although I'd been busy the previous day having a heart attack and all, I'd made sure that there'd been no messages left on my answer phone. I'd therefore assumed that he no longer wanted to speak to me. When I'd eventually finished pottering and was once more firmly ensconced in my office, imagine how surprised I was to find an email from my boss, Marco Balacci. A very nasty email it was too, accusing me of going off on shopping trips whilst I was supposed to be working. Now, it's not that I don't go off on the odd shopping trip occasionally; it was more the fact that on that day, I had been stuck at home, bored out of my skull and had had to resort to gardening in the hope of passing some time.

I immediately rang him on his private line.

"Marco Balacci."

"Hi Marco, it's Kate, I hear you wanted a word."

"Oh, so you are in then? What's wrong? Shopping at the Trafford Centre not up to its usual standards?" He spat down the phone.

Don't get me wrong, I was extremely irritated at his tone, and were it not for the fact that I had mortgage payments to make, I would have told him where he could stick his job.

But somehow I managed to remain calm enough to say quietly, "Actually Marco, I've been here all day."

"So why weren't you answering the phone earlier? Still in bed, eh?"

"I have been up and available for work since nine o'clock this morning, waiting for instructions, as usual. Can I help it if I'm not fully utilised? You know I'm always available to do your bidding, O Great One." I continued, as I really didn't want to give him the opportunity to get his teeth into that comment, "You probably can't tell, but I'm curtseying so low, my skirt is touching the ground. By the way, when will I be getting my next assignment, O Lord and Master?"

"We need to talk about that. We seem to be having a sourcing problem in your area."

Don't ask me what that was supposed to mean, but it sounded suitably ominous, so I simply muttered, "Um, OK, what should I do then?"

"Leave it with me and we'll meet up when you come over for your team briefing next week."

That was so typical of the man. Ring up, drop a bombshell and just piss off leaving me to wonder what he had up his sleeve. Still, something good had come out of the call. He'd reminded me about the team briefing. These are meetings, which happen every couple of months, where all the company's consultants leave their individual countries and converge on Berlin. The irony of it all is that they are delightful wastes of time, held in the capital city of a country which holds time-wasting on a par with puking up on someone's sofa – sure it happens, but no one particularly wants to see it. The job-related crap was on the whole, totally worthless, but it gave us the opportunity to get together and have a damn good piss-up, often on the company's money.

I knew that Marco had never liked me on a personal level, but I had always been aware that he'd reluctantly admitted that I was spectacular at my job and was therefore unlikely to get rid of me. I'd also heard that he was a really great guy, but even after three years of working, I was still unsure of the accuracy of this statement. With me, he was always gruff and blunt, with a hint of annoyance never far from his expression. His manner was brisk and strictly professional and I had only seen him smile once in my presence and that was when we'd had a complaint from one of my clients. So it wasn't surprising, given this history, that I had a few concerns as to the nature of our meeting. Just in case of any deviousness on his part, I decided the wisest course of action was to clarify my position legally. I photocopied my contract of employment and hotfooted it to the citizen's advice bureau.

The frighteningly young employment law advisor told me confidently: "You've got him by the short and curlies."

"And that's a legal term is it?"

"Yeah, why not? Anyway he can't fire you, at least not legally, not without a few verbal and written warnings."

"So what happens if he does then? Does that mean I've got him . . ."

"By the bollocks, yes."

Buoyed by the unflinching confidence of this apparent thirteen-year-old, I left the office with a smile and returned home.

I'm not going to hold you in suspense. I'll tell you now that the meeting in Berlin was not as worrying as I'd convinced myself it would be.

Marco was there, all six-foot of him, wearing his trademark Versace suit and Armani tie. I was once more incredibly aware of his strong presence and were it not for the fact that I loathed him, I could have been really attracted to him. He was then, and still is by the way, an exceptionally good-looking man. He was always nicely bronzed, not in a Bob-Monkhouse-orange way, but in a healthy I-regularly-holiday-somewhere-warm-and-sunny kind of way. His ebony hair and piercing blue eyes hinted at his Italian heritage. He describes himself as an Italian American and is immensely proud of the fact that that his family had built the corporation up from its origins as a small construction company. There were always totally unsubstantiated, but gloriously gossipy rumours flying around the office about mafia connections and money laundering. The Balacci Corporation was now a large global concern, with Marco spearheading the IT consultancy branch and protecting it as his own little baby.

When we sat down for the meeting, there was no mention of my termination (far nicer than 'being fired', don't you think?) and Marco even managed a little light-hearted banter. Or at least as close to it as someone as socially inept as Marco could get.

"Kate, how would you like to be in control of your own destiny?"

"I'd love to, but how?"

"I thought you might like to try to use your considerable um . . ." He was struggling to find the right words and I'd decided not to help him out in any way, "considerable talents to find your own assignments."

"And what exactly did you have in mind, when you speak of my 'talents'?"

To my great shock, he began to blush. "Well, obviously, I'm not suggesting that you take yourself off onto the streets or anything like that."

"Excuse me?" I spluttered; this discussion was definitely not what I'd been expecting. And I'd just taken a rather large gulp of coffee.

"What I'm suggesting is that you find yourself some clients in Manchester. You are, so I've been told, a good saleswoman, so here's your chance to prove it to me. Someone of your skill should have no trouble finding assignments." He allowed himself a grin, which began to take on Machiavellian proportions, the longer I stared at it.

So there it was, I'd been given a licence. To what exactly, I wasn't quite sure? But I was certain that if Marco was involved, it had to be one of the fail variety.

I was determined not to fail. In fact it then became my number one concern. Operation wipe-that-stupid-smile-off-Marco's-face began. OK, maybe it didn't actually begin at that precise moment. I went out with my colleagues, got spectacularly drunk and passed out in the hotel lobby first. But I'd made up my mind to get on the case immediately upon my return to England. As soon as I stepped off the plane, I had a message from Jane on my mobile, reminding me that we were having one of our regular 'get togethers'.

After a night out with the girls, I woke up with a stinking hangover and was capable of destroying anything that made a sound louder than a pin drop. I dragged myself to my office and attempted to start finding some work to do. Now I'd show that Marco a thing or two about my talents.

Chapter Two

Specific Worry Mode

I feel embarrassed admitting this openly, but sometimes, late at night, I used to worry. Often I had nothing specific to worry about – I just provided myself with a general worry topic and let myself go. Other times I would worry about things that I have no cause concerning myself with. I had one of those nights back in November, I remember it as clear as day. When I was in town, going down the high street, surrounded by thousands of people, I caught the eye of a man who was walking towards me. He was a complete stranger, but for a split second our eyes locked and just as instantly it was over. Believe it or not, this was what set me off. I woke up at 3.00 a.m. with the horrid feeling that I'd missed him. You're probably asking yourself who had I missed, aren't you? Dress me in pink chiffon and call me Barbara Cartland if you like, but I still believed in HIM. The Man. The perfect Yang to my Ying. My spiritual other half. Catch me on a brave day and I'd deny this completely, but at 3.00 a.m. in 'specific worry mode', I was happy to admit it. I asked myself, what if that man was The One? Should I be penalised for not having the wits about me to even smile at him? What if I'd found him and let him get away? When I was in the mood for a serious fester, I used to love unanswerable questions like that. Believe me, even the mysteries of the ancient Egyptians are a doddle compared to the sort of questions I posed myself. In the past, I managed to figure out how they built the pyramids (pyramids are actually alien spacecraft which crash-landed on earth) and the real use of Stonehenge (a really really easy maze), merely as a warm-up to my more significant fretting activities.

It wasn't just me either – I remember Sandi complaining about it as well.

"You know what, Kate. I think I'm giving up for good. There are no decent men on the planet. Nowadays they're all too busy living down to the *Loaded*-laddish thing that not one of them is presentable enough to introduce to your favourite maiden aunt, let alone your friends and family. And the ones who have enough eloquence to string together a sentence of more than five words are too busy sitting at home, chatting up Americans on the Internet."

"Yeah, there just aren't enough men to go around."

"No, that's just it, Kate; it's not the quantity that bothers me, it's the deplorable lack of quality."

Jane took a different view, but she was never allowed to actually voice it when we were together in a group. Whenever we were discussing the subject, i.e. every time we met up, Jane was excluded because she'd 'found one of the decent ones, so she wouldn't understand'. But, when we were alone, she was always banging on about fate and destiny, saying that she'd never have met Craig if it wasn't for the fact that she had dyscalculia, which is a form of number dyslexia.

She'd had problems with numbers all her life. She'd even met a few previous boyfriends through ringing telephone numbers wrong. But a couple of years ago, her dyscalculia changed her life forever. Jane had just started her own business. She was mainly doing the rounds of the spiritualist fairs which are running all over the country – you'd be amazed at how many of them there are. Anyway, she'd been so busy that she didn't have time to find a proper accountant and decided that it couldn't be that difficult to do it herself. Why pay a fortune for some 'suited bod' to fill out a simple well-explained form? She was absolutely buzzing when she'd finished so she'd come round to my place with a bottle of champagne to celebrate. The only problem was that instead of declaring an income of £15,000, she'd written £51,000 and caused quite a stir in the relevant Inland Revenue department. This caused them to schedule her for an audit. Upon hearing the news, she was distraught and began scouring for an accountant to help her out. She wasn't having much luck until one night when she'd stopped by at her Auntie Freda's house to find her aunt deep in conversation with the satellite repairman. After a long and apparently confusing chat, it turned out that the repairman's brother was an accountant. He'd rung his brother and arranged for him to meet Jane to sort out her financial difficulties. Jane says it was all that late-night poring over receipts and invoices that did it – I just think she was lucky. She often says to us that in life you get what you need and not what you want. She believes in the idea that we all have a pre-ordained path. Even if we make the wrong choices along the way, fate will always find a way to get you back on that path. So if you stop fighting it and simply go with the flow, life is much easier. Apparently there's an eastern religion which uses this as their main tenet.

I'd love to believe her, because it means that even if we make mistakes we all get there in the end. I can't make up my mind, I just grow more and more confused every day, especially since . . . Oops! I nearly let it slip out just then. Look, I realise you're probably still dying to know why I'm sitting in this café, but I'm determined at least to try to get this in the right order. So you'll just have to be patient, won't you?

November crept up on me like an opportunistic thief, stealing away the year while I wasn't looking. Before I knew it, it was mid-month. Things were going along pretty well all told. I'd managed to find four rather comfortable assignments with local Manchester companies. I'd done this by scaring the pants off them about the millennium bug. Most people didn't know this, and I suppose now it can't harm if I let the secret out, now that the millennium eve is but a distant memory. The millennium bug did not exist! It was a rather nasty wheeze dreamt up by computer programmers who thought it would be 'cool' to ensure that their year 2000 got off to a great start. The whole process was like this: programmers in the 1970s were young hotshots who recognised that if they wrote programmes with in-built flaws which would become apparent in say, thirty years, when they were approaching retirement, they would be the only ones able to fix them and therefore would be able to earn enough to retire comfortably. Unlike many of their programmes, this idea worked beautifully and by late 1999, it was up to the remaining programmers and opportunists like me to help terrified companies sort themselves out.

This was when I achieved 'in the black' status with my bank. All of a sudden, my bank manager was asking me if there was anything he could do for me. Up until that point, I hadn't realised that he could in fact write nice letters. I'd grown so used to being scared when he wrote to me that it took a while to get used to it. Not that the new development wasn't scary: it was just scary in a different have-another-credit-card-while-you're-here way.

So it was a normal day a couple of weeks after bonfire night. I woke up as usual and went into the shower. As I was working up a good old lather, I felt a strange lump on my right boob. Like most women, I tried to check myself for lumps on a semi-regular basis, but had completely forgotten for a few months. Not totally believing what I'd felt, I started off quite light-heartedly. But as I attempted to investigate further, I became more and more anxious.

"Medical centre."

"Good morning. Can I have an emergency appointment please?"

"Emergency, eh? Doctor is really busy today. Are you sure you mean emergency?"

"I'm positive."

"Is that Miss Townsend?" she enquired suspiciously.

"Yes, it is."

"So is this a heart-attack-style emergency?"

"No, this is a lump-in-my-tit emergency, if you must know." That should shut her up; I congratulated myself.

"Well, why didn't you just say so in the first place?" she announced irritably.

I didn't get a bloody chance, I mentally fumed. "So can I have an appointment then?"

"Of course. Come in at twelve and I'll make sure that Doctor sees you."

Somehow, I managed to stay calm. My mind kept trying to list all the possibilities and fly through all the different scenarios, but I managed to rein it in long enough to function until midday, when I went in to see my doctor.

Dr Nichols was and still is the perfect 'have-it-all' woman. Just thinking about her, even now, makes me feel inadequate. She is my age, she's gorgeous, a Cindy Crawford look-a-like, all blonde hair and (completely natural) boobs. She's taller than me (about five foot eight) and younger looking than me – which I find completely unnatural because she's got three young kids and by rights she should look totally knackered. Not only that, but around the time of the breast-prodding appointment, it had just come out that her husband had left her a few months previously for a red car and a predictably young bimbette, but she was so sorted that no one even suspected that she'd had problems at home. How's that for a superwoman? Apparently she divorced him, got herself a decent housekeeper and has never looked back.

I was grateful for the fact that she didn't think that I'd overreacted. The lump was still there when she examined me. Which, by the way, is a really peculiar thing, sitting there topless having another woman feeling your breasts. The whole time she was prodding around, I was desperately trying not to burst out laughing. Fortunately, Dr Nichols wasn't one for talking while she prodded about. Not for the first time I wished that the surgery's procedures allowed her to do the smear tests, because the 'smear test nurse' always insisted on having major, but alarmingly trivial conversations while she was 'down there'. That's just not right. Call me a prude, but as far as I'm concerned, the rule is: if your face is closer to my 'bits' than my head, don't talk, just get on with your business and try not to involve me more than necessary. This rule has been known to apply to a few boyfriends as well, by the way.

Anyway, where was I? Oh yes, Dr Nichols, kind, lovely, caring, amazing and, more relevantly, gentle, Dr Nichols.

"Well, Miss Townsend –" she said whilst having a final feel.

"Call me Kate – it's the least you can do considering where your hand is."

"Quite. Well, Kate, it's definitely in a strange place."

"Oh, is it?"

"And it does seem less solid than a normal growth."

"And that's good, is it?"

"I'm not sure."

Wait a minute – this was not the time for her to be unsure. As long as I'd known her, Dr Nichols had always been very definite with her diagnoses. Now, for the first time, I needed this assuredness. No wishy-washy 'I can't be sures'.

"So what do I do?"

"Well, I do think it warrants a visit to the clinic at the hospital. You may have to stay there the entire day as they pride themselves in giving a full diagnosis."

"What does that mean?"

"They will do all the tests in one go and by the end of the day, you will know exactly what it is."

23

"What it is?"

"Yes, whether it's malignant or benign."

"How can they be sure?"

"Look, don't worry. Cancerous cells are easily identifiable."

There, it was said. The C word had been mentioned at last. Oddly, I felt extremely calm. As soon as the word had been uttered, a sense of tranquillity passed over me.

"It'll probably be a couple of weeks until you get an appointment and most of all, don't worry. Chances are it's just an enlarged cyst."

"OK, doctor." Suddenly I was doing impressions of the receptionist. I was numb from the fact that I actually had a health scare which warranted a visit to the hospital.

On my way home, I attempted to rationalise it all away. Obviously, the doctor's not too worried. If she was, I'd be in the hospital in double-quick time, surely. The fact that she thinks it can wait a few weeks must mean that there's probably nothing to worry about.

By the time I got to my house, my fears had begun to dissipate. I opened the door of my mock-Tudor house – alright, alright, some white paint and a couple of planks of wood disguised as beams, does not mock-Tudor make, but it was a bad day and who wants to be reminded that they live in a dodgy-looking semi in a dubious part of Manchester? Anyway, fuelled by months of watching morose and yet strangely life-affirming films on the Lifetime channel, I set out to prove that, yes, all women are alike when it comes to a crisis. No, I don't mean I got out the Ben & Jerry's and proceeded to consume enough ice cream to keep a small continent chilled in the summer months. I got out the rubber gloves and started cleaning. Not only that, but when the place was spotless and after a short trip to the local DIY store, I began painting. I was like a mad artist type, using the walls of my entire house as a huge canvas waiting for the full expression of my emotions (OK, I admit, I only managed the living room, but pretend for the moment I was slightly fitter and less prone to lower back twinges and so managed to do the whole house). In fact I was so manic, that my right earlobe only escaped removal because I found my lost favourite earring – the one that I thought I'd lost when I had an afternoon romp with the crazy as a loon, but remarkably sexy receptionist at my local fitness centre. That was the closest I'd ever got to working out at the gym! Anyway, the earring was under the sofa and there was no way I'd do away with an earlobe when I finally had a matching pair of diamanté hearts again. I rearranged all my furniture, putting the comfy IKEA sofa against the opposite wall and moving the rocking chair around, so that it had enough room to rock without taking huge chunks out of the wall. Then I proceeded to do something that I'd never done before. I walked slowly around my house surveying my possessions.

My house is charming (small) and possesses interesting architectural features (weird sticky-out things on the wall that I put candleholders on – God knows what they're actually for) and I love it to bits. It is supposedly a three-bedroomed house, but one of the bedrooms, I swear, is not big enough to actually accommodate a bed, but can just about manage a desk and computer stuff, so I like to call it my office. And the small room off the landing is no longer described as a broom cupboard, it's now referred to as a very comfy, yet compact den. I wandered into the kitchen. I

25

gazed lovingly at my washing machine, stroked my invaluable dishwasher, blew the cobwebs off my white casserole dish with the roses on it that I got free with a set of recipe cards and, not for the first time, pondered whether the art of casserole making is a lost skill, seeing as I'd never in my adult life had the unmistakable urge to 'do' a casserole. I tried out all the chairs in my dining room, just to make certain that they were equally comfy (they were), then I went upstairs and rooted around in my spare room. Armed with a shoebox full of old photos and even older love letters from long-forgotten boyfriends, I sat on my sofa trying not to think of anything remotely related to nasty illnesses and lumpy bits.

I was so deep in the sea of nostalgia and yearning for my lost youth that the phone made me jump when it rang.

"Miss Townsend?"

"Yes, speaking."

"This is Jean, from the Well Woman Clinic at Hope Hospital. I've been speaking to your doctor."

Wow, they worked quickly. "I thought she said that it'd take a few weeks?" Before I knew it, I was up and pacing the length of my 'bijoux' living room.

"Sometimes these things go quicker." Jean gave a small cough and suddenly her voice sounded different as she explained the mysteries of the appointment-making world.

Not that I heard much of it. I felt as if I was underwater and was too frightened to breathe in case I drowned. Then Jean's voice came back as if in an air bubble.

"Would it be possible to come in on Friday?"

That was two days away. "Um . . . er . . . I suppose . . ." I held the phone away from my ear and made that strange 'Scream' painting gesture that was popularised in one of those stupid Hollywood films featuring that little kid, whose name dropped immediately out of my mind when I heard the next sentence.

"I'm sorry it's such short notice, but we thought you'd appreciate being seen quickly."

What was I supposed to make of that? Why on earth would I appreciate being seen quickly? The words 'hastening death' popped briefly into my mind and I dropped the phone through my shaking fingers. Have you ever tried to pick something off the floor when your hands won't stay still? Well, it must have taken me a long time because when I got it back up against my ear, Jean was speaking again.

"Miss Townsend? Are you still there?"

"Yes, yes, of course, sorry, yes, I can make Friday."

"There's an open slot at 8.30 a.m. Would that be suitable?"

"Yes. Thank you." I always love getting life-changing news at some ridiculous hour of the morning. I'd worn a discernable groove into my carpet, so I sat down and tried to breathe calmly.

Dr Nichols must have rung them up. She said that she'd contact them, but for her to ring them obviously she was concerned. Which meant that I, too, should be concerned. Friday? I had two days to get used to the fact that I might have cancer. Jane came round almost immediately. She started laying out a tarot-card spread on my coffee table.

"Jane, stop. I don't want to know."

"Well I do, so shut up, go and make a brew. Don't use tea bags though. Use real tea."

"Why? Do you want to read my tea leaves?"

"No, it just tastes better when you make it with loose tea."

27

"Oh." I wandered off into the kitchen.

It was her sharp intake of breath and half-smothered screech that brought me prematurely into the living room.

"What is it? Am I going to die?" I was almost climbing the walls with worry.

"No, Craig and I are going to have a fight."

"I thought you were doing my cards?"

"Oh them. I did them at home. You're going to be fine. Although I could be wrong."

"What's the point of you doing them then?"

"You know that tarot cards can't do timings very well. You're definitely going into hospital, and there are a lot of medical matters which could be discussed, so that's probably Friday, but the timing is always a bit screwy."

"So, basically, what you're saying is that I am definitely going into hospital and, as for anything else, you can't be certain."

"Yep." Jane nodded one of her knowing, I'm-so-bloody-mystical-I-surprise-myself-sometimes nods, shrugged her shoulders and continued fussing around with her cards.

"Well, Sherlock, I told you that I was definitely going into hospital. Fat lot of good your cards are!" I turned away from her and recommenced my pacing. I don't know why I was hoping that her cards would provide some deep insight, but in the true spirit of grasping at straws, I suppose I thought Jane would be able to give me an answer. I went back into the kitchen and completed the tea making. I even got out the caramel chocolate digestives that I save for very special occasions and/or instances of deep depression. Bringing everything back into the living room, I could tell that Jane was still bristling over my last comment.

She was itching to have a go, so I said, "Go on then, you know you want to."

"You shouldn't mock."

"I wasn't mocking. I was saying quite plainly that it's a load of bollocks!"

"Shhh!" She picked up her cards and cradled them like a baby. "They'll hear you."

"For God's sake! They are inanimate objects. They are bits of pulped trees. They do not have feelings."

I gave an exasperated harrumph and reeled away from her. My mind seemed to be working overtime, but not actually coming up with anything constructive at all.

"Look, I'm off if you're going to be like that."

Jane's face looked seriously hurt and I felt the familiar guilty nudging of my conscience, which was also wagging a finger and reminding me that I was being a complete bitch.

"I'm sorry. What else can you tell me?"

"There's definitely a warning, but I don't think it applies to Friday. Take a card, just to make sure."

I picked out a card and laid it on the table. Jane turned it over and, I swear, I jumped when I saw what it was. It was the death card. Yeah, predictable right? Well, it still made me shiver. Jane was quick to point out that it didn't actually mean death and it was probably not referring to Friday.

"The death card simply means the death of a situation or state. For example, if you are depressed, the death card could mean that the state of depression will end. That sort of thing."

"And what does it mean for someone going to the hospital to have a potentially life-threatening lump in the boob checked out?"

29

"Probably that there will be a few big changes in your life in the near future."

"Yeah? Well, death would be a pretty big change in my life right now."

"Don't be silly."

That was as far as the conversation was going to go for one day. Jane refused to talk about it any more. Instead we just drank our tea and gossiped about Sandi and her amazing love life. She seems to accrue men like most people accrue interest at the bank. We both shook our heads in disbelief at her sheer front, but both secretly wished that we had such front, both figuratively and literally. Sandi really does have a magnificent pair. None of us quite understand how she manages to keep them so perky, but we discuss it at length at every opportunity. Despite Sandi's earnest assurances, we still refuse to rule out the possibility of her having had a sneaky boob job on one of her trips abroad.

After a few hours of pure bitchiness (but in a 'nice' way, of course) Jane picked up her cards and said her goodbyes, leaving me more upbeat, but still emotionally top-heavy.

* * *

In a way I was really glad that Friday turned out to be a horrid, grey winter's day. It was one of those days where the clouds were black and threatening rain at any moment. I bundled myself up in a couple of layers of clothing and ventured out into the cold.

I walked into the clinic fifteen minutes later and found myself surrounded by stricken women, some with and others without partners clasping their hands in support. The one common link between all of us was a sense of dread.

I'd put together a 'hospital waiting-room survival pack' containing snacks, two novels (funny ones, obviously), an assortment of mellow chill-out George Michael music for the Walkman (I'd selected 'Older' for extra calmness) and copious amounts of chocolate. Despite all of this, the first thirty minutes found me surreptitiously inspecting the other occupants of the waiting room. All voices were hushed and solemn and each time a treatment-room door opened, you could feel the anxiety level rise. Each departing woman wore one of two possible faces, utter devastation or pure joy and relief. It was difficult to tell which face upset the waiting women more.

Personally, I found myself having strange thoughts. When a devastated woman emerged, I looked deeply into her eyes, thinking 'In a few hours that could be me' and I just wished she would leave quicker so that I didn't have to think about it any longer than necessary. Whenever a happy woman departed, I thought 'You lucky cow, why isn't it you? Why do I have to be here?' I was desperately trying to remember the statistics: was it one in ten women or one in eight? I'd already counted three devastateds and six happys. There were fifteen women waiting, which meant that out of twenty-four there were already three affected which, statistically speaking, had to be good for me, surely? Oh, but what if it were one in five? My mind was so busy calculating that I almost missed my name being called. As I walked towards the little room, I felt the eyes staring at me, assessing my and therefore their own chances.

There was a nurse in the room, fussing with bits and pieces on a cupboard top. She was small, plump and kind-looking, just perfect for the situation. She seemed exactly the sort of person I always wanted my mum to be instead of the over-the-top, pushy, irritating, melodramatic, drag-queen-in-bad-drag that I actually have for a mother.

"Come in, take a seat. Dr Lawrence won't be long."

I nodded silently, secretly astonished that she had a southern accent (quite posh too), when all the outward signs plus the geographical location of the hospital suggested that she'd have one of those Lancashire dialects like that strange butcher from *Coronation Street*.

"That's right, lie down there and take off your top please." She smiled warmly and pointed to the bed covered with a disposable paper blanket.

I'd been lying there for about five minutes trying desperately to forget why I was there. Which was particularly difficult when you're lying in a small room, topless, with a nurse studiously avoiding eye-contact. Suddenly the other door into the room opened and in walked an Amazon of a woman. Not only was she tall, but her personality and therefore voice was larger (or should that be louder) than life.

"So, Miss Townsend," she boomed, "let's see what we have here."

With that, she grabbed my breast and started prodding. She then proceeded to do the same thing that dentists do. She started up a conversation, asking totally unrelated questions when the etiquette clearly states that silence is required.

"So rotten weather we're having, eh?"

"Yes, really . . . OW . . . changeable." My words were punctuated by yelps of pain, as she manhandled (doctorhandled?) my breast. I hesitated while I considered when would be the right moment to tell her that the lump was in the other boob. "Erm, ow actually, it's ow in the other ow erm . . ."

"Yes, yes, I need to check this one for comparison."

"Oh."

Eventually, she got on to the examination of the lump. After thoroughly exhausting topics of conversation such as the weather and Millennium Eve plans, she announced: "A-ha."

"You've found something?" My heart was pounding like mad.

"Yes, just sit still a second please."

She went off to pick up a pair of sterile gloves and a dressing pack. "So, what is it you do for a living, Miss Townsend?"

As I wasn't sure if this information was relevant or simply another topic to keep me occupied, I answered truthfully.

"I'm an IT con . . . ARGH!"

Yes, you've guessed it – she lulled me into inconsequential discussion and then squeezed my boob as hard as she could.

Now, before I tell you what actually happened, I would suggest that if you are eating right at this moment, you should close the book now and only return when the food has safely settled in your stomach. If you intend to ignore this advice, just remember that I warned you. Right, where was I?

She was squeezing my breast like an old lemon and I looked down to see her squeezing a thick stream of yucky yellowy-green puss from my nipple. Painful? Definitely. Stomach turning? Yep, that too. But the knowledge that the lump had merely been a blocked duct came as a shower of relief washing over me.

I don't remember how I left the room: I was floating. No doubt the waiting women were all totally pissed off with me, but I didn't care. I didn't have cancer, all I had was a . . .

"Tit zit," Jane announced authoritatively later, when I'd explained the day's events to her. "You had a zit in your tit!"

"Alright, alright, let's not go on about it."

Jane started giggling. "Why not? It's funny."

"Actually, no, it's not. What if it wasn't . . ."

"I'm sorry."

"Everything happened so fast. I don't know what I would have done if . . ." I shook my head.

Jane obviously decided that it was time to get back to the mickey-taking. She chuckled once more.

"Let me get this right. So far, you've had a heart attack that never was and a lumpy boob. Quite a medical-intensive couple of months, all told. Any more health scares in there?" She tapped my head. "You are going to get so much stick for this. You wait till the girls hear about your tit zit."

"Blocked duct."

"Zit!" she chuckled. "Acne of the breast!"

Chapter Three

Dancing My Socks Off

Sometimes you've got to dance like no one is watching. I read that in a book somewhere and I once spent all night thinking how fantastic that sentence was. I wished I could think up something so profound – unfortunately I'm not that deep. The best I could come up with was: sometimes the sun is just too bright. It doesn't have the same resonance, does it? So there we go: another thing that keeps me awake at nights. Some people would take one look at me and my situation and assume that I have more important things to worry about. But as I keep saying, it's the little things.

December 1999. One of the best months of my life. It was the month that I met Matthew. Matt Silver. What a fabulous name! Just imagine what someone called Matt Silver would look like. It was a name pregnant with imagery, rugged, tough and ridiculously sexy. Trust me, he was that good.

I was in the Crown and Speckled Pheasant just off Deansgate, passing the time until my meeting. I have a huge problem with time. Some say I am even obsessive about it. I tend to arrive at least half an hour early for everything. So there I was carefully sipping my mineral water, trying to focus on my upcoming meeting, when I decided that I should nip off to the loo. I put down my drink and swivelled off my stool, straight into the sexiest arms on the planet, spilling his beer to kingdom come and completely trashing his suit.

"Oh my god! I'm really, really, really sorry!" I gushed like some out-of-control fountain, watching the stain spread down his trousers (nice package, I observed by-the-by).

"It's OK, it could have happened to anyone. I shouldn't have been walking so close anyway."

"You're just being polite, aren't you?"

"No, honestly, I've had much worse."

"I'm so sorry! Let me buy you another."

The thought of me being in charge of another pint of liquid made him physically recoil. "No, it's alright. I don't think I'll bother," he said hastily.

I had to do something; I'd ruined his suit and probably ruined his entire day too. Plus the fact that he made Tom Cruise look like a hideous swamp creature.

"Let me give you my card. You can send me your dry-cleaning bill." Phew, really sexy. You're a right vamp, Kate. So what if it was a bit unromantic and over the top – bugger-me he was gorgeous. I'd have done absolutely anything to give him my phone number.

"It's really not that bad," he shrugged.

I looked at him with the closest I could get to puppy-dog eyes and he accepted the receipt of my business card. I looked pointedly at his empty hand and willed him to get the message.

Jane's always telling me how strong the human mind can be. She says that everyone has telepathic ability; it was merely a question of concentration. I was standing in front of a soggy Adonis in a pub, desperately concentrating on the one thought: give me your phone number!

All of a sudden, everything was moving in slow motion. I saw a quizzical look pass fleetingly across his face, as if he didn't really know why he was doing it and his hand moved achingly slowly towards his inside pocket.

It worked, it worked! I couldn't believe it; he was actually going to give me his phone number. I reminded myself to give Jane a huge sloppy kiss for this. I was so busy congratulating myself that I didn't notice him bringing out a handkerchief and walking away, wiping his face. So I was stood there holding out my hand in thin air, looking like an idiot and feeling one hundred times worse.

Remember what I told you about fate and my life? Well, that wasn't the last time I met Matt.

It was my turn to choose the destination for the next girls' night out, so I chose Chicanas, a really nice Mexican restaurant where they had a tendency to clear away the tables after midnight and indulge in a little sexy salsa-type dancing. I thought, given enough cheap red wine and decent food, we'll have a whale of a time.

All members of the coven were accounted for and after spiking Louise's drink with mineral water for the fifth time, Jane thought it safe to suggest a little boogie. We were crazy women, shaking our bits like there was no tomorrow. Then the dancemaster (the head chef, Javier) suggested a group dance. We were all lined up along one wall and the guys were lined up opposite. Basically the idea was that you grab a guy, do a bit of wiggling and move on to the next. Halfway through, my feet were a bit tired, but I thought to myself, one more guy and I'll stop. So would you be at all surprised to find out that the next guy happened to be the soggy Adonis from the pub? I thought not. At that stage I didn't know his name, so after getting over my shock, I asked him. I swear I hadn't planned it this way, but the music was so loud that he had to get really close to my ear, which by the way is one of my most powerful erogenous zones, and he said, "Matt Silver".

I nearly fainted, but kept moving in the hope that I'd get my strength back eventually. I was unable to speak so I just carried on wiggling in his arms, until Gen tapped me on the shoulder and suggested that we help get Louise back home. I looked across the room to see her half-naked and slumped over a table. Apparently some mischievous waiter had been feeding her tequila.

So I turned to Matt and shouted (it was loud, remember?): "Can I call you?"

He nodded and pulled out a card, with his name and number on it. If I hadn't been so muddled, I would have thought about this a lot deeper, but I was, so I didn't. And before I knew it I was sitting in a cab, being puked on by Louise.

The next morning, I sat in front of the phone trying to get up the courage to ring him. Unfortunately, every time I attempted to pick up the receiver, someone rang me.

"Kate, you up for breakfast? We can go to The Nose and I'll pay." That was Jane. I declined her kind offer on the grounds that I had things to do in the house. Plus the fact that I had lunch plans with a cookbook and a nice portion of British lamb.

"Kate, tell me I didn't throw up on you last night. Gen said I did, but I don't believe her." Obviously, that was Louise. She was mortified when I admitted that yes, she'd chucked up her stomach contents over my favourite dress, but the only reason she was still alive was that it didn't reach my shoes. After her 'one thousand apologies' I assured her that it didn't matter and I had been meaning to choose a new favourite anyhow.

I couldn't resist winding her up, so I added, "It'll be months before I can afford it though . . ."

"Listen, we can go shopping and I'll buy you your new favourite dress!"

"I couldn't possibly," I said, totally without conviction.

"Please, I insist."

"I dunno . . ."

I guess Louise could feel me faltering so she hastily added, "And some shoes to match."

"Sold to the lady who can't hold her drink." I was just so predictable – offer me a pair of shoes and I was anyone's.

"Deal then?" Louise said with relief.

"Deal."

"Great, I'll see you next week."

It was at this point I decided to stop trying to ring Matt and got into the shower instead. You may be interested to learn that there were no calls for me, and therefore no naked rushing out of the shower to get to the phone, just to find that the person had rung off. Which was a first; usually that was a guaranteed occurrence as soon as I stepped under the water.

I'd been consulting Delia on the best way to prepare lamb, and was in the garden cutting some rosemary, just as she'd suggested, when I was certain that I heard the faint tinkle of my phone ringing in the house. I'd decided that I wasn't up to Sandi and her Sunday-morning moans (more of these later) and Gen was just too butch for that morning, so I forced myself to allow the answer phone to pick up. What was an answer phone for, if not to screen calls? I continued my selection of the perfect sprig of rosemary. As I casually returned to the kitchen I heard the tail-end of a message.

". . . so, I'm just off to kill myself now. Don't try to stop me, I've decided. See you next week. Bye."

Sandi gets so emotional on Sundays. It's the one day of the week when she wishes that she hadn't got rid of that crazy husband of hers. She said that she can't stand the thought that everyone in the country is sitting happily in bed with their partners, eating croissants and reading the Sunday papers. While she sits miserably watching the *Heaven and Earth Show* wondering why Toyah Wilcox, the person with the worst voice on television, does her own voice-overs. At least that was her complaint that particular Sunday, which I discovered when I'd listened to the full message. While I was at the answer phone, I noticed that there was another message waiting for me so I played it, expecting to hear Gen ordering me to join her for brunch. Instead I was stunned.

"Kate, I'm pregnant. I wanted to tell you earlier, but I didn't know what to say. I hope you're not angry and I realise that I'll never see you once the baby's born, so that's why I wanted to go for breakfast. That's all." It was Jane, the original, Mrs I-Hate-Babies-And-Will-Never-Ever-Have-One-Trust-Me.

I couldn't get to the phone quick enough. I dialled her number and got the engaged signal. I then went through that paranoid stage when you think, 'Oh, they're trying to call me'. So I put down the receiver and waited for it to ring. And ring it did.

"Jane, that's brilliant!"

"Erm, actually, it's not Jane." The voice was undeniably masculine and extremely Matt-like.

"Oh." I didn't mean to feel deflated, honestly I didn't. Any other time and I would have been 100 per cent over the moon to hear his voice, but MY BEST FRIEND WAS GOING TO HAVE A BABY! This was perhaps the worst time, in the history of all the worst times in the world, for him to call. "Sorry, Matt, but can I call you back? I've just had some amazing news."

"Sure, I'm out this afternoon, but I'm in this evening."

"Fine, I'll call you tonight."

Without wasting another moment, I grabbed my car keys and rushed out the door.

Before I go on, maybe I should explain the 'I realise that I'll never see you once the baby's born' comment. I know that you probably won't understand me and this knowledge might put you off me for good, but I hate babies! I actually feel a bit queasy when I see one. It doesn't matter if they are supposedly the most gorgeous baby in the world, I can't face looking at them. Anyway, I think they all look the same – like Ian Hislop, when he's been given a particularly taxing question on *Have I Got News For You*, especially when they're just about to crap in their nappy. My friends know that it's nothing personal. They know that I won't come round to have a look when it's been born, and they know

41

not to expect me to be excited by the actual baby itself. I can get really excited if my friends are having one – you know the lead up to the birth, that sort of thing. I can go shopping for baby clothes as well as the next person – who wouldn't find the miniature clothes adorable? Let me put it this way: if populating the planet was up to me, the buck would definitely stop here.

By the time I rolled up at Jane's house, Louise and Gen were already there. I could hear the delighted squeals even before I got out of my car. A departing Craig met me at the door. Craig is a typical ginger (hard G – Mancunian style): pale complexion, almost-white eyebrows and a multitude of freckles. He's not a typically weedy-looking accountant; he's stockily built, with a nice smattering of muscle definition (or so Jane assures us). He usually walked with a jolly spring to his step, but despite the happy news, the spring had obviously been sprung. He was running slightly trembling fingers through his floppy ginger fringe and muttering to himself about 'bloody women'. His usually calm exterior showed signs of obvious strain, his boyish face contained a few extra lines.

"Not another one! They're in there, Kate. Driving me nuts. Not one person has noticed me. I mean, I did have something to do with it, you know. The way they're acting, it's as if it was an immaculate conception or divine intervention. I'm off to the pub, if anyone's interested." He began plodding sadly away from the house. "It's my baby too."

"Have a good time," I offered as some consolation. "And Craig, congratulations, Daddy!"

Craig turned and smiled a huge toothful grin. "Thanks." He only just managed to avoid being run over by a speeding Mini, driven by Sandi. She was talking to me before she'd even extracted herself from her vehicle. "Isn't it fab news? I'm so excited, I'm going to be an auntie! Well, maybe not a real auntie, but an honorary auntie! I can't wait to get shopping!"

"Hi Sandi. Glad to see you didn't succeed in killing yourself after all."

"Kill myself? Don't be silly. I'm going to be an auntie. Give me a hand."

She reached into the car to retrieve a five-foot teddy bear, and countless bags of baby things. I was astounded that she'd managed to get so many things in the short time that had been available to her between her phone call to me and her arrival at Jane's house.

"How on earth did you manage to get all these?"

"The Trafford Centre. The world and her husband was there today. I couldn't get a proper shop done. Nightmare."

I looked down at the bags in my hand and decided not to find out what exactly a 'proper shop' was.

* * *

"I shuppose Jo is a good name for a baby, jusht add a 'e' and itsh a boysh name." Sandi slurred.

We'd been at Jane's for the best part of six hours and had consumed a creditable amount of champagne. Unfortunately Louise and Jane were completely sober, both for obvious reasons. Craig had long since returned from the pub and was holed up in his study which, with the arrival of the baby, would have to be turned into a nursery. So he was determined to make good use of it while it was still there. I can only remember snatches of conversation. We'd been trying out babies' names and thinking about how things would necessarily have to change once the baby came.

"So you'll still come on girls' nights?" Louise enquired.

"Of course. Craig will have to get used to looking after the baby."

"And you're really happy?" Gen asked.

"Unbelievably happy. Who'd have thought it?"

"I wouldn't have in a million years. D'you remember that night we were baby-sitting for your sister? You were so bad with the kids. I'm surprised she didn't disown you. How long were you in casualty?"

"Four hours." Jane giggled.

"And exactly how did Jack get the saucepan stuck?"

Jane groaned and covered her eyes. Peeking through her fingers she cringed. "Don't. I get nightmares just thinking about it."

We chuckled for a little while and in a pause to give our stomach muscles a rest, Jane began shaking her head. "Can you believe I'm going to be a mother? I hope I do a better job than mine did."

There was silence while each one of us contemplated the maternal abilities of our respective mothers. None of us actually gets on with our parents. We'd all agreed years ago that that was what friends were for: to reduce the amount of time one actually had to spend in the company of the folks. It seemed really weird that one of us was actually going to be one. A mother. Obviously, it had to happen eventually. You couldn't have a group of five women going into their thirties without one of them getting preggers at some point. Still, it had been good while it lasted.

I never did cook that lamb.

Chapter Four

New Year and Relationship Beasts

If it wasn't for bad luck, I'd have no luck at all. That's a line from the song that is playing in the café now. I laughed, but only because it was so true. I think you can take it as read that that sums up my life for the moment. But maybe I'm being a bit too coy. I should probably get on with my tale, but I keep looking around at the other occupants of the café and to tell you the truth it's depressing. There's such an atmosphere of drudgery. I can't believe that I'm in here at all watching people just getting on with their lives, not really seeming to live them. I suppose anyone looking at my life at the beginning of this year would have said the same thing about me. The problem comes when you actually decide to start living – things just aren't as easy as that. You would think that the difficulty is making the decision, but I can tell you from experience that that is the easy part. Being brave enough to make the change: now that's what separates the wheat from the wussies. Oh well, I'd better get on with it before you give up and go and make a cup of tea. Although, now I think of it, why not go and make a cup anyway. I'll wait for you . . .

Right, are you comfy now?

Alrighty, January started in the exact same way that January has started for the past eight or nine years, with a stinking headache. And every year I think the same thought: next year, I'm going to stay in on New Year's Eve and start the New Year off with a clear head. The one difference was that when I crawled out of bed, I was forced to climb over the sleeping form of Matt on the way. Yep, Matt, my official boyfriend. No, I couldn't believe it at first either, but it was working out surprisingly well. He'd almost moved in by then. We were spending so much time in my house, that bar making the actual decision to 'move in together' we were there. By the time that the Millennium Eve party invites came around, we'd already metamorphosed into the dreaded KateMatt beast – even worse, people started calling me Katt, simply because it rhymed with his name. I soon stopped that bit of nonsense. However much I fought against the merger, our names were inextricably interlinked. Of course we still did the girls' nights and that was the only time that I heard my name said on its own. Luckily, by the end of December, everyone had found themselves someone to cling on to as 1999 turned into 2000.

Sandi's bloke had the unfortunate nickname of Mr December because not only did he look like one of those calendar models, but we also knew that as sure as eggs is eggs, when dawn rolled over the country on January first, he'd be out on his ear. Sandi had admitted as much when she first mentioned him to us. He was simply there to get

46

her through the disheartening Christmas/New Year period.

Louise had started seeing a taxi driver. But not just any old taxi driver – it was actually the driver of the cab she'd puked up in. Apparently he'd gone to her house a week later to get her to pay for the cleaning and had stayed for three days. Not only did this amaze and astound us all, but they were extremely happy together. Louise had even started making marriage noises and buying *Bride* magazine.

Gen had finally introduced us to her Italian lover. We'd been hearing about him for years, but had never met him. Normally, she'd disappear to Italy for a few weeks and come back tanned, happy and more than a little flushed. Finally, she'd managed to convince him to come to the UK and she was remarkably occupied for the entire time he was around, coming up briefly for air once a week. We knew that he wasn't her 'one true love', but he was definitely her 'one true lover' as she liked to say. So there was no doubt that marriage was not on their cards.

Jane and Craig were still coming to terms with their impending parenthood.

And me? Well I had Matt.

"I'm going to get some aspirin and some water," I whispered.

"Get me some too," Matt croaked back.

"OK."

I creaked wearily out to the bathroom and rested my pounding head on the cool mirror for a while in that I-want-to-die-God-I-promise-I'll-never-drink-again-if-you-just-get-rid-of-this-headache sort of way. After forcing down a few Nurofen, I creaked back to the bedroom again, passing Matt some pills and collapsing back into bed. Sometime later, I was prodded awake by Matt's morning monster.

Usually I like its arrival because sex is a great way to start the day, but New Year's Day had to be an exception.

"Leave me alone." I turned over and pushed him away.

"Come on, babe, just a quickie?"

"No, I'm still a bit queasy."

"Suit yourself." He eased his tall frame out of bed and wandered to the bathroom.

Not what you could call the epitome of semi-marital bliss, or maybe it was too much like the behaviour of an old married couple. Whatever, it was hardly a satisfying start to the year, although, knowing Matt, he was probably feeling perfectly self-satisfied in the shower.

So before I knew it, I was back at work. The next few weeks kept me busy, just going around all my clients making sure their systems were ticking over nicely. My bank balance was overflowing with good cheer and retainer payments. Life just couldn't get any better. Or could it?

* * *

"Did you want another cuppa, love?" The waitress points at my empty cup.

"Yeah, I think I'd better." I refocus on my surroundings. The minestrone soup-eater has long since left the tatty café. Her place is now taken by two raucous ⅼfootball fans, obviously on their way to a match by the sound of optimism in their voices. They remind me of how I was that January: optimistic, not even the vaguest thought of sadness or worry around the corner.

I don't actually know what happened on that day. The day that changed my life. I remember that it was really, really busy. Both my phone lines were ringing non-stop. I remember hearing my mobile ringing downstairs and telling Marco, who was moaning at me on the phone upstairs, in my office, that I should go and get it. I put down the phone with a 'hang on, I'll go and get my mobile' and went towards the stairs. After that there wasn't much.

I was falling through the air. I remember the pain, but it seemed so far away that it couldn't have been happening to me. I felt a ping, like someone was flicking an enormous rubber band in my leg. I knew I was hurt, but I couldn't focus. Then there was a thick black fog. You'll be very glad to hear that there was no white rooms or ghostly figures guiding me into the light.

There was just a thick black fog.

Chapter Five

Drugs and the Single Girl

I always thought that childbirth was the only time that you could scream for drugs and actually get them. I found out in the accident and emergency room that if you scream loud enough, they'll give you all the drugs you could ever want, and not some namby-pamby sissy drugs either: morphine, the mother of all narcotic substances – much like legal heroin. Actually I don't really remember what went on in casualty. All I remember is floating away and feeling happy. It seemed to me that everyone was as white as pristine hospital sheets. At first I thought this might be an effect of the drugs on my eyesight, but then I realised that everyone who came near me, including the doctors, was in some form of shock. It was funny really: doctors would come into the cubicle speaking as they entered.

"Good afternoon, Miss Townsend, let's . . ."

That was as far as they'd get because at this point they'd

have spotted my leg. Then they'd turn white . . . then green and leave clutching their stomachs.

Despite this, no one was particularly panicking. The nurses kept coming in and prodding me in some way, either taking blood or taking a pulse, so I wasn't too surprised to find yet another one fussing around my ankles. She pressed her fingers up against my foot and gave a very sharp intake of breath and rushed out. She returned with a doctor.

"I can't get a pulse."

I was astounded. Was that it? Was I dead? Was that what it was like? I've seen *The Sixth Sense* – dead people don't know they're dead. I still felt alive, in fact so alive that the pain had somehow increased. Maybe this was like when people have a leg amputated – they say that you can still feel it afterwards. Maybe I was dead. I tried to speak, to tell them that I was still alive, but I couldn't move my lips. In fact, after taking a short inventory, I found that I couldn't move anything.

When I was little my Auntie died. My mother explained to me that her spirit had gone away and her body would be put in the ground. I remember thinking: but what if she comes back? What if she comes back and finds herself stuck underground? I had nightmares about it for months. They were all about being buried alive and not being able to get out. My worst nightmare was coming true. They were going to bury me alive.

"Yes, you're right. There's definitely no pulse." The doctor sounded so sure. And he should know, shouldn't he? This was my last chance – I had to force myself to move. I concentrated all my effort on my right arm, which hadn't been injured in the fall. With a final mental push, I felt my arm move. There, they'd definitely notice that, wouldn't they? I tried my voice.

"Hello!" At least that's what I wanted to say. I think it came out as more of a croak though.

The nurse prodded the doctor, who then enquired, "Are you comfortable?"

Well, they could have been just a little bit more excited, couldn't they? After all, it's not everyday that someone comes back from the dead. Or maybe it happened more often than I thought, because they weren't at all amazed by it.

"Ah, Miss Townsend, there seems to be a slight complication – we're just calling the vascular team now."

"What . . .?" I couldn't articulate very well so he went straight on to explain.

"You may have severed an artery in your leg. It's the main one that supplies blood to the foot."

As I write this I am physically shaking, just thinking about what that means. But what you have to remember is that I was on the biggest and longest drug-induced trip of my life. The doctor was so calm and off-hand that it just didn't register. I know it sounds unbelievable, but I swear that even if he'd said, "You have five arms and have grown a penis," I would have reacted the same.

I think my actual response was "Oh," in a kind of I-sever-arteries-every-day-and-twice-on-Sundays nonchalance.

For a short while afterwards there was a flurry of activity in my cubicle. I felt like a kumquat in a Wythenshawe Tesco, everyone poking me as if they were trying to work out what I was. I'd never seen so many students in my life. They were all there listening to the vascular consultant with rapt attention. I tried to follow his explanations, but a green giraffe kept popping up and wanting me to talk to it.

One by one the girls appeared, except Sandi of course, but more about her later. All three of them (in order of appearance: Louise, Jane and Gen) managed to lose all traces of facial colour within seconds of their arrival as the news of my injuries was passed on. I lay there surrounded by my favourite people and all I could think of was "Cheer up, you miserable gits".

"Do you think she's going to be alright?" Jane whispered to Louise.

"The doctors say they don't know. We'll have to wait and see." Louise made a shrugging gesture as if in despair.

"Do you think she's comfortable enough? Should I get her another blanket, do you think?"

Jane sounded so solemn that I almost expected her to break down in tears any second. I wanted to giggle, but nothing came out.

"Will you all stop talking about her as if she's not here. She's hurt her leg not her brain. She can hear you, you know." Go on Gen, you tell 'em!

I summoned up the strength to utter some words.

"Look, she's awake. Kate, darling, what is it?" Gen cooed.

"Farm chilli me."

"What did she say?" The three voices merged into one as they tried to make out my sentence.

"I think she said, 'Farming is chilli for me'," Louise announced authoritatively.

"Don't be so daft. Why would she be talking about farming? Kate darling, say it again."

Gen spoke so slowly I wanted to be witty and tell her that I might be hurt, but I wasn't stupid. I forced myself to form the words once more.

"My . . . arm . . . killing . . . me."

"Her arm's hurting her." Gen immediately took control. "Nurse, my friend is in pain, can you do something?"

The passing nurse tutted and came to check my charts. "I'm sorry, but she's had as much morphine as we are allowed to give her. Any more and it would be dangerous." She shook her head briefly and walked out of the cubicle.

I'd never really thought about the sayings we use. How many times every day do we say things like, 'my feet are killing me' or 'my head was so bad, I thought I was going to die'. Unfortunately, in my case, it was not the arm, but the leg that was killing me. The blood was pumping out of the ruptured artery into the surrounding tissue. My life force was leaving me and I couldn't really grasp the idea. Looking back now I can't explain the feelings I have knowing I was so close to popping off. All I could think of at the time was 'Thank God I made that will'. I'm sure if you were in my position, you'd have thought up something more interesting, a suitable epitaph or last words, which could be quoted forever and a day, like, 'Damn, I'll never get to the gym now'. Anyway, my final memory of that day was being wheeled away from the cubicle waving sadly to my friends, feeling like it might be the last time I saw them.

* * *

Eight hours and rather a lot of surgery later, I felt a tap-tap on my shoulder.

"Katherine? Katherine?"

54

I was really confused. What was my mother doing in the recovery room? I felt the tapping again.

"Katherine? Wake up, Katherine."

"Go away, I don't want to go to school today, Mum." I mumbled in my semi-delirious state.

"No, Katherine, you're in the hospital."

"Oh." I mean, it was an easy mistake to make. Only my mother called me Katherine. I opened my eyes and found myself eyeball to eyeball with a rather young-looking nurse. I know that this isn't exactly the right time or place to get into this sort of thinking, but is it me or are these doctors and nurses getting younger by the second? I mean this one looked like a well-endowed twelve-year-old. I felt like asking her if her parents knew that she was out so late. But then again, I wasn't quite sure how late or early it was.

"There you go," she smiled. "Welcome back."

At first I speculated on where I'd been, but then I remembered that I might have more pressing worries. The nurse had a faint look of concern on her face and I immediately wondered if I should check that all my limbs were present and accounted for. I slowly edged my good arm down my leg, there was definitely something still below the knee and I smiled, but I didn't feel brave enough to do a visual reccy.

"We're just going to take you back to ICU. Try not to worry, you're a light."

My head was still a bit of a mess, so that was what I heard. She may have been telling me that I was alright, but I heard what I heard.

When I woke up the second time, I saw my family gathered around me, all taking on that white tinge in their faces. I moved my arm.

"Look, she moved her arm." That was my ever-observant brother. It was said in the same way someone would look up at the sky and say 'Look, there's a comet!'

"Katherine, darling, Mummy's here."

Yeah, I know. But trust me, she doesn't appear much in this story so you'll have to sit through her while she is here, OK? "Are you awake, darling?"

I lifted up my arm. "Look, she's lifting up her arm." That was Benny again giving the full commentary. I didn't feel there was sufficient cause to be completely amazed by every movement I made, so I decided to have some fun.

"Look, she's moving her leg!"

"Ooh, she's drumming her fingers."

"She's lifting the third finger of her left hand."

Some obscure and occasionally obscene gestures later, I'd had enough. I opened my eyes and uttered, "I'm fine, you can go now."

"Don't be silly, darling. Mumsie will stay for as long as you want me to."

God, I wished 'Mumsie' would push off. I felt like saying, 'In that case, I want you to go now', but decided against it on the grounds that if I started being mean, they'd think I had psychological troubles and have me sectioned before I could say 'utter nutter'.

"You look tired, Mum. You should go home and get some sleep." And don't ever ever darken my hospital curtain again. No, of course I didn't say that last bit out loud.

"Aren't you Mummy's brave little bunny?" Mum looked over at Dad and Benny and said tearfully: "She's so lovely. She's concerned about me, in her situation. You can learn a lot from your sister, Benjamin." She never gives up an opportunity to put down her children. In fact sometimes I wondered whether she'd have actually had us put down, if she'd had the chance. But in hospital situations, there's no one better than my mum for sheer motherhood acting ability. You'd never guess that this was the same woman who, when I was eight, told me 'Never have any children, darling. They suck all the life force out of you and you'll regret it later. Trust me, I know.'

My mother moved away and for the first time I saw it. A huge metal bar attached to four pins sticking out of my leg. My voice disappeared down the back of my throat and I made a very strange gurgling noise.

"What is it, darling?" My mother cooed rather like a startled pigeon.

I was completely unable to form words. Instead I just peered in terror at the metal structure emerging from my lower limb.

"What's wrong with her?" Benny asked my mother, who in turn shrugged as if it was a complete mystery.

I wanted to shout out, 'I seem to have acquired some alien scaffolding, you fucking morons! What the hell do you think is wrong with me?' But instead all I could summon was enough energy to point at the hunk of metal.

"Oh that, darling, it's just an . . ." My mother looked at my father for assistance in finding the correct term for the device.

"External fixator." He nodded knowingly. The first words my father had been allowed to utter. I was still none the wiser.

"Of course, an external fixator. It's holding your leg together, it's quite handy really." She was so casual, you'd almost think she was discussing a new melon-baller or a new design of cheese grater. "Now would you like something to drink? Go get her a glass, Benjamin."

And with that all further discussion of my newly acquired steelwork was dismissed.

Chapter Six

Apparitions

Eventually, after three mind-numbing and excruciating hours, my family finally left the ward. The only good thing for me in that time was that I kept drifting off as I got more shots of morphine from the little machine by my bed. The machine in question was hooked up to an IV, which delivered a dose every few hours or so. But the best thing about it was that at the press of a button, it delivered an extra boosting dose, up to the maximum permitted dosage, after which it simply clicked at me. Trust me, it was a definite sanity-saver. Thank goodness for the appliance of science.

Sometime later that day, or it could have been the next day . . . Drugs are great for merging days into one another. Not only do you not know if you are coming or going, you also have doubts about whether you're there at all and why the green giraffe had to eat all the biscuits? Luckily all the narcotics ensured that I didn't really know what was going on in ICU. Now that I think about it, it was approximately a week after the major operation and after another four minor 'tinkering' procedures, I was moved to an orthopaedic ward.

The ward had eight beds and each bed was surrounded by a curtain which could be pulled closed to create the illusion of a private enclave. In this little enclave, the hospital allows each patient three basic items of furniture: a strange wardrobe/night-table, which has an array of drawers and little cupboards, a trolley table, which can be raised or lowered and is mostly used for eating meals, and finally a rather comfy-looking, but in actual fact hideously uncomfortable, armchair for the patient to spend all day 'sitting out'.

As soon as I hit the ward, they took my little machine pal away from me. I suppose they thought I was having far too much fun – either that or they calculated that after weeks of maximum dose morphine, I was liable to turn into a junkie – so I was forced to take my medicine in the boring pill form. The haze began to lift and I was forced to slowly return to earth.

Not that I didn't have the odd relapse into a dream state. One day, I was completely convinced that I saw Sandi walking down the ward towards me. I was so positive that I was hallucinating that I began giggling like a maniac and it wasn't until she stood in front of me smiling and patting my arm in that poor-little-sick-person way as people tend to do, that I realised I wasn't dreaming. And believe me, it was a shocker. Of all the girls, Sandi was the last one I expected. Sandi hates hospitals. She especially hated the one I was in, because both her parents had died here: her mother from cancer and her father from a stroke. As a consequence, she never visits hospitals. So to see her turn up as bold as brass was astounding.

"Hi, Kate."

"Sandi, what are you doing here?"

"I thought I'd visit that old biddy over there. What d'you think I'm doing here? You stupid cow!"

"I didn't mean it like that. I'm really glad you came. What you got there?"

Sandi was holding a large box, which she took from under her arm and gave to me. "It's a present, open it."

I ripped off the paper with as much energy as I could summon, which turned out to be a piddling little whimper so Sandi helped.

"Oh my God, it's a Playstation!"

"Yep, and I got you three games."

"Crash Bandicoot 1, 2 & 3. Oh Sandi, you're absolutely fantastic. I love you loads and loads."

"Yeah, well, I'll set it up for you."

Just after New Year, I'd gone to stay at Matt's flat for a weekend and got completely addicted to his Playstation, especially Crash Bandicoot. The girls were sick of me going on about it. I'd spent nearly all of my time there, fighting with Matt for possession of the control pad.

"There you go." Sandi made it sound as if she'd successfully completed brain-surgery rather than just plugging a few cables into my telly.

"Thanks. I can't believe you bought me a Playstation."

"Well, enjoy. I've got to go – it's just a short visit I'm afraid. I have a meeting."

"No, that's fine. And thanks again, I don't know what to say . . ."

"What are friends for?" Sandi turned and left and if it wasn't for the gleaming new Playstation on my telly, I'd never have thought she'd been there at all.

Chapter Seven

Top Dog and Dead Beasts

I'm trying to remember all of this in the right order, but forgive me if it's not 100 per cent chronological. The early days in the hospital were pretty mushed up together really and it was only when they took me off the heavy drugs that I was able to start experiencing clarity once more. It's amazing how resilient the human body is. My vascular surgeon said this to me just after the big op. But I think the body's resilience is a mere trifle compared to the resilience of the mind. For the body, repairing a wound is simply a series of processes, a pre-defined sequence. But for the mind to repair a psychological wound, there are an infinite number of processes and it uses them in a myriad of different ways. Damn! I'm getting good at this thinking lark.

Anyway there I was in Ward 5H, surveying my surroundings. I realised I was in an eight-bed ward, but it looked as though only five of the beds might be occupied.

"Fancy a sherbet lemon, love?"

I looked around to see a little old lady lying in the bed next to mine. Her lined face wrinkled in a smile, but all I could think of was that she looked like a huge walnut.

"No thanks, I'm fine."

"You've been in the wars 'aven't you, love?"

"Yes, I suppose I have, a bit."

"Feeling woozy, are you?"

"Yeah, a bit."

"That'll be the drugs," she said authoritatively. "We've been waiting for you to join us. Renee wanted to 'ave a chat to you yesterday, but I told 'er to 'ang off for a little while. Still, you look a lot better today."

"Renee?" Obviously, this being North Manchester, the name was pronounced without even the slightest hint of a French accent, and rhymed with 'beanie'.

"Bed six. Fractured 'er 'ip getting out of the bath." She extended a bony finger and pointed at the bed opposite me.

I looked over and saw nothing more than a small pile of bedclothes. For a fleeting moment, I wondered whether my family had actually had me sectioned. Maybe I'd been moved to a psych ward and I was surrounded by hallucinating maddos.

"Give 'er a wave, Renee."

The bedclothes were pulled back to reveal a shock of ginger hair and a huge smile. "Can I talk to her now, Doris?"

"Can't you see I'm talking to 'er now? You wait your turn. Just give 'er a wave like I said."

The smile faded slightly as her bony arm extended and waved vaguely in my direction. I turned and looked at Doris, thinking thank God I wasn't in prison right now, cos this little old lady was obviously 'top dog' on this ward and if we had been in Holloway or something, she'd be making me her bitch right about now.

"I'm Doris. I've been 'ere months, seen everyone come and go, you know. Fell down the stairs – they 'ad to whip my leg off in the end." She lifted her blanket to reveal a stump where her left leg should have been.

With no warning whatsoever the curtain on the other side of my bed let out a screech which would have put a foghorn to shame.

"Oh well, Eva's up." Doris rolled her watery blue eyes and went on to explain. "We'll 'ave no peace now. She carries on like that, no one knows why. Screams all day like a bleeding parrot and 'alf the night too. Until the sleeping pills kick in, then at least she shuts up. But some nights she refuses to take 'er pill. God 'elp you then, love. I 'ope you've got some earplugs, that's all I can say. We're all used to it now, aren't we Sarah?"

Doris pulled back the curtain on the other side of her bed to reveal a large sad-looking woman maybe in her late forties, who'd obviously been crying. "Say hello, Sarah."

Sarah looked up, wiping a stray tear and said venomously: "Piss off, you nosy old bitch!" With that she dragged her curtain closed.

"Don't mind 'er, they lopped both 'er legs off." For the first time, Doris lowered her voice and continued, "Fell in 'er kitchen. It was nearly a week before they found 'er. The legs were too far gone, see. If it wasn't for *The Puzzler*, she'd probably still be there."

The puzzler? My mind scoured its memory banks for North Manchester slang. Was that a local word for a loan shark? I needed to know. "Sorry, the puzzler?"

"You know, that monthly magazine, full of puzzles? She had it every month, regular as clockwork. Apparently, Mrs Khan, from the corner shop, got suspicious when she didn't come in for it and sent 'er son round to check 'er out. 'E called the police when 'e saw all the post mounting up by the front door. She never even thanked 'im, you know, but some people are just born rude, I reckon. So what do you think of our little ward then?"

"I thought they were always banging on about not having enough beds, and here we are with a ward that's half empty."

"It won't be for long though, love. We're expecting two more today and the girl next to Renee is 'aving x-rays done. You'll like 'er, you will, she's about your age. She doesn't say much: she keeps 'erself to 'erself mostly. A fireman, don't you know. She was putting out a fire and fell through some floorboards, broke 'er leg in four places – she's got one of them same things you've got there." She pointed at my ex-fix and continued without even taking breath, "And 'er 'usband's a fireman too, or maybe he's 'er fiancé, anyway they're involved at any rate, if them kisses they 'ave are anything to go by. Julie 'er name is."

I stared at Doris, astounded. I wondered whether MI5 knew about her abilities to extract information, but instead I simply uttered a standard: "Oh."

"Do you fancy a sherbet lemon, love?" Doris held out the bag once more.

"No, thanks, I'm still fine."

So there we had it – a full tour of the ward and back to the beginning again.

* * *

The more observant of you may have spotted that one, fairly important-ish member of my entourage had been missing. Later on, the same day as my grand tour of 5H and approximately two weeks after my accident, Matt Silver, my boyfriend, fidgeted onto the ward. As he walked empty-handed towards my bed, his eyes darted from side to side, as if preparing himself in case one of the old ladies took it upon themselves to mug him. Forgive me if I'm going off on one again, but I'm certain that the universal rules of common decency dictate that when visiting a poorly person in hospital, the very least one should bring is a bag of grapes – or am I wrong? Anyway, he sat down beside me and smiled a thin frailty of a smile and began to speak. Guess what his exact first words to me were? After me nearly dying in a fall and being in hospital for around two weeks, guess what the man said? You lose twenty points if you guessed that he asked after my health in any way. You lose ten points if you thought he may have said some form of hello followed by a term of endearment (Hi, love, Hello, sweetie etc.). A whopping fifty points go to you, now, this second, if you said: "God, I hate these places."

"Is that it Mr Silver? I'm almost at death's door, very nearly lost a limb and all I get from you is the information that you hate hospitals? My boss, you know, the horrid Marco of the 'I hate Marco' fame? Well, he positively detests me and guess what? I've had two bunches of flowers from him already this week alone. Aren't you even going to kiss me?"

"Oh yeah." Matt twitched and stood up to approach me. He then proceeded to kiss me as if I was carrying some form of contagious disease.

That's when the warning bells sounded and a red light started flashing above my head.

No, I mean literally, not metaphorically. Matt must have pushed the emergency-call alarm-bell as he leant forward on the bed. Three nurses came running towards me prepared to save my life, if required. They seemed almost despondent to find that I was perfectly fine and nowhere near a crisis of any kind.

"Just be careful next time, young man," the irritated sister lectured. "This is no place for people to be setting off alarms willy-nilly you know." And with that she turned and swished down the ward.

After such a start, you would have thought that the only way to go was up. But seeing him there twitching away looking less like a boyfriend and more like someone having an epileptic episode, I realised that our time had passed. After nearly an hour of stilted (me) and uncomfortable (him) inconsequential (both) chat, I decided to broach the subject of our relationship, but not before asking him to close the curtains. Obviously I knew that this would have no effect on Doris's ability to eavesdrop. She'd not turned a single page of her *Chat!* magazine since he'd arrived and normally she'd have read it cover to cover before she'd finished her cup of tea, which at that moment was cooling rapidly, untouched, on her trolley table. It was obvious that my visitor had caused a bit of a stir and would probably be topic of conversation par excellence for quite a while on our little ward, but closed curtains at least gave the appearance of privacy.

"Matt?"

"Yeah?"

"I think it'd be better if we just left things, for now."

"Huh?"

"You know, I'm going to have loads of stuff on my mind and I don't think I can handle a relationship." And you didn't even bring me any grapes, you tight-arsed pillock.

"Oh . . . er . . . OK."

All of a sudden, he looked somehow smaller and less sexy and he was getting more weasel-like with each second that passed.

"Maybe when I get out of here we should get together or something." Either that or I can get Doris to send someone round to break your legs, you weak-willed piece of . . .

"Yeah . . . er . . . OK." He looked at me and a brief flash of relief passed over his face. "If you're sure?"

"Yeah, I'm sure. It's for the best. I'll give you a call . . ." When hell freezes over, I thought to myself, but instead I simply said, "When I get out of here."

And apart from a half-hearted attempt on his part to kiss me goodbye, that was the demise of the KateMatt beast.

"Good on yer, love." Doris smiled just after giving Matt the evil eye on the way out. "Just like my old dad used to say, cut out the dead wood before it kills the tree."

I smiled at the thought of Doris's father being a tree surgeon in between shifts 'down't pit' (did they have pits in Manchester back then?) and found myself cheered up by the sight of two huge thumbs up and wide-toothed grin coming from Renee in the bed opposite.

I know you think that I'm just being brave and covering up my heartache with light banter, but to tell you the truth I really was relieved to end things with Matt. I really did have more important things to think about.

Chapter Eight

Bad News and Thai Food

"Are you waiting for someone?" the waitress with the life-worn face enquires as she passes my table on her way back to the kitchen, arms piled high with the remains of the lorry drivers' breakfasts: greasy plates and mugs with oil-marked lip-outlines.

"Aren't we all?" I say mischievously.

"Not me," she says with a breezy smile that lights up her eyes.

"Amen to that!" I call after her.

She returns a moment later with a disinfectant dish-cloth and starts wiping down tables. The sterile smell returns me instantaneously to the hospital ward . . .

* * *

"You'll never walk again."

Devastating words, granted, but when you actually hear them they take you by surprise, even if you are expecting

69

them. That morning, the words seemed to drift over my head like smoke, wisping in and around, never seeming to touch any part of me. My immediate response was: "Oh really?"

I'd been so used to doctors coming up to me and saying stuff that I didn't quite understand that I'd already amassed an entire store of ready-to-use platitudes ('Oh really' and 'Oh, OK' being by far the most popular).

"Miss Townsend, I don't think you heard me. Although we try to be positive in our prognoses, the sheer devastation caused by the complete dislocation of your right knee leaves us with no other option than to explore the reality that you will never walk again." My consultant, Mr Holland, repeated, this time much more firmly.

Before I responded, I surreptitiously checked that they hadn't whipped off both my legs in the night while I was sleeping. Having been introduced to the other occupants of the ward, I knew that there was a slight possibility that they may have got a bit carried away with the limb removals. No, they were both definitely still there and my hand felt the now-familiar cold metal of the ex-fix. I looked up at Mr Holland. I was speechless for a moment.

"B-b-but . . . why not?" I eventually managed to stutter, "I-I-I've got my legs still – why c-c-can't I use them?"

He looked down at me as if I were a particularly dumb child. "Well, for starters, even if your body were to eventually get over the trauma, it's highly unlikely that your knee will ever be stable enough to actually carry your body-weight and enable you to walk. The top half of your leg was almost completely separated from the bottom half. It was quite astonishing really. There was only a centimetre or two of the anterior ligament holding the two halves together. We had to completely reconstruct your knee. Perhaps if you were less . . .um . . . perhaps if you were carrying a tad less um . . ."

"You mean, if I wasn't such a fat porker?"

"Er. . . um . . . yes . . . quite." To my surprise, my young, but exceedingly venerable consultant blushed, coughed self-consciously and continued. "Although, if we're really investigating the miraculous, and of course a certain optimisim could be appropriate at this juncture, we might be able to fix up a brace and maybe then you could learn to walk again."

All in all I thought he managed to recover quite well, under the circumstances. I was so busy giving him an internal round of applause for maintaining his composure that it took a while for his words to actually penetrate my brain. That was the best-case scenario? I was utterly numb. Eva started her ritual screaming once more and for the first time since this nightmare began, I felt like screaming along with her. I took a very slow, deep breath to steady myself mentally and looked at Mr Holland in confusion.

"But on a practical level, even the brace would be highly unlikely given your . . . um . . . proportions.

"I don't understand. Why do I have this metal thing then, if it's not actually going to get any better?"

"You must remember, Miss Townsend, that 'metal thing' saved your leg. You have to admit your chances, however slim, of actual mobility are far increased with your limb intact. At least that way you may be able to stand up." His voice suddenly softened and he went on. "You had a serious fall, more serious than anything I have ever encountered. You have had massive trauma to your leg and your knee was

71

completely dislocated. The fact that you are still alive after the substantial blood loss from the artery is a big plus. No one knows exactly how a body will heal. The external fixator will give you the best possible chance of getting out and about again, but we have to be realistic. You will probably need a wheelchair for the rest of your life."

"Oh, OK." I mumbled.

"I'll be round again tomorrow, Miss Townsend." And with that he turned and strode over to Renee's bedside. I looked at my watch. Soul-destroying news and it wasn't even 9.00 a.m.

* * *

It could have been five minutes, it could have been an hour: time is meaningless when it is the only thing you have left, an indefinite amount of time stretching in front of you like one of those never-ending highways in Texas. But for a while, I understood Eva. I felt the misery and inner pain which is so acute that the only way it can be vocalised is in agonised screams. I still didn't know what news Eva had been given to make her feel such terror, but I finally knew why she kept the whole ward awake with her racket during the night. In fact I was seriously considering doing a bit of screaming of my own. Luckily, one of the nurses had insightfully assessed the situation and had taken it upon herself to make me a strong, sweet cup of tea and close my curtains to allow me the only privacy a hospital ward affords. I don't know which nurse or when she did it, but I was glad she had.

It must have been around lunch time as I could hear the metal trolleys full of food cunningly disguised as grey mush trundle into the ward. Knowing that at any minute a nursing assistant would be popping her head through the curtains and asking me if I fancied some lunch, I was preparing my Greta Garbo 'I-vant-to-be-alone' face to show her. When, as expected, I heard the curtain swish, I turned my face to my pillow and mumbled, "Go away."

"Oh, OK, then." Jane's voice wafted over.

"Jane?" I turned to see the only person who could possibly make me feel better. "Oh, Jane!" It was more of a guttural choke than actual words and immediately the up-until-now-suspiciously-absent tears arrived and coursed in huge rivers down my cheeks.

Jane moved quickly over to the bed and grabbed me in a tight hug.

"Gen told me what the doctors said. She talked to them this morning. We'll get through this." Jane's voice was getting thicker and thicker and I could tell that she was also crying. "We'll get through this together."

It turned into one of those awful, but strangely cleansing, crying sessions, with snot and everything. I don't know how long we were snivelling, but eventually we located my box of tissues and started to sort ourselves out.

"I have Thai food."

I couldn't help but laugh at the matter-of-fact way in which she said these words. It is at times like these that I truly believe that Jane really is psychic. She always knows the perfect thing to say at dodgy times. There were perhaps a hundred things that could have or should have been said given the news, but who else would choose that particular moment to inform me that she's brought an entire Thai banquet?

"Green curry?" I laughed/cried.

"Green curry, red curry – when Anil heard you were in hospital, I swear he even wanted to try and make a purple curry, just for you."

She manoeuvred the wheelie-table in front of me and started unpacking the feast. She even produced plates, chopsticks and the special serviettes in the shape of swans that always made me smile. "Anil says whenever you need another fix, you should ring him from the hospital phone and he'll send his no-good-lazy-nephew, who by the way is staying in Manchester for a while, over with all your favourites – no charge as long as you persuade the layabout nephew to get himself a proper job."

I laughed out loud, and for a brief moment I was back in Anil's restaurant listening to him moaning about his family problems and more specifically his sister's youngest son, who has a job which as far as Anil was concerned would 'bring shame upon whole family'. He'd never got as far as actually saying what this heinous job was, but the way he moaned about it, I'd always imagined that he was something excitingly unspeakable like a porn star or a dentist.

"This smells amazing – you have no idea what the food is like here."

"I can imagine, but don't you worry, Gen has made a rota. Starting Saturday, we've all been assigned days to bring you proper stuff to eat. She said that we couldn't condemn you to having to eat the hospital slush. Remember, she was here to have her appendix taken out and she's never recovered from the mashed potato." She giggled more to herself than anyone else, then turned to me and smiled. "Plus we've decided to bring our girls' nights to you here.

Obviously we won't be able to dance the night away, but we'll definitely smuggle some booze in."

Not for the first time, I remembered why I loved those girls so much.

"What's going on here then?"

Jane and I looked guiltily at the owner of the voice.

"Looks like you two are having a party." Mr Holland said disapprovingly.

"I-I-I . . . er . . . well, it's . . . um . . . her fault." I pointed a finger at Jane and tried to hide under my covers.

"Thanks, you grass," Jane mumbled under her breath. "You see doctor . . . um . . . I just thought she might . . . er . . . ." She threw a terrified glance in my direction which translated meant: can you get thrown out of hospitals for bringing Thai food?

"Well, ladies, I'd be prepared to overlook it this time as long as you save me some of the red curry and a healthy portion of that jasmine rice." Mr Holland grinned a huge grin. "I've just got to check up on Mrs Spence and I'll be back."

"Who was that?"

"My consultant, Mr Holland, why?"

"He's scrummy."

"You're married."

"You're not."

"Neither the time, nor the place."

"Don't tell me you've not thought about it."

"I've not."

"Liar."

"I've had other things to think about."

"Liar."

75

"He's my doctor, it's against the rules."

"I knew it. He's not married, though, so there might be a chance, you know." Jane winked at me cheekily.

"How do you know he's not married?"

"No ring."

"Not all blokes wear –"

"Scenario: You are married to a gorgeous hunk of a doctor –"

"Consultant," I interrupted.

"Even better, a gorgeous hunk of a 'consultant', who spends his whole time wandering sexily around hospital wards, meeting god knows how many different women every day. Would you give him the option of 'not' wearing a ring?"

"Point taken, but this really isn't the time."

"Put it away for the future."

"OK."

"Promise?"

"Promised."

"So what happened with Matt then?"

"How do you know something happened with Matt?"

"You didn't mention him as a reason not to get jiggy with Mr Sexy Consultant."

I was both irritated and impressed with Jane's ability to grasp even the tiniest nuance in every conversation regardless of the speed with which it was conducted.

"You know," I shrugged.

"Didn't bring you any grapes, eh?"

"Yeah, that sort of thing."

"You're better off without him. I never liked him that much anyway . . ."

Don't you hate it when you get out of a relationship and

then all your friends start telling you how they really couldn't stand the guy and then go off on a marathon let's-list-all-the-ways-I-disliked-him session. Jane had only just got started: ". . . and he never bought a round at the pub, did you notice? OK, he bought the odd round, but he only ever went when most people still had loads left and he only had to buy one or two. You completely changed when you were with him."

"No, I did not!" I was indignant now.

"Oh yes, you did – you ask the girls. And," she announced triumphantly as if it were her pièce-de-résistance, "he used to snort at the news! Whenever Trevor Macdonald mentioned anything to do with banking, he'd snort at the telly and shake his head. Did you notice that?"

Actually I hadn't. I knew we spent a lot of time with Jane and Craig, but she must have been studying him constantly. I had no idea what she was talking about, but I never got a chance to interrogate her as, just at that moment, Mr Holland strode back through the curtains.

"I've brought my own plate."

"So we see." Jane made even these words sound suggestive.

I butted in before she could say any more. "Help yourself. I think she brought enough to feed an army," I said, as Jane made space for him by vacating the chair and hopping up onto the end of my bed.

We watched in silence as he filled his plate. "Never usually get to eat Thai during the day – what a great idea!"

"Thank you, I had it all by myself, you know."

I kicked Jane with my good leg and said to Mr Holland. "So it's not against the rules to bring food in?"

"Not at all. Some of the sisters don't like it, but they all make exceptions, especially for long-termers like yourself."

"Long-termers?" Jane sought clarification. We all knew I should be prepared for a long stay in hospital, but up until this point no one had actually come right out and confirmed it.

"What she's asking is how long will I be here?"

He finished off his mouthful of curry and composed his doctor face. "Well, as you know, you had a serious –"

"Yeah, yeah, I know, I had a serious fall, blah, blah, blah – cut to the chase. How long?"

"Well, it's difficult to say . . ."

"Make an educated guess . . . please."

"Somewhere between four and six months. I'd guess nearer six, though."

I know this should have upset me, but how could it when the man giving me this news had a napkin stuck under his chin covered in red curry and rice on his cheek? Imagine how it would have been if we'd had spaghetti. Maybe this is a perfect way to lessen the effect of distressing news: make all doctors eat a bowl of spaghetti bolognese when delivering such information. That would make the world a better place, I mused.

Before I could refocus on Mr Holland, his bleeper went off. He made his excuses and disappeared. I looked over at Jane and shrugged.

"Oh well. It could be worse." She attempted an optimistic, but wry smile.

Eva began her wailing and I smiled sadly back.

"How?"

Jane swished open the curtains surrounding my bed and looked over towards Sarah's bed, I followed her gaze.

Together we watched in silence as the nurses helped Sarah out of bed and into her armchair. A thin hospital blanket was draped on her lap covering an empty space where her legs should have been.

Chapter Nine

Interlude

The advantages of being in hospital are few and far between. The most useful thing it gives you is time. You have plenty of time to do things that you normally put off because you're too busy doing stuff like cleaning your toilet or watching a fascinating documentary on the nesting instinct of lesser spotted Juju birds or whatever. So there you are with plenty of time and, as in my case, you are somewhat limited on options of how to use it. I used the time to think. Loads and loads of thinking. Now, if you'd been paying attention, you'll probably be saying to yourself, at least now she has something to lay awake at night worrying about. But would it surprise you to discover that not once in the entire time I was in hospital did I lie awake worrying. A deathly experience removes all need for angst. When you've been that close nothing really worries you that much. No, I used to lie in my hospital bed, on that crazy ward, and I would give myself thinking topics. What do I want out of my life?

Am I happy? Do I like myself? Do I like my friends? Sometimes I'd be really efficient and set a specific time period for each thought. I'd time it by Eva's screams. For example: What do I want out of life? That one was a three-scream-er. After her third scream, I'd change thinking topic.

* * *

So now that we're edging towards the end of January in my little story, do you feel that you know me yet? I know I've not really told you much about me physically, but is that the important bit? People get too caught up in that whole appearance thing. Would you feel more sympathetic to my story if I told you that I had blue eyes and blonde hair? Would it make any difference to my pain if I had green eyes and ginger hair? If I was Scottish? Welsh? Chinese? West Indian? Asian? The reason that I haven't told you is that it's not important what I look like.

Now I'll say something that might frighten you. I am you.

I am the you that is going along quite happily until you have an accident that almost kills you. Now I'm not telling you this out of spite, nor am I saying this to worry you. I'm simply saying that last year I had a job that I moaned about to my friends. I spent my time working, resting or playing. I passed most of my twenties oscillating between being terrified that I wouldn't get married and terrified that I might. I'd begun my thirties knowing exactly what I wanted out of life, but unsure how to get it. Most of my money went on clothes, shoes or drinking. My friends and I worked hard and behaved badly on 'Friday nights out with the girls'. I knew how to chat up guys if I wanted and how to get rid of them if I didn't. I'd had my fair share of boyfriends, one-night stands and hopeless but passionate assignations with men who I should have left well enough alone. But all of that past history, all of my life before the accident, faded away. By the end of my third week on the ward, my previous life was no more than a vague recollection. All I, and those around me, were concerned about was circulation, medication and bowel movements.

"Have you moved your bowels today?" the nurse boomed across the ward.

I looked over at her and nodded.

"What's that?" she bellowed.

"Er . . . no," I said in a hushed but firm voice.

"Did you say you had? 'Cos if you haven't we'll have to give you something to help it along."

"Um . . . what sort of something?" I tried to keep my voice just slightly above a whisper, to encourage a modicum of decorum to what was essentially a very private matter.

"I'll get you some." With that she stuck her head out of my curtains and roared down the ward: "Helen, can you get me some Fybogel – she's constipated in here." I suppose I'm lucky she didn't call out for an enema.

That's when I realised that things were never going to be the same again.

That sentence was a lie.

The actual point when I realised that things had irrevocably changed was the evening after I had my catheter removed. The evening I experienced 'THE BEDPAN'. But that can wait as I'll probably need to work up to it, so let's just pretend for now that the overly loud nurse shouting out my bowel movements was the point of no return.

Chapter Ten

The Doctor – Eminem Combination

I very soon learned that hospitals were all about routine. The nurses had so much to do that they had to get all their patients in some form of order. It's just like new mothers forcing their babies into a routine that bears no resemblance to what the child needs or wants; it's all about getting it into a routine that fits in with the mother.

At the stroke of 7.00 a.m., all the lights would go on (it was winter, remember?) and the breakfast-cereal trolley would come trundling in, followed by a few nurses. As I was at the far end of the ward, I kept my eyes closed and listened to them working their way up to me.

"Would you like a cuppa, Sarah?"

"Fuck off!"

"That's a lovely way to talk to me, isn't it? How about I put your cuppa here and I go get you some cornflakes?"

"Piss off, and leave me alone!"

"There you go, cornflakes, with just a little bit of sugar."

"Bitch."

On the other side of the ward I heard, "How about you, Renee? Would you like a cup of coffee?"

"Oh, Nurse, you know I don't like coffee. It's tea for me or nothing."

"Black, no sugar?" the nurse asks with a smile in her voice.

"Ooh, Nurse, you're playing games again. White with three, just like yesterday."

"Just thought you might like a change today, Renee, that's all."

"I like it how I like it, Nurse."

This was going to be a good day – the voice talking to Renee was Suzanne, one of the nicer nurses on the ward. She was almost always on duty with Karen. They were both around my age and were full of fun. They seemed to realise that there was enough sadness in a hospital without the staff adding to it unnecessarily. I could have a good laugh with them and they made me feel somehow normal again. Yep, this was going to be a good day.

"Wake up, sleepy-head, breakfast's here."

"I'd like the eggs benedict and the smoked salmon please." I joked.

"Yeah, and I'd like a millionaire and a private jet, but you'll have cornflakes and I'll go home to my boring old man tonight." Karen chuckled and handed me a bowl of cornflakes and a strong black coffee.

"Thanks, Karen. How's your day so far?"

"Fine, fine, I stumbled around my house in the dark this morning, couldn't even find a matching pair of socks." She lifted up her uniform trousers to reveal a sports sock on one foot and a cartoon character on the other. She chuckled, "Still, it makes life interesting, doesn't it? How're you doing today?"

"I'm getting by. Things could be worse."

Karen squeezed my hand and smiled. "That's the spirit, girly. Ooh, guess what?"

She sounded so excited, I had to ask, "Go on then, what?"

"Mr Holland is coming to see you today after rounds. He wants to have a chat."

"Something wrong?"

"No, that's just it! There's nothing medical for him to talk about. He said he just wants to have a chat."

"So what's so exciting about that?"

"He usually never comes back to the wards after rounds." Karen had a glint in her eye. "You lucky, lucky thing!"

"Karen, I'm shocked. Just exactly what are you trying to suggest? As a medical professional you should know better," I tutted. "I'm sure he just wants to pop by to let me know that I only have a week to live or something. That's about all I get from him these days."

"Whatever," she smiled and started to turn away, but turned back and winked. "He's not married, you know . . . Right, Doris, what would you like for breakfast?"

And with that she moved on leaving me wondering why everyone around me seemed to be so intent on informing me of the marital status of my consultant. Surely they could see that at this juncture in my life, the last thing I wanted to do was have any sort of romantic involvement. Plus how much more of a clichéd, doomed romance could there be than doctor and patient? There were laws against it surely?

After breakfast there was a lull for a couple of hours, while everyone was washed and dressed. Being bedridden, I needed help with my morning ablutions. I was still too physically weak to do much of anything for myself really and as for getting dressed, forget it – they just helped me out of one nightie and into another one. In a way, I was glad of it. It was liberating. I hadn't obsessed about the state of my hair, make-up, clothing or anything at all for weeks and the world hadn't come to an end. Although, if you think about it, maybe it was because the world had very nearly come to an end that I no longer needed to obsess about these things.

Anyway at 9.00 a.m., the doctor's rounds began. This was when all the fun started. Junior doctors, registrars and consultants, not forgetting student-doctors, all gathered round each bed in turn, discussing the occupants in that official/medical/dismissive way that doctors have. At the beginning I used to pipe up and say: "I am here, you know, there's no need to talk about me as if I'm not here!" But it made no difference and the nurses really didn't like it when you, the patient, had the nerve to interrupt the consultant. After my initial outbursts, I was kept firmly in check by the staff nurse's evil eye, daring me in that 'go ahead, punk, make my day' sort of way to open my mouth.

The consultant would rehash the injuries, a little daily reminder of how my life as I knew it was over. Then they spent a little while prodding and probing, lifting up dressings and either frowning or smiling depending on what they saw. They inspected the ex-fix to ensure that everything was shipshape and then they addressed me directly.

"So, Miss Townsend, how are we feeling today?"

Again, at first I used to say cute little things like 'I dunno about you, but I feel like crap warmed up and served on toast' or 'I'm kept awake most nights by a screaming banshee, I have to listen to old women droning on for hours on end about Mrs Jackson's piles and I've been offered more boiled sweets than any one person can take, but apart from that I'm fine and dandy, how about you?' Then I realised one small thing. They don't really want to know. The only reason they ask is to make sure that you haven't actually expired while they've been discussing you. All they needed from you as an answer is a sign of life, however vague.

So I simply said, "Fine, thanks, Doctor."

They then all nodded quite happily and continued with the discussion of future prognosis. At the beginning, I used to listen avidly, but after a while I realised that it's just too depressing, so I picked up my Walkman and played some loud angry music – Eminem is wonderful for this. In fact I think they should issue Eminem CDs to all patients. Not being as confident in my profanity as Sarah, I found it therapeutic to be able to sing/rap along with him and swear to my heart's content. I especially enjoyed being able to shout 'I just don't give a fuck!' quite loudly and watch the shocked faces of the students before lifting the earphones and announcing innocently: "I'm sorry, did I say that out loud?"

After the doctor's rounds, the medication trolley was wheeled in. All conversation would cease, everyone would stop what they were doing and watch the trolley's progress like vultures waiting for lions to finish with a carcass. It wasn't a great loss, trust me. Mostly the conversation was a meaningless discussion on some form of bodily function – do old women talk about anything else? I might discuss this later, because I have a lot to say on this subject, but now's not the time. Hospitals turn normal people into the closest approximation of the junkies that you see hanging around parks in the undesirable parts of town. We were all dependant on the medication trolley and needed the pain-killers just as keenly as we needed water and food. I really didn't want to imagine how much pain I would have been in if I didn't receive, every four hours on the dot, those five tablets of varying colours and sizes. And every time I heard the trolley being wheeled in I put my hands together and thanked the heavens for the wonders of modern medicine. Even Sarah found it in herself to be very nice indeed to the nurse wheeling the meds trolley.

At 11.00 a.m. precisely, physiotherapists swarmed onto the wards like a plague of locusts. Two to a bed, they gathered round and started inflicting the most awful torture upon the incumbents. At least what with all the noise emanating from behind the curtains, I'd always assumed that it was torture. Luckily they always left me alone, so I was never quite sure what pain they were actually inflicting. Somehow by the time they opened the curtains the patients were always out of bed and sitting in the armchairs with pained expressions on their faces. They would then remain in the armchairs for the rest of the day until, in the early evening, a different set of physios would return to inflict more agony and deposit them back into bed.

They say that somewhere there's a bullet with your name on it. Well, that day was the day that my number came up. For the first time I took off my headphones to see two physios standing beside me. Surely they were next to the wrong bed? They didn't want me, did they? I looked around, panic-stricken. DID THEY?

When the male physio opened his mouth what he said sounded like one word: "MissTownsendcanIcallyouKatherine?-It'stimetogetyouuup."

"Huh?"

He was big and brawny, and in fact my first thought was that he looked like a bouncer or an enforcer of some kind. Were it not for the fact that this colossal man was dressed in the standard physio's uniform it wouldn't have been too far-fetched to assume that Doris had sent one of her boys round to see to me.

The female physio, a rather athletic-looking, extremely pretty, blonde-haired woman of about twenty-five leant over the bed and said with a friendly smile: "Katherine, we need to get you up now." They were playing good cop/bad cop.

Couldn't they see that I was very poorly? I'd had a very severe injury. They couldn't seriously be considering moving me at this delicate stage, could they? In fact this is exactly what I asked them, to which they both smiled their physio smiles and repeated, "It's time for you to get up now, Katherine."

The female, who introduced herself as Lynn, began removing the bedclothes from around me and spent a short while examining the external fixator. It was attached to my leg with four longish pins, two of which were approximately two inches apart and fixed into the top part of my shinbone, just below the knee. The other two were fixed two inches apart into my lower thighbone. These four pins were connected horizontally with a complicated but essentially sturdy titanium bar. After her inspection, Lynn pronounced me ready.

"Right, very slowly now, can you sit up for me?"

I tried to voice my doubts that this was actually possible

at this stage, but the firm hand of the male physio (who I later found out was called Chris as most male physios seem to be called) encouraged me on my way.

Now I don't know if you have ever spent nearly three weeks on your back in bed, but just the raising of my head sent me into a dizzy spin and I thought I was going to die, faint and throw up, not necessarily in that order, more like at the very same time. Chris allowed me to fall back into my prone position and I felt like saying, 'See, I told you I'm just not ready'. But strangely I wasn't able to speak.

Lynn and Chris stood away from the bed for a few minutes and I thought that they'd leave and try again another day when I was feeling better, but instead, Lynn came back to me and said, "Right, let's have another go."

I felt the hand on my arm once more and that masculine, whole-sentence-in-one-word voice said: "Onetwothreego," and he hauled me upright. "Thereyougohowyoufeeling?"

The air came rushing out of my lungs so quickly my whole chest seemed to crack in half. "I'm a bit dizzy, but I think I'm OK – my chest hurts though."

There I was thinking that this was the end of their torture. They wanted me up and here I was sitting upright. They could go now. Unfortunately they made no move to leave my bedside.

"Right now, let's get you out of bed."

OUT OF BED! They must be kidding. With what must have been the most terrified expression seen since a Comms controller in Texas heard the words 'Houston, we have a problem' I squeaked: "You're joking, right?"

"Oh Katherine," Lynn sent a patronising smile in my direction, "you'll soon learn that we never joke about these things." Chris grunted his concurrence and grabbed a firm hold on my shoulder.

"Right, when I count to three, I want you to move your good leg so that it is hanging off your bed." As she mentioned my good leg, she gave me a comforting pat. "Are you ready?"

"No!"

"One, two, three, go!"

With an incredible amount of effort, I managed to heave my leg round. I could feel the blood rushing down to my toes and my leg started to tingle, not an altogether unpleasant feeling so my confidence grew slightly. This wasn't going to be as bad as I thought.

"Right, now this time you need to move your bad leg, and swing it round, OK?"

"But it won't bend, will it? I mean it's fixed straight." I was willing to try anything to stop this from happening, but realised that with these two, it was only delaying the inevitable.

"Don'tworryI'llsupportitalltheway." Chris attempted a smile, but it really didn't make me feel any better.

"Are you ready? One, two, three!"

With Chris's hand under my leg I heaved the muscle and lifted it round.

Now, I have never had a baby, but people tell me it's the most excruciating pain you can ever experience and the only way I can describe the amount of pain that I felt at that moment would be to liken it to giving birth to a baby the size of Wales.

I heard what I thought was Eva starting up again and it wasn't until I heard Lynn's soothing voice saying, "Hush now, you're OK. We've got you," that I realised that the screaming was emanating from me.

Chapter Eleven

Dough Balls and Slanging Matches

I read somewhere that friends are the new family. Remember I had plenty of time on my hands, so I read a lot. Not books though. Curiously, I could not manage to read more than two pages of a novel. Every time I started, I'd end up reading the same sentence over and over again. This phenomenon I called 'Hospital Brain' – a condition where your mind becomes unable to concentrate on anything for any period longer than five minutes. Thoughts rush into and out of your head with such speed and regularity that it simply becomes easier not to dwell on anything lengthy at all. I don't know why this occurred: there was no official explanation for it. I asked Mr Holland once during his rounds. He'd asked me if I'd been experiencing any unusual reactions to my medication. Having never before imbibed a combination of morphine derivatives, paracetamol, ibuprofen, diclofenac, amitriptyline and sleeping pills on a regular basis – I didn't know what the 'usual' reactions were.

But seeing as he'd asked I thought I should say something. Although I knew that it might not be completely relevant, I mentioned my lack of concentration and he just grunted something along the lines of 'It's to be expected really, don't you think?' and then focused his students' attention on more important matters (the state of my anterior and posterior ligaments to be precise).

Therefore, having no formal explanation for my lack of concentration, I decided to make the best of it. I devoured entire articles from the magazines provided on a regular basis by Gen and Jane, so I am now full to the brim with completely useless information and interesting conversational titbits. Thanks to my reading material, I know how to snare a man, seduce him, excite him sexually, cook him meals, spice up his working day, buy him new clothes, discover if he is having an affair, confront him, and dump him: an entire course of a romantic liaison guided by the psychologists and relationship experts of *Cosmopolitan*, *New Woman* and *Marie Claire*. Am I the only person to notice that these women's magazines don't actually talk much about women at all? They all seemed obsessed with things to help women deal with men. They should really call them men's magazines.

With the help of Louise's selection – *Elle*, *Vogue* and *Harpers* (she's a sophisticated lady, don't you know) – I explored page upon page of clothes that I could never ever afford and even if I could afford them, I would never fit into them and even if I could afford and fit into them, I would rather walk around naked than be seen dead wearing them. But I poured over them as intently as if they were a cure for cancer or a new way to turn tinfoil into gold.

So, friends the new family, eh? Well, on my ward, I was

the only one who took this literally. Two weeks after her first visit, my mother had tired of playing the concerned parent role and slinked back off home taking my father with her. My nineteen-year-old brother had 'kindly' offered to stay in my house, 'to make sure it's OK', but we both knew that it had more to do with his feelings of freedom from my mother than any feelings of concern for my home's safety. My one stipulation was that all breakages must be paid for and all stains must be professionally cleaned. Let him have his moment in the sun, I thought to myself.

Jane, Gen and Louise visited me on a regular basis, bringing provisions and reading matter. I had a varied diet of both. The nurses quickly dubbed my cubicle 'Katherine's Brasserie' and Mr Holland was often among the valued clientele, stopping by whenever he smelt something interesting wafting from behind my curtains. I don't know what I would have done without the girls, especially in the early days.

Of course, as expected, I hadn't seen Sandi since the Playstation delivery. I wasn't upset: I understood how much effort that visit alone had cost her. But sometimes, in my lowest moments, I craved her insatiable sense of humour and energy. Jane tried to make up for it, but we all knew that the five of us were friends for a reason. All the individual ingredients made up something that works – like the secret recipe of Coke – no one knows what it is, it's just right. Without Sandi, we were the 'New Coke': it looks the same, it smells the same, but it's missing something.

So it was a Friday night in the second week of February and Louise had brought a full spread from Giovanni's: dough-balls, garlic bread, four different types of pasta and a pizza with everything. As was usual on Friday nights, the nurses had rearranged my painkillers so that I could drink a smidgen of alcohol (unofficially, of course). Jane, even though she herself was unable to drink, had selflessly brought a few bottles of a cheeky Chilean red and I was having a ball. For those few hours on a Friday, I could almost forget that I was injured.

I told them all about the funny events of the week in the hospital.

"So, there I was, sat there under the x-ray and the guy was arranging my knee underneath, like I was some bizarre still life. Then he asks me the strangest question."

"Would you like something for the weekend?" Gen giggled.

"Are you going anywhere nice this year?" Louise suggested with a smirk.

"Want some hot 'n' sexy beef action?" Jane cackled.

"Nope. He says, do ya fancy having a look at something else while you're here?"

"What did he mean by that?" Louise piped up, as ever the stickler for correct explanations.

"He just wanted to know if there was any other part of my anatomy that I fancied taking a peek at while he had me under the x-ray."

"Huh?" all three girls said in unison.

"I swear. Apparently he's a trainee and he's allowed to do three films per week, for training purposes, as long as the patient doesn't mind. He had one left, was just about to go off shift and wondered if there was specific bit of my insides I fancied seeing 'up close and personal'."

"So what did you do?" Gen was gobsmacked, but laughing.

"I asked him to check whether I had child-bearing hips!"

We chuckled together for a while until Louise piped up, "And have you?"

"Well, apparently so. He reckons with my bits, it'd be like whizzing down the slide at one of them waterparks. *Wheeeee!*"

We were laughing so hard that we didn't notice the curtain being pulled back.

"So the witches' coven is in session, is it?" Mr Holland enquired. "Miss Townsend, I'm shocked. I assume that's not red wine I see in your hand."

Four pairs of eyes alighted on his smirking face and as one we sighed in wonder.

I'd heard that sort of sigh before. I was at my local cinema watching *Legends of the Fall*, the place was packed to the rafters with women and their uncomfortable fidgeting boyfriends, the story had just started and in about the fifth scene, Brad Pitt's character appeared. At first we saw him from behind in a long sweeping shot. But then the camera closed in on him and he turned around. His face filled the entire screen. That was when I heard the collective sigh. It was a sigh that combined longing and lust, desire and ecstasy: in essence it spelt SEX (double underlined with capitals).

Even though my consultant was a fairly frequent visitor, he never failed to cause this kind of stir. I'm sure there's a logical explanation. It could probably be explained chemically, the introduction of testosterone immediately causing a rapid increase in the oestrogen levels or something, but all we knew was that whenever he appeared, we all felt hot and flushed.

Gen, as always, was the first to recover, "Mr Holland, nice, er, to see you. Do sit down . . . um . . . balls?" She held out the bag of dough-balls oblivious to the double meaning and the rest of us giggled like naughty schoolkids. "What?!" She glared at us and then comprehension dawned and she burst out laughing.

"So," I ventured once we'd all calmed down a little, "to what do we owe the pleasure of this visit, Mr Consultant?"

"Oh, I've been catching up on my paperwork and just thought I'd pop in."

"Yeah, right. Give him a bowl of pasta, Gen."

"No, actually I can't, I'm having a late dinner tonight."

"A hot date?" I teased. Despite myself I was praying, 'please say no, please say no'.

"Actually, no."

Phew! Now we were all intrigued.

"Out with the lads?" Jane piped up.

"Nope."

"Old girlfriend?"

"Nope."

"Old wife?"

"Never married."

"Oh, for God's sake, just tell us, won't you?" The exasperation oozed out of Louise's voice – she never was any good at guessing games. I remember she threatened to stab me once, on a drunken night at college, during a game of animal, vegetable and mineral.

"Now where's the fun in that?" He smiled and stood up. "Goodnight, ladies."

After he'd excused himself, the mood went a bit flat, so I thought it would be fun to hear about Sandi's adventures.

"How's Sandi?" I asked the girls.

Jane and Louise looked at Gen. Obviously something was up and Gen had drawn the short straw.

"She's gone."

"Gone where?"

"To Australia."

At first I thought the red wine was reacting badly with the drugs still in my system. I could have sworn she'd said Australia. "Did you just say Aust –"

"Australia, yes."

"Why is she in Australia?"

Again Jane and Louise tried to pretend they weren't in the room.

"Because she's stupid."

"Huh?"

"It's all Jane's fault."

You have to hand it to Gen, she's brilliant at passing the buck when she needs to.

Jane suddenly snapped to attention. "What d'you mean my fault?"

"You're the one who did the cards." Gen looked at her with that 'go on tell me I'm wrong' look she has sometimes.

"Only 'cos Louise told me that Sandi was driving her crazy and if I didn't do them, she'd sue me for pain and suffering." Jane pointed an accusing finger at Louise.

"That's not fair. You weren't the one who was being kept up all hours of the night listening to her depressing whining and moaning. All you had to do was do her cards, say something positive and she'd have been fine. You know how worried she was." Louise's voice was getting higher and higher pitched: uh-oh, storm's a-brewing.

"And whose fault is that?" Jane shouted, glaring at Gen, "Certainly not mine! I wasn't the one who told her about worst-case scenarios."

(From that point on it got a bit confusing – it was like one of those *Eastenders* fights. For Gen, Louise and Jane – read Peggy Mitchell, Pauline Fowler and Pat Evans).

Gen: "She asked me, I told her."

Jane: "You didn't have to tell her everything, you know what she's like."

Louise: "You can bloody talk, you and your, 'ooh, let me get my cards!' As if they've been any good to anyone ever." (Louise should have known not to get involved when Jane and Gen were at each other's throats).

Gen: "There's no need to be nasty."

Louise: "And why not – you've never been backward in coming forward."

Jane: "And who asked you, Miss I-don't-care-about-anyone-enough-to-worry-when-my-best-friend-nearly-dies cold-faced cow!"

Louise: "Now that's not fair. I was the first one to get to casualty. I didn't roll up half an hour later like some people."

Gen: "And what's that supposed to mean?"

Jane: "Well, you have to admit, it did take you bloody ages to get here."

Gen: "I was working in Sheffield. I didn't know the dozy cow was going to fall down her stairs, did I? Some of us have real jobs, you know. We can't all fanny around with bloody playing cards, now can we?"

Jane: "They are tarot cards, as well you know, (dramatic pause) Imogen."

Cue sharp intake of breath from the rest of us while

Gen simply went bright red and speechless with rage. Unfortunately Jane hadn't finished.

Jane: "And fanny around? You didn't call it fannying around when I told you not to go to Cuba, that time just before that bloody great hurricane hit. You'd have been slap bang in the middle of it if it wasn't for me."

Louise: "You could have got that information from the weather channel, anyway."

Gen: "Who the bloody hell asked you to stick your nose in? I can argue for myself, you know."

"SHUT UP, ALL OF YOU!" That was me, shouting. I'd heard enough. Obviously I'd been involved in a sufficient number of these arguments to realise that if I'd let it go on any further, there'd be bloodshed. A tense hush descended.

"Alright. Someone tell me what has happened to Sandi." I looked at the girls one by one and finally prompted: "Gen?"

Louise started to complain. "Why her? I'm . . ."

I silenced her with a withering look.

Gen drew a deep breath and began: "Well, you know her history with this hospital?"

I nodded.

"I told her about what your consultant told you about worst-case scenarios and she went off on one. You know how she gets . . . well, she was convinced that something bad was going to happen to you."

"Something bad did happen. That's why I'm here."

"No. She thinks that something will happen to you here, in this hospital. She thinks the hospital is possessed or something and that you'll die here, like everyone else."

"But that's stupid. I haven't got cancer, I had an accident. And although I admit the level of conversation available on this ward is frustratingly banal and fluffy, I'm hardly a candidate for a stroke, not yet at any rate."

"That's what I told her, but it didn't make any difference. She wanted Jane to check the cards."

I looked at Jane, for clarification, "Jane?"

"I told her that I couldn't do them, 'cos it's your future not hers. It wouldn't work unless you cut the cards." Jane looked at me sadly. "In the end I did them and the bloody death card came up first, bold as bleeding brass. Typical!"

"So what's all this about Australia?" I looked at Louise.

"She said that there was no way that she's going to stay around and watch another person she loves die in this bloody morgue of a hospital. One day, she announced that she was going to visit you here and the next thing we knew she was ringing Gen from a Sydney hotel room."

"Why didn't you tell me all this was going on? All of you."

"We didn't want to worry you. You had enough on your plate," Gen mumbled. Jane and Louise nodded in agreement.

"So when's she coming back?"

"She said she'll come back when you're out of danger."

"Danger? I'm not in any bleeding danger."

Famous last words – I think you'll agree.

Jane had always warned me about tempting fate and I immediately wished those words hadn't been said out loud. But in the event, they were the last words spoken that night, because at that moment the nurse came through the curtains and basically threw the girls out for making such a commotion while the other ladies on the ward were trying to sleep. The girls whispered their apologies and sheepishly crept off the ward, promising to visit again soon.

Chapter Twelve

Bleach and Blood Samples

"Looks like you've taken root here, Missy." The waitress taps me on my shoulder, bringing me back to the present. The bad attempt at a 'deep south' American accent threw me for a moment and I look up at her, blinking.

"Huh?"

"Sorry, love, I watched a film last night and you just reminded me of a girl in it."

"What film was that?"

"I can't remember the title exactly, something about cafés. It was a good film; the young girl in it was just like you. She sat in the café for hours." She smiles a knowing smile, "She didn't say much either."

I don't know what to say so I just mumble an 'Oh'.

"You're not after a job, are you? It's just that the girl in the film was after a job, that's why she sat there so –"

"No, I'm not after a job," I interrupt.

"That's good, 'cos we ain't got no jobs here, apart from mine and I'm not about to let you . . ."

"Don't worry, your job is perfectly safe."

She peers at me suspiciously, "You've not just come out of prison, have you?"

"Huh?" She's completely lost me now.

"It's just that the girl, from the film, she'd just got out of prison and –"

"No, I've not just got out of prison. Although . . ." I paused, maybe I have in a way.

"Well, not that it's any of my business, of course . . . don't mind me, love, I'm just a bit nosy sometimes. People are always telling me that I should stop . . ."

She carries on talking and I tune her out, another useful skill learnt in the ward. Occasionally I nod, just to let her think that I am listening, but my mind is elsewhere. I look out of the café window and see my darling Harris glinting at me, waiting for me. I must look extremely sad at this point because the waitress taps me on the shoulder once more and says, "Cheer up, love. You know what they say, don't you?"

"Sorry? What?"

"If you're at the bottom, the only way left to go is up." She smiles once more and walks back towards the kitchen.

It's funny how when things are bad, we convince ourselves that it can only get better. Well, if there's one lesson I learnt from hospital it was this: when things are bad, there's always room for them to get just that little bit worse.

* * *

February 14th, Valentine's Day, and the Monday following my confident 'I'm not in any danger' remark. I'd spent most of the morning sucking up to Doris, who had overheard the 'banal and fluffy conversation' remark I'd made to the girls the night before and had taken it very personally indeed. After bribing her with a selection of upmarket women's magazines from the stockpile in my cabinet, I managed to appease her enough to stop her rounding up a geriatric posse to run me out of the ward.

So there I was lying in my bed in dread waiting for the physios to arrive, to inflict more pain and get me out of bed for the day, when Karen, the lovely nurse, came through my curtains. At least I thought it was Karen; I wasn't immediately sure because she was wrapped up in a papery-plastic-looking-gown-type-thingy, wearing gloves and a mask which covered her mouth and nose.

"It's Valentine's Day, Karen, not Halloween," I joked, but quickly realised that Karen wasn't smiling with me. "What's going on?"

"Look, Kate, don't worry, Mr Holland wants to take a look at your leg. I've just got to remove the dressings for him."

I hate it when they say things like 'don't worry', because it invariably means that there's something very real to worry about.

"Why the get-up then?"

"Just a precaution."

"What's going on?"

"Mr Holland will be here in just a sec."

Karen was avoiding my questions and she was having difficulty looking me in the eye – she always looked me in the eye. She was so distant and business-like that I began to fear that something serious was about to happen. I was starting to panic.

Mr Holland arrived and he too was dressed up in the same gear as Karen. His normally luminous eyes were dull and despite wearing a face-mask I could tell there was no hint of a smile on his usually charming face. He was solemn. He acknowledged my presence with a brief nod of the head and stared at the wound on my leg. I saw him shake his head and look over at Karen, shaking it once more for her benefit. Immediately Karen turned and left the cubicle.

"Miss Townsend, Katherine . . ." He'd never used that ominous tone before. Come to think of it, he'd never even used my first name before – never, not even when he was stealing my sweet and sour pork. It was strictly Miss Townsend. He was serious and I was frightened.

He paused for such a long time, I wanted to shake him and say 'tell me, tell me, tell me now', but no words left my suddenly dry mouth. I just stared intently at his face.

"Katherine, I have some bad news."

I think at this point I actually squeaked. It was an anguished noise that came from the back of my throat.

"You have developed MRSA in your wound here on your calf." He pointed to the spot where Karen had removed the dressing. "We'll have to take swabs from the pin-sites, here and here, to see if it has spread."

I looked at the point where the ex-fix entered my thigh and I swear I saw the skin crawl away from the pins in fear. "MRSA?"

"It's a bacterium; some call it 'the hospital bug'. It's fairly serious in a hospital situation."

Somewhere from the depths of my memory, I remembered reading about it in one of the magazines under the headline 'Superbugs – The Silent Killers'. It was all about how hospitals were the breeding-grounds for superbugs which were resistant to most known forms of antibiotics. And I'd managed to get one. Fear was swarming around my brain. I could feel it behind my eyes, in my temples. It was like a tiny insect eating away at me. I felt it in my nose; it began inching its way to the back of my throat. My windpipe started to constrict and I couldn't catch my breath.

Tears started forming and before I knew it I was crying in rivers. "Am I going to die?"

"Shh." Mr Holland grabbed a tissue and wiped away the tears. "Of course you're not going to die, silly. We can treat it. We're just going to have to move you out of the ward."

"Move me? Where? I don't want to go." Panic was hitting me in huge waves now. Leave the ward? Move me out? I felt like my world was being destroyed once more. This ward, this stupid, irritating ward, full of rubbish-uttering, sweet-offering old women, was the only place I felt safe and now they were taking me away because I had a superbug.

Before I knew it, Karen had returned with two other nurses I didn't recognise, all of them in gloves, masks and those stupid papery-plastic gowns. I felt like a leper, an unwanted, radioactive piece of detritus. Without warning they put down the wheels of my bed and began wheeling me out of the ward. As soon as we vacated the space, a similarly gowned cleaner began emptying my little cupboard and clearing the trolley table of my posessions. As we exited the ward I saw another cleaner begin mopping with such a strong bleach solution that even at a distance, the smell reached my senses and stayed with me as they wheeled me into a side room.

I looked around me. It was about the size of the second bedroom in my house – not tiny but by no means huge. It had walls the colour of strained sick and watery sunlight was filtering through the dusty blinds. This was to be my home for the next, well, however long it was going to be. Karen and the other nurses made several trips bringing all my stuff from the cubicle. A couple of nurses were fluttering around various parts of my body, taking my blood pressure, dressing my wounds, prodding around in my pin-sites with overlarge cotton buds taking swabs. They even stuck a few in my nose to make sure it hadn't got up there. Then a new type of medical person, dressed in a pink uniform, arrived and started inspecting my arm.

"Who are you?" I peered suspiciously at her.

"I'm a phlebotomist."

"Don't tell me, I've got fleas as well."

The woman laughed a patronising laugh and smirked. "No, I'm here to take some blood."

I know it sounds stupid to admit this now, bearing in mind that by this point I must have had six or seven surgeries, I'd had all sorts of stuff attached to some part of my body since the accident and they'd definitely drawn enough blood in the first couple of weeks to keep a vampire feasting for a few years, but I feel that this is the time to admit that I'm terrified of needles. How can this be? Well, think about it. Up until now, I had been full to the brim with morphine and feeling nothing much at all. They could have (and probably did) stuck needles in my eyeballs for all I cared. Hell, I would have even volunteered for acupuncture back then. But now, compos mentis and fairly clearheaded, the sight of this pink woman with a needle the size of the

Empire State building sent shivers down my spine and sweat oozing from my brow. I know, I know, it was stupid. Now, looking back, I know how silly it was. Even back then, I really had more pressing things to think about, but no one can really explain a phobia. So many things had been out of control. I'd had no say about any part of my life since January. So to the utter shock of the phlebotomist, I began to take back control.

"NO!" I bellowed.

"Er . . ." The woman's eyes flicked from side to side in confusion, "but . . ."

"I said, no!" I was still yelling – my mouth seemed to have a mind of its own. "No needles, no prodding, no blood. Sod off!"

"But . . ." She looked at the two other nurses in the room, who had both stopped their fluttering in shock.

"And you two can piss off out of it as well! Leave me in peace." I glared at them all with venom and bile, if that was possible. "Go on, fuck off, the lot of you! GO!"

The last word came out as a roar and the women seemed to react like silent-movie heroines who were in deep peril. They picked up their petticoats and ran for their lives. I felt elated, I felt a surge of power, I felt alive. I had taken control, I had experienced a brain rush, I had once more taken charge of my life. I had . . . I felt . . . I . . . I . . .

A tiny voice began to prod me in the most sensitive part of my brain: my conscience. I had screamed at three innocent women who were just doing their job. I felt terrible.

There was a gentle knock on the door. Karen poked her head through and extended her hand. A white handkerchief unfolded and she waved it in mock terror. "Is it OK to come in?"

"Yeah," I said with a defeated sigh.

Karen came into the room and sat down on the bottom of my bed. She held my hand and squeezed it reassuringly.

"Katherine? Um . . . Kate? I know you're frightened, but there are a few things that we need to do. I'll talk everything through with you in a little while, but first things first – we really need to take some blood. What with the MRSA and everything, we need to run some tests."

"I know, I know," I sighed.

"So can she come back in?"

"Yeah."

"Be nice to her, OK?"

"OK."

Karen gently got off the bed and returned to the door. Opening it, she poked her head out, "It's alright, you can come back in now."

There was a slight hesitation and then two pink women entered.

"Karen?" I tried to speak quietly and calmly, but my voice jarred even me. The pink women flinched. "I'm a bit . . . um . . . could you possibly . . . er?"

"Of course, that's what I'm here for." She came around the other side of the bed and held my right hand while the phlebotomist began tying a rubber-tube-type thingy around the top half of my left arm.

She tapped the inside of my arm a few times and prodded about trying to find a vein. Thinking she'd found one, she prepared her needles. I looked away and braced myself.

Remember what I said about things getting worse? Well,

surprise, sur-bloody-prise, she couldn't get the vein. She tried again, probing around, but seemed to draw a blank. The other pink woman stepped forward and took over. She worked with a bit more assurance and confidently plunged the needle in. Nothing. Nada. Missed again.

Four phlebotomists, a junior doctor, a ward sister and one supercilious registrar later, the vials remained empty. I felt like a cheap prossie at King's Cross – I'd had so many pricks and I was still no closer to being left alone. It was worse – by this time there were about eight people in my room, all inspecting my arms – one of them was even checking out my foot in desperation. Both arms were full of holes and bruised and still my veins were refusing to give up their blood.

"Someone call down to A&E." Karen's suggestion seemed to pass around the room getting more and more approval from the collected throng until finally the highest ranked (the arrogant registrar) nodded and a junior doctor was dispatched. Karen looked down at my panicked face. "Don't worry – if anyone can find a vein, an A&E doc can. You'll be done in no time."

Unfortunately, after my experiences so far, I didn't share her confidence, but along with the others in my room, I nervously waited for the arrival of the A&E doc. After twenty agonising minutes, a breezy young – frighteningly young, in fact – doctor came swishing into the room.

"OK, what do we have here? I've got ten minutes and I'm on my break."

Karen outlined the problem to him and he inspected my arms while I was trying to get the courage to vocalise my concern. He looked about twelve years old, for goodness sakes.

"Er . . . Karen?"

"It's OK, give him a chance."

I motioned for her to get closer and I began whispering in her ear, "But he's so . . . um . . . so very . . . um . . ."

"There you go!" The triumph in his voice very nearly outweighed his confidence. He waved three vials of blood at Karen and swooshed out of the room. I hadn't felt a thing.

"Wow," I gushed, "he's good."

"Yep," Karen nodded with a smile playing on her lips, "he sure is."

* * *

"So, how's my favourite patient? Rounds are finished – I'm all yours, for a while at least. No food today?"

Mr Holland's voice shook me out of the doze into which I'd slipped since the blood incident.

"Huh?"

"No chow mein? No pizza? Have your friends deserted you?"

"No, someone'll probably be in later."

"Oh, OK." He looked disappointed, but then remembered why he'd come. "So, here I am. I'm all yours."

"Huh?"

"Ask away!"

"Huh?"

"Katherine," he groaned. "Alright, let's start from the beginning again. You must have many, many questions floating around your mind. I'm here to answer anything you want to know."

"Anything?"

"Yes, anything."

"What's your first name?"

"I meant about MRSA, Katherine."

"It's Kate. Only my mother calls me Katherine. Anyway, you said anything I wanted to know."

"Are you sure you don't want to know that the full name is methicillin-resistant staphylococcus aureus?"

"Not particularly," I shrugged.

"I suppose it wouldn't amaze you to discover that according to some estimates as many as 80,000 patients a year get an MRSA infection after they enter the hospital, would it?"

"Not really."

"You know, Kate, I studied for a very long time to gather all this useful information – the least you could do is try and be interested."

"Oh, but I'm really interested," I smiled, "to know your first name."

He gave a big sigh. "Daniel."

"Can I call you Danny?"

"Nope.

"Dan-Dan? D?"

"You can call me Daniel. How's that?"

"Well, Daniel, I'm very pleased to make your acquaintance." I stuck out my hand to shake his, but he just laughed.

"Trust me, Kate, I'm already acquainted with parts of you that you've never seen."

"Why, Daniel, that's illegal surely? Can I report you?"

"I've been inside your knee, remember?"

"Oh, yeah. I forgot."

We smiled at each other and for a while, we sat in companionable silence. Eventually Daniel spoke: "Kate, it's not that bad really. Honest."

"So why have I been moved?"

"Not everything's about you, you know."

"Sorry?"

"It's all me, me, me with you, isn't it?" he chuckled. "We moved you for the safety of the other patients. In case you hadn't noticed, they are fairly elderly and it could be potentially dangerous if any of them contracted MRSA."

"So why isn't it dangerous for me? I'm the one with the superbug."

"You are a fairly, um . . . robust." He coughed. Do you think the cute consultant had difficulty broaching the 'weight' subject? Whenever he had to refer to it, he broke out in a coughing fit. "You're a comparatively um . . . healthy young woman. We'll just pump you full of antibiotics and you'll be fine."

"Can my friends still visit?"

"Of course, unless they're in the habit of fiddling around in your wounds and then touching up the elderly patients."

"No, I think they might be able to restrain themselves. It might be difficult for Louise once she's had a few, but I'm sure we can control her."

"Louise?"

"Blonde hair, sexy eyes?"

"Oh, the lawyer. Very protective of you."

"Yeah, well, they all are. How did you know she's a lawyer?"

"She threatened to ruin my career and, I think her exact words were, 'sue me until I was nothing more than a stain in the gutter', if anything untoward happened to you in the operating theatre. I've never seen her drink alcohol though."

"She doesn't, not here anyway. She can get a bit wild. Can you imagine the havoc she could wreak? No, she's only allowed the one glass of wine unless it's a special occasion."

"What's the story with the redhead? She doesn't drink either."

"That'll be Jane – she's preggers."

"OK." He sat back in the chair, literally twiddled his thumbs for a brief while, then looked back in my direction. "So, how are you feeling, now?"

"Better. Thanks, Daniel."

"My pleasure."

"By the way, do my friends have to wear gowns and gloves when they visit?"

"No. They'll need to wash their hands with an alcohol solution when they leave, but the staff will explain when they get here. Also, the nurses will run you through the cleaning procedure so you can prevent it spreading to any of your other wounds."

"How about pregnant Jane?"

"Tell her not to go near your wounds and she'll be fine."

A insistent beep sounded. It appeared to come from his crotch and I couldn't help laughing.

"Your bits are beeping."

"Thank you, Miss Townsend. I heard it." He pulled his beeper from his pocket and got up. "I'll have to go. I'll see you later on this week."

Before I knew it, I was alone once more. I listened to the silence and smiled. I hadn't been offered a boiled sweet in at least four hours. Maybe this wasn't going to be that bad after all.

Chapter Thirteen

Life's Not Like That

When I woke up the next morning, two things shocked me.

The first shock came when I opened my eyes and peered at my watch to see it was after eleven. I'd slept for more than fifteen hours and, for the first time, I hadn't been dragged awake at the crack of dawn. The second shock hit me when I looked around my room and saw the biggest bunch of flowers I'd ever seen in my life. There was a small envelope and a note from Karen, which explained that the flowers had been delivered late the previous evening, and rather than wake me, she'd taken the liberty of arranging them in a vase. I picked up the small envelope and opened it. It said: *Happy Valentine's Day, Love* X. At first I smiled – it had to be the girls and I was touched – but then I considered it more carefully. It couldn't be the girls; they would have signed off with 'The Coven' or 'The Witches' not 'X'. The more I thought about it, the more irritated I got. Don't get me wrong – I realise that that was the whole point of Valentine's Day and everything, but who on earth spends a small fortune on flowers and gives no clue as to their identity? Not even a slight vague hint. NOTHING!

I was reminded of one of those mid-nineties Hollywood romantic films, where the female lead, a cold businesslike-but-hiding-a-sad-childhood woman, inevitably played by a stunning and impossibly skinny brat-packer, receives a bunch of flowers from a complete stranger who doesn't sign his name. The stranger turns out to be a sensitive, romantic, caring, thoughtful, unavoidably full of inner sadness, but predictably rich gorgeous hunk, played by a teen-dream actor who, as he got older, moved into action movies. The film spun a seductive web of Romeo and Juliet-esque love and supplied the predictable happy-ever-after ending. If you weren't careful, you could believe that the world was really as warm and fuzzy as it is in the movies. But it's important to remember this tiny little fact: life is not really like that.

Most likely, the actors couldn't stand the sight of each other and spent most of their time in their trailers bitching about each other's halitosis. Later, the actor probably got locked up for slapping his girlfriend around and the actress probably spent the time between her various failed marriages flitting between rehab and liposuction.

What am I trying to say? I'm saying that I very nearly fell into that Hollywood romance trap and nearly started fantasising about who could have sent me the flowers, but I stopped myself and instead I simply spent around an hour just admiring their beauty and scent.

I literally stopped and smelt the flowers.

A nurse came in and brought me out of my contemplation. "Time for you to have a wash," she informed me and began assembling the required items. A washbowl was filled with warm water, my face-cloth was placed next to the bowl on the trolley table and my towel was located and handed to me. Then without warning, the end of the bed was raised, so that I was suddenly thrust into an upright position. Every action was executed with the utmost efficiency.

"Do you need any help?"

"No, I think I'll have a go at doing it myself today."

"Suit yourself. Oh, I nearly forgot," she retrieved a sachet of an orange and suspiciously smelly liquid from her pocket, cut the top off and emptied it into my water, "you have to use this. It's antibiotic and will stop the MRSA spreading to your other sites. Give me a buzz if you can't manage." She turned and was gone.

It wasn't as easy as I'd thought, but I won't go into details – you might be eating or something. Just imagine trying to have a wash when you're too weak to lift yourself up and your right leg is stretched out straight in front of you with bits of metal sticking out of it and you are completely unable to move in any direction without a major pain shooting up and down your leg. But I'm pleased to report that eventually I managed to cleanse myself sufficiently to feel slightly fresher.

Another funny thing is that I hadn't worn underwear since the accident. It was the first time in my life that I had gone without 'down under' for any longer than a close encounter with a member of the opposite sex. My breasts had been unrestrained for over a month and I was starting to fear that they were enjoying their freedom just a little bit too much. I laid there and jiggled them around for a while and obviously lost track of time, because that was the position that Gen found me in, when she arrived with a massive bag of jumbo haddock and chips (with extra vinegar) direct from the frying pans of Harry Ramsden's.

"Ooh, excuse me!"

"Didn't your mother teach you to knock before you enter a room?"

"I did knock, Miss Jiggly. You were obviously too wrapped up in your breasts."

"You're just jealous 'cos you'd need a microscope to find yours!"

We looked at each other and burst into a cacophony of mirth. We laughed and munched on our fish and chips, remembering old adventures and generally having a great time. Somehow it really didn't feel as if we were in a hospital. At least not until an ache appeared in my pin-sites and I remembered that I must have slept through the morning medication run.

"What's wrong? Are you alright? Should I get a nurse?" Gen's voice was full of concern. Even though I'd tried to hide the pain from her, it was no use: she was acutely insightful and immediately went in search of medication for me. In no more than five minutes, she returned with a tiny plastic cup filled with tablets. "They said that you were asleep when they came round this morning and the nurse was a bit frightened of waking you up. What's that all about?"

"I, well, I got a bit frustrated yesterday and, don't quote me on this, but I may have possibly, um, shouted a little at a few nurses." I sheepishly looked out from under my eyelashes in what I hoped was a cute 'Princess Diana' kind of way in an attempt to head off a Gen lecture on the injustice of public sector pay.

"So you threw a hissy fit and scared some poor nurses. You are such a bitch sometimes."

Oh well, the 'Diana' look didn't work, so I tried a faint groan.

"Don't you groan at me. You know that they're only trying to do their best. They get paid a pittance and have to do all the crappy jobs that this society asks of them. Did you know that they work long hours and are subjected to the most frightening violence from people that they are trying to help, for goodness sakes . . ." Gen sighed her I-don't-know-what-the-world-is-coming-to sigh.

"I know, I know. I'm really sorry. I did apologise, I'd been having a really tough day." I began telling her all about the virus, but she interrupted.

"Oh I know all about that. I rang your young Mr Holland last night. Actually . . ." It was Gen's turn to look sheepish. "I ring most days, just to make sure you're alright."

"You do?" My heart felt a tiny tug and tears started welling up. "That is so lovely."

God knows what was wrong with me – my emotions were so messed up, I was bursting into tears left, right and centre. In the previous thirty-odd years, I could only remember having cried a handful of times. But in hospital, I was single-handedly keeping the Kleenex company in business. I looked at Gen and because she hates mushy stuff, she gazed intently at her skirt-seam while shrugging her shoulders in that don't-even-think-about-mentioning-it-it-was-very-definitely-nothing way she has when she's embarrassed.

"Anyway," she coughed, "don't worry about the medication in the mornings. I've told them never to leave

119

you without it again. If you're sleeping, they'll leave the plastic cup on your table. OK?"

"Yeah, thanks Gen." I paused: "You know I really –" I was going to say 'love you', but she glared at me with a 'don't you dare' look and I changed my mind.

Gen coughed uncomfortably and after a brief pause, started chatting again. "They've changed the clothing ranges in Fashion Boutique again."

I knew exactly what was coming – as I may have mentioned before, Gen is very very petite and is forced to shop in the children's section of most shops. The only shop she likes is a small place called Fashion Boutique because they forgo sizing based on age and use a simple XS, S, M, L sizing structure, thus allowing her to pretend that they are 'normal' adult clothes. These clothing rants can last for ages, so I just got myself comfortable and fixed a sympathetic smile on my face.

"They've decided to call it Little Miss. Do you know how embarrassing it is to realise that you're a Little Miss 2? They've even got stupid bleeding cartoons on the labels. I can't go back there. I'll have to find somewhere else to go, it's horrifying!"

"Yeah, it sounds awful." I briefly considered changing the subject, but remembered that she'd not had one of these seething fits for quite a while, so it would probably do her good to get it out of her system.

"Someone told me that Dorothy Perkins have started doing stuff in a size four, so I went in and asked, but all the salesgirl did was laugh. Then, while still giggling she suggested that I try the petite kiddies section at Mothercare. Mothercare! I swear if she wasn't about six foot tall and I could have reached it, I'd have strung the bitch up by her ridiculous swan-like neck."

"Gen?"

"What?" Gen pouted.

"What does it matter? As long as the clothes fit, who cares if they're child sizes? What bloke in the heat of passion is gonna check out your labels?"

"That's not the point and you know it."

"There are plenty of small people. Everyone knows that Kylie Minogue is tiny and look at how popular she is. Do you think that all those blokes who slobber over her care where she buys her clothes?"

"It's alright for her, she's got a stylist who buys everything. She doesn't have to face the indignity of actually going in herself. Besides, she gets her stuff direct from the designers. They make it especially to her size. There's no way I could find someone who'd do that for me."

"All you have to do is find someone famous who is about your size and ask her who does her clothes."

"Like who?"

"Barbie?" I giggled.

"Ha-bleeding-ha." Gen glared at me. "Everyone's a comedian. Your Mr Holland seems to think that he's one as well, doesn't he?"

Does he? I hadn't really noticed. But then again he's not had too many amusing things to say to me, what with wheelchairs and superbugs. And I wished she wouldn't keep saying 'your Mr Holland' as if it was the 1950s and he was my betrothed. Oops, Gen was staring at me waiting for some kind of response. Another thought occurred to me. "How did you get him to tell you that kind of stuff? They're only allowed to tell family all the medical details, aren't they?"

"Yeah, that's what he said to me at the beginning. But I asked him if he'd actually met your mother? And then I asked him if he really wanted to have you finding out all the bad news from her? At least he had the good grace to agree with me. We've been in touch since then."

"I'm not sure I like you talking about me to my consultant. You are sticking to medical matters?"

"What else would we be talking about?" She had a mischievous glint in her eye as she spoke the next words. "He's not married you know."

"For the positively last time, ever, I know he's not married." I rolled my eyes in exasperation. Gen was still smiling and I became suspicious. "What else have you told him?"

"I may have mentioned somewhere along the line that you're not with Matt any more. Just to get his medical opinion on how sadness might affect you, of course."

"But I wasn't sad."

"Yeah, I know, I may have mentioned that too at some point." Gen smiled and then looked at her watch. "Oh well, I'd better be getting off. I have to go to Rochdale for a meeting. Jane said she'll be in tomorrow. She says she's bringing a surprise, although I'm not sure I should have told you that. She's starting to show now, you know. She'll probably bore you to tears with all her scan stuff. That's probably the surprise. Damn, I'll be late. I'm off."

"OK, then. You drive carefully," I called to her departing back. When Gen makes the decision to leave a room, she doesn't hang around – she's off quicker than a tart's knickers.

* * *

122

Later that afternoon, I was waiting for the physios to arrive to extricate me from my bed and deposit me into the chair. It's strange, but the act of sitting up, with my leg resting on a stool, had caused me incredible pain. I didn't know why or how it was so painful, but once sat in that chair, the only thought in my mind was when I could get back into bed. The throbbing pain came in longish waves, much as I imagined contractions to feel like, but unfortunately there was no bundle of joy at the end of it for me. Each time I sat out, I would send a nurse in search of the single solitary payphone which served the telecommunications needs for two entire wards. When the nurse returned, bearing the phone like a precious treasure, I would then ring Jane and explain to her in detail how horrible the pain was, in an attempt to prepare her for the unavoidable pain of childbirth. I imagined that I was a kind of public service for pregnant women, but Jane didn't seem to see it the same way.

After the first few times, the pain of sitting up had lessened, but even so, the longest I'd been able to sit out was around an hour.

When the physios eventually arrived, they had me out and sitting up in less than five, relatively pain-free, minutes. Before I had an opportunity to buzz the nurses to ask for it, one of them brought the phone to me. As I said before, hospitals are all about routine and the nurses thrive on it.

On the phone to Jane, I embellished slightly the amount of pain I was in and added, purely for effect, you understand: "Oh, but don't worry, you'll know soon enough just how much agony a body can stand without passing out."

That was when she finally snapped. "Why are you intent

on scaring the pants off me every day? I realise that it's going to hurt and I'm terrified enough already without you sticking your oar in and making it worse, thank you very much. It's not as if I'm getting that much sleep as it is. God knows, I won't get that much once the baby's here."

In the face of such naked angst, there was nothing I could do but apologise profusely and, drawing on my 'old women on ward' experiences, I proceeded to explain in graphic detail the latest condition of my wounds.

"Why are you telling me this?"

"Because it's all the news I have. I'm hardly going to start telling you about some great new club that I've visited, am I? What with me being stuck in this godforsaken place. I'm bored, Jane, I'm bored silly and stuck. I have no life and nothing to do. I want to go home." The last words came out in a choke. I hadn't realised just how much I missed my little house until those words had left my mouth. I began to sob like a child.

"Oh, honey, I know, but there's nothing anyone can do. You just have to be patient. Listen, I'll have a think. I'm coming in tomorrow – we can come up with something then, OK?"

"'K," I sniffed.

"Don't worry, we'll think of something. Take care, honey."

"'K, bye."

I put the phone down and cried. Then I must have dozed off, because the next thing I remember is Chris the physio tapping me on the shoulder and apologising for taking so long to get back to me.

I looked out of my tiny window and saw that it was dark

outside. I'd done it! I'd managed to sit out the entire day. I'd not been troubled by the pain – my body had finally adjusted to sitting in an upright position. This was a major milestone and for the first time I realised that I was actually getting better. Slowly, agonisingly slowly, in fact, but the reality was that I was getting there. I laughed out loud. Chris, who had up until now only experienced a sullen, whingeing, complaining Kate Townsend, was slightly taken aback, but soon realised also that I'd turned a corner. He then did two things that I'd never seen him do. He smiled a beaming, glorious smile and uttered two words as clear as crystal.

"Well done."

Chapter Fourteen

Bedpan Interlude

I did say that I would tell you all about the day I realised that my life was irrevocably changed. The day itself started fairly innocuously. I was lying in bed, thinking about nothing much at all, humming to myself and floating off on an imaginary pink cloud. It was about the time that I was being weaned off my lovely little morphine machine and slowly beginning to come round. I was minding my own business and enjoying the remnants of the floaty feeling, when all of a sudden I had a severe pain in my stomach area. It felt as if I was being attacked by a very small assassin who was trying to kill me by stabbing repeatedly with a tiny, tiny knife. Even in my fuzzy state I realised that this was not a particularly normal feeling to have, so I pressed the call button. Almost immediately Suzanne (the other lovely nurse, remember?) appeared and, taking in my agonised expression, asked me what was wrong.

"Is it possible that Lilliputians have a contract out on my head?"

"Lilliputians? I don't know, let's see. Have you ever tried overthrowing the Lilliputian government?"

"I don't think so."

"OK, have you ever had a bar-room brawl with a really, really small person?"

"No, never."

"OK then, I think we can discount the Lilliputian vendetta theory. Where's the pain?"

"Down there." I pointed to my nether regions and scowled. "It's really painful."

"I'll take a look – it's probably something simple." She lifted my bedclothes and began to inspect the different tubes that sprung from various parts of my anatomy. I don't know what she did next, but whatever it was caused me to issue a cry which sounded remarkably like a hyena that had been slapped on the backside with a cricket bat. (Obviously, having never met a hyena, I am merely surmising that this is what one would sound like in the unlikely event that they came into close contact with someone who had just hit a six).

"OK, I think I see the problem. Your catheter is blocked. I need to have a word with sister. I'll be right back."

Within minutes Suzanne had returned with a small package. I was going to ask what the package was, but I realised that I'd probably be better off not knowing.

"Sister thinks it might be a good idea to remove the catheter." She busied herself around my midriff and then proceeded to say something that I knew was a complete lie, but I accepted it because I really wanted it to be true, like when your mother tells you that a wasp won't bother you if you just ignore it.

"It'll feel like a small scratch."

I nodded and smiled, then, much like when the wasp that you've been attempting to ignore turns around and stings you on the eyelid, Suzanne proceeded to rip my insides out and squeeze them through a tiny hole around the size of an eye of a needle. I screamed the scream of a torture victim.

"There you go, all done." Suzanne tidied up and disappeared. I comforted myself with the knowledge that the miniature assassin had gone and my stomach felt much better.

The day continued quite normally, or at least what passed for normality back then – floating stuff and disembodied voices – and I thought that things were fine, until, later on in the evening, I felt a strange sensation. Something I hadn't been aware of, something that I had a vague recollection of but strangely hadn't encountered since the accident. I needed to go to the loo. Not number twos obviously 'cos I had problems with my bowel movements (see chapter nine). All that was required was a very simple (HA!) wee. I rang the bell and mentioned my problem to the nurse, who proceeded to open the curtain and scream, "Jackie, bedpan needed in bed five!"

This was when I started thinking. Hang on, I was completely unable to move. I couldn't even sit up at that point. I had no strength to do anything more than lie there like a beached whale and somehow, I had to use a bedpan. I didn't even know what one looked like.

It didn't take long until at least one of these concerns were soothed as the nurse returned with a cardboard oval-shaped bowl. She took one look at me and called out, "I'm gonna need some help with bed five. It'll take four at least."

She may as well have put on a Captain Ahab voice and screamed 'Moby Dick ahoy!' Luckily I was too woozy to be sensitive about such things.

One by one, three other nurses appeared. When the final one arrived, I looked at them and said, "He's not going to be staying, is he?", eyeing the male nurse suspiciously.

"Well, it depends how desperately you need to urinate," Nurse Loudmouth boomed.

Uh-oh. I needed to go really badly at this point so I hoped for a compromise. "He'll have to do the top end then, eh?"

"Well, he'll go where he's needed." She turned away from me and addressed the assembled throng. "Right, Shaz, you take the top half, Jackie and Alan, you take the bottom and I'll do the sliding."

Sliding? What was she talking about? This wasn't a school playground and I didn't want to slide anywhere, but I thought it best not to mention this out loud.

"Right, Katherine, can you lift up your nightie?"

"But there's a man in the room. I couldn't possibly."

"OK, guys, let's go then, she obviously –" They all started to leave.

"No, don't . . . OK, I'll do it, but can he at least look in the other direction or something?"

"Well, you've not got anything he's not seen before. But if you insist. Alan . . ." Alan nodded his head and looked away.

I quickly lifted up my nightie and covered myself with my sheet. "OK, done."

"Right, everyone, after three, tip and roll to the left. One, two and three!"

I felt my whole body being heaved and the cardboard bowl being thrust roughly underneath my bottom.

"Is it in the right position, Katherine?"

How on earth was I supposed to know? This was the first time I'd peed into a cardboard bowl. "I think so."

"OK, we'll let you get on with your business and give a buzz when you're finished," she bellowed at me for the last time and then the assorted nurses silently left my cubicle.

As soon as I was alone a thin trickle began, which turned into a long stream – I'd obviously been holding in quite a bit of liquid. I gave a satisfied sigh and felt a huge feeling of relief. Unfortunately the relief didn't last long, because very soon I felt a strange warmth spreading around my leg, a warmth which very quickly cooled against my thigh. I'd missed the bowl almost completely. Now as far as I could remember, I had never in my life wet the bed. My mother always held me up as an amazing example to my brother Benny. Whenever he had a late-night accident, the refrain was always 'your sister never wet the bed'. So I was completely unprepared for the feelings which welled up inside me at this new development at age thirty. Humiliation mixed in equal amounts with embarrassment and shame coursed through my body and I started to cry. The more I cried the more stupid I felt and the more I wanted to cry. I was far too embarrassed to call the nurses, unwilling to face the likelihood that the hollering nurse would shout out 'Incontinent wretch in bed five!' I couldn't even summon the energy to find my box of tissues, so I just sat there wet at both ends, feeling so miserable I wanted the ground to open up and swallow me whole.

I don't know how long I sat there in the disgustingly sopping sheets, but it must have been long enough for the previous shift to end, because the next thing I knew was that Karen appeared at my curtain, having just started her shift.

"You'll never guess what happened to me today in the –" She began and stopped when she saw the wretched look on my face. "What's wrong?"

"I missed the bedpan," I whimpered and continued my dejected weeping. "My bed's wet."

Karen came over to my side and used her very best soothing voice. "Don't worry, everyone does it the first time. It's not as easy as it looks."

I sniffed an extremely large and snotty sniff and said, "Really?"

"Yep. Don't worry, I'll get you cleaned up."

True to her word, within fifteen minutes, she'd cleaned me up, changed my sheets from under me, and dressed me in a brand-new, clean nightie. I still felt mortified at what had happened, but thanks to Karen, I was at least dry.

I had always felt a certain pride at my independence and that was why the whole hospital experience was made ten times worse. Thanks to a fairly decent education and the presence of a pretty good financial situation, I'd never had to ask anyone for anything in my whole life. In a matter of seconds, the time it took to fall down about twenty steps in my house, my independence was snatched away from me and I had no idea when or if I would ever get it back again. I wasn't even capable of wiping myself after my toilet activities. In time, I would get the hang of the bedpan, but with that first disaster, something had been irretrievably lost from my life, something I could not define because it was nothing concrete, nothing you can touch. You could almost say that a tiny piece of me died that day.

Chapter Fifteen

Blue Peter and Deception

The day after my revelation with the physio, I once again found myself in a black mood – or maybe it was just a dark-grey mood – brought on by the fact that although I had been making progress, the progress was not happening fast enough for my liking. I was so bored that I'd resorted to throwing rolled-up bits of newspaper at my rubbish-bin. I was getting quite good at it (35/50 – it was a loooong morning!) when Jane bounded into my room with a carrier bag. Soundlessly, I watched her extract from it a small tin of paint, a paintbrush, an extremely long ruler, a furry pencil case and a huge pile of brightly coloured cards.

"What's all that for?" I eyed her with suspicion.

"We're having a *Blue Peter* day."

"A what?"

"*Blue Peter* day. Only we're going to have to do without the glitter, the shop had sold out, but I'm sure we can manage."

"Manage without glitter? We couldn't possibly!"

"Stop being so sarky. I'm doing this for you, you know. You could at least give me a little smile."

I teased the corners of my mouth into a vague upwards direction. "OK, but I want to be John Noakes. You'll have to be Valerie Singleton or Peter Purves."

"But I'm always . . . alright, but just this once."

I'd won a famous victory. Jane never usually let anyone else be John Noakes – usually I had to be Peter or Valerie. I smiled a massive smile and unzipped the pencil case to find a dazzling array of felt-tips, metallic markers and other artistic goodies.

"So tell me again why we're doing this?"

"You've forgotten, haven't you?"

"No," I bluffed. Of course I had no idea what it was I was supposed to have forgotten.

"What happens every year?"

"Oh my God!" I exclaimed. "I've forgotten to register for the London Marathon."

"Ha ha, Kate. What is the date?"

"Jane, at the moment, I'm having difficulty remembering what day it is – now you're telling me I need to remember months too?"

"Saturday will be February 19."

"Oh really." I didn't think I wanted to hear what she was going to say next. Should I tune her out now or wait until she got really annoying?

"You know what that means, don't you?"

"The 19th is a Saturday?"

"KATE!" I couldn't believe it, she actually stamped her foot. "It's your birthday."

"Oh, is it indeed?"

"Yes. Why aren't you excited?"

"What have I got to celebrate?"

"Your birthday, you miserable git. It's party time."

"I'm not having one this year."

"A party?"

"No, a birthday."

"Kate Townsend, stop being such a cow! You said you were bored. This'll be perfect."

"Perfect? How?"

"You're going to have a party and we're going to make the invitations."

"What do we need invitations for? There's only two other people to invite. There's no way I can –"

"Stop being a sourpuss – it'll be fun."

"What will?"

"A party. I've talked to that nice nurse and she said that you can have as many visitors as you like as long as they don't spill out onto the ward and bother the other patients."

Why are my friends spending all their time chatting to my medical people behind my back? I was beginning to feel a little left out. After all, they were my medical professionals and it seemed that they hardly ever talked to me.

I was trying to keep up with Jane who was by this time whizzing around my room measuring out squares on my walls. The pregnancy had obviously filled her with an incredible amount of energy. She was showing now and her normally slender stomach showed a bulge like a half-deflated football. What was wrong with her? Didn't she know that she was meant to be feeling like crap and throwing up all the time? Why couldn't she do anything the way she was meant to? I'd read that pregnant women were meant to have rubbish hair and spots due to all the hormones, but Jane had never looked better. Her very-nearly-ginger hair had changed to a gorgeous rich auburn colour and her face had never been so lusciously smooth. Damn, she was talking to me again. In fact, she'd not stopped wittering on since entering the room, but I was certain that she'd just asked me a question of some sort. "What? What? Um . . ."

"I asked her if we could paint stuff on your walls and she checked with the nurse in charge and she said we could as long as we agreed to paint it over when you leave."

"But . . . but . . ."

"It's alright. Apparently this room was due to be repainted anyway, so when I offered to pay for it to be redecorated after you've gone, she perked right up and agreed. She's probably out there now thinking of new ways to spend the money they've saved."

"But . . ."

"You get started on the invites. I'll start marking out the borders."

"Oh, OK. Get down, Shep!" I chuckled and looked down at the card in front of me. "What should I write?"

"Just think of something interesting."

"Interesting, how?"

"I dunno, make it fun."

"Fun, how?"

Jane gave an irritated tut and growled: "Just get on with it!"

* * *

135

You are cordially invited to
KATE TOWNSEND'S BIRTHDAY PARTY
on
Saturday, 19 February 2000 at 8pm

SEE her fabulous new living space
WONDER at the appalling colour on the walls
SMILE at her hilarious stories
HELP to make it a better place for her to live
RSVP to Jane via astral projection*

Bring food, alcohol, paints, paintbrushes, yourself

*If the Heavens are not aligned give her a ring instead

An hour later, my walls had fairly large, black, square outlines painted on them, ready for my friends to come along and fill the boxes with works of artistic significance. Jane was covered in tiny flecks of black paint, which I thought was pretty incredible seeing as she'd hardly done enough painting to warrant such a stunning Dalmatian-like appearance. She was sat on the end of my bed, still talking nineteen to the dozen and colouring in the little stars that I'd drawn on the invitations.

"And I thought we could invite the guys from Chicanas. They keep asking about you. Ooh and Anil wants to visit as well, just to make sure you're eating properly and he wants to bring the no-good-lazy-nephew with him. Apparently he wants you to marry the nephew and make him a better man or something."

"But he's only about twenty-six years old!" I spluttered.

"Yeah, but you're thirty and Anil thinks you should be married."

"To his no-good-lazy-nephew? I've never even met the guy and the stuff that Anil's told me about him is hardly a great recommendation."

"It sounds as if all he needs is the love of a good woman to straighten him out. That's what Anil says anyway. I think he thinks he could kill two birds with one stone. You know what he's always saying,"

"Yeah. 'Katie, you too lovely to be dried-on old spinistery,' I know."

"He means well."

"Alright, invite him along as well then, but don't let him bring the nephew. You don't think he really is a porn star, do you?"

"No idea, but we could get him here and ask him."

"No, definitely not."

"Can Craig bring his mate Kevin? His wife's just left him and he's a terrible mess. Craig's been round there nearly every day this week. I said to him that he might as well move in with us, so I could at least catch a glimpse of my husband every now and again."

"What did he say?"

"He said that I should hush-up or he might end up moving in with Kevin."

I smiled what I considered to be an inscrutable smile and changed the subject delicately. "Anyone heard from Sandi?"

"What's wrong?"

"What d'you mean what's wrong?"

"Why did you just change the subject? Why don't you want to talk about Craig?"

"I do want to talk about Craig. Let's talk about him now. How is he?"

"What's going on?"

I was completely stuck now. Anything I'd been hoping

to keep from Jane (and you, my darling reader) was just seconds away from being revealed. Jane smelt a secret and once smelt, always discovered. I was done for.

"What's going on between you and my husband?" Jane stood up and towered over me.

"Nothing's going on."

"Katherine Townsend," Jane's voice was rising so steeply and getting so loud it was practically unintelligible, "you better tell me this!"

"What on earth is going on in here?" The ward sister came barging into the room. "I will not have such noise! You are upsetting the patients – you'd better go."

"But . . ." Jane's face was red from the exertion.

"No buts, you should leave now." The ward sister stood between Jane and my bed and firmly encouraged her towards the door.

"This isn't over!" Jane yelled as she was pushed out of the room.

As soon as she'd gone, I sent a nursing assistant off in search of the payphone. I needed to call Craig.

"Kate, what's wrong?"

"Craig, you'll have to tell her."

"Tell her? Why?"

"She was here. She smelt the secret."

"Kate! You know what she's like. I told you not to talk about me."

"She brought you up, not me, and by that time, I couldn't get out of it."

"Oh well, I suppose there's nothing for it. I'll tell her tonight. Should I cook, d'you think?"

"No, she already knows something's up. If you cooked a

meal the shock would probably kill her." I smiled despite myself. "Good luck, Craigy."

"Thanks. I think I'll need it."

* * *

I know, I know, you just want me to get on with it and let you in on what had been going on with Craig and me. All I have to say for the moment is this: it started out above board and completely innocently.

See, you thought you knew me, didn't you and now I've shocked the hell out of you.

Oh, for goodness sakes, close your mouth and put your eyes back in their sockets. You haven't even heard the story and you're judging me. That is so unfair and you should be ashamed of yourself. Let me tell you what happened.

Practically from the first day after the accident, Craig, being the only accountant in our midst, was assigned to take care of all my financial matters. So about a week before the *Blue Peter* day, Craig appeared at my bedside with a whole briefcase full of my bills and bank statements. We spent around an hour sorting out what needed to be done, I signed a few forms and letters so that he could send them off to relevant people and he brought me up to date with what had been going on. Then we started chatting about other stuff. Naturally at some point Jane came up in our discussions and Craig began to moan that she hardly ever talked to him about anything else but the baby. It was always the baby this and the baby that. I listened to his complaints with a growing sense of alarm. Obviously Jane was completely unaware of the workings of his brain. She was so engrossed in her pregnancy that she was excluding her husband. Then he mentioned that his friend and colleague Kevin had recently split up from his wife and instead of being devastated, he was having the best time of his life. This, in the way only a man could rationalise, had led him to yearn for a small chunk of freedom of his own. Before he had a chance to elaborate further, he was ousted by the afternoon arrival of the physios. I needed to get deeper into what was really going on, so I told him to come back the next day so we could talk it through. If Jane and Craig's marriage was going to go down the pan it wouldn't be for the lack of my efforts.

The following evening, Craig appeared and after the usual '3W' small talk (work, weather, ward anecdotes) I asked him.

"What's going on, Craig?"

"I dunno, Kate. It's just, you know, stuff," was his exceedingly eloquent answer.

"You really frightened me yesterday. Tell me."

His reply basically came in the form of 'my wife doesn't understand me' and how he wished he'd married someone like me.

"What d'you mean 'someone like me'?"

"Someone independent, you know, easygoing, but focused."

"Someone stuck in a hospital unable to move?"

"You know what I mean – someone with your strength."

I was beginning to understand what was going on. Craig was having a breakdown. Anyone who would compare me with Jane and figure out that I was the strong one had to have a fairly major screw loose somewhere. If I were to relate our relative strengths in beer form, I would be a

Shandy Bass (spiked with extra lemonade especially for very young kids) and Jane would have to be Tennants Super (with a shot of vodka to add that little zing).

"Stop right there, Mister. You have five minutes to tell me what's really going on before I ring for a nurse and have you committed. You're out of your tiny little warped, self-absorbed mind. She's having YOUR baby – you should be getting down on your knees and thanking her, not moaning like a six-year-old!" (Apologies to any six-year-olds out there).

His next words, shocked me. I mean they really shocked me. They reverberated around my brain and left me shaken to the core. And do you know what the worst thing was? He said them so quietly, I only just about caught them.

"I don't want a baby."

The silence in the room was palpable. I'm not going to say 'you could cut it with a knife' because really, who ever heard of cutting silence with a knife? What sort of knife would you use anyway? All I can say is that the silence was suffocating. It took a couple of seconds before it occurred to me to breathe.

Then I remembered something. "Wait a minute. You were over the bloody moon when she told you. Jane said you were jumping up and down on the bed like a kid at Christmas."

"I know, but I've had a chance to think about it – I don't want to have a baby."

Damn, he'd said it again, this time loud enough so I couldn't even pretend that he hadn't. "It's not as if you actually have to do much, is it? All you have to do is stand there, hold her hand and do a bit of cheerleading. Jane's the one who'll have her insides stretched to capacity and then ripped open. You've got it pretty easy as far as I can see."

"Easy? If it's so easy, why do most parents screw it up? I mean look at mine. Look at yours, for God's sake."

He had a point, I had to admit.

I needed to try a different tack. "But, Craig, you and Jane are nothing like your parents. And you're about a million miles away from mine."

"What if I'm like him?"

"You're nothing like him. You would never ever hit Jane."

"But what if we have a baby and I –"

"Listen, Craig, you would never hit Jane and you certainly would never hit a child. You are not him."

It seemed that the more he thought about the baby, the more he thought of himself as a father. This in turn brought back memories of his own father, a particularly nasty specimen of fatherhood, who relentlessly beat and battered his wife and children until one drizzly day in May when Craig was thirteen years old, his mother packed their things, picked him, his younger brother and sister up from school and took them all off to a shelter. With the help of the women at the shelter, they moved to the other end of the country (from Southampton to Manchester) and started a new life.

"Craig."

"Yeah?"

"You will be the best father a child could ever hope for. You are kind, loving and caring. You could no more be like your father than I could be like Kate Moss. It's physically impossible. So stop your moaning and whining and go home."

"I will." Craig got up and kissed me on the cheek.

I dunno what happened, but Craig somehow got into the habit of coming in on his way home from work. Usually to tell me about another one of his worries about his impending fatherhood.

"Kate, I hate babies! They cry all the time and they're more than a little yucky."

"Are you kidding, Craig? They're lovely, they have those gorgeous big eyes and they have such soft skin. And yours is bound to have the most wonderful green eyes. He or she will be so adorable." Did I actually say that? I am ashamed to say that I did and half of me believed it.

The reason that I kept this entire episode a secret has nothing to do with the fact that Craig had been to visit practically every night since then, under the guise of 'working late' or 'visiting Kevin'. I had kept this secret because I found myself having to defend babies on a daily basis and it occurred to me that I didn't detest them as much as I thought I did. To my utter horror, I realised that having one would not be the horrendous experience I used to think it was. Now obviously I'm not saying that I would have wanted to go out immediately and get knocked up, but, in hospital, having a completely new view of the world, talking way into the night to a nervous wreck of a father-to-be, I realised that babies aren't too bad. Per se.

Can you imagine the fallout if any of my friends ever got to find out about it? I would never hear the last of it and my ability to win any argument with the girls would be forever destroyed. I could see it now; whenever I got the upper hand in any discussion, arguing my point with conviction and vigour, it would pop up and I would have to concede that maybe my beliefs were not all as strong as I thought. This is why I couldn't bring myself to mention it to Jane.

So there you have it. It wasn't half as bad as you thought, was it? I can't believe you even considered for a second that I could have anything even approaching an affair with my best friend's husband. Not that I could have even if I'd wanted to – and I didn't, of course – I could only just about sit upright for goodness sakes.

Don't worry, I'll wait for you to apologise.

Go on then, I'm waiting.

Chapter Sixteen

Smoked Salmon and Steve McQueen

The day of the party arrived and I woke up in a strange, light-headed mood. The excitement had been welling up for days and I was so ready to have some fun.

"Good morning, Birthday Girl," a voice drifted into my thoughts.

"Morning, Suzanne. What have you got for me this morning?"

"Well, seeing as it is a special day for you, I thought we'd give you —"

"Don't tell me! Cornflakes? No. I know, special occasion, it must be Frosties!"

"Actually," she brought a covered plate out from behind her back and placed it on the table in front of me, "take a look."

I lifted the cover to see a split bagel, topped with piping hot scrambled egg, nestling on a bed of creamy pink smoked salmon. "Oh my God!"

"It's not exactly eggs benedict, but Karen and I thought it'd do. By the way, Karen will be in at midday, but she's got to go to 5G for the shift. She said to tell you she'll stop by afterwards. She hates to miss a party, our Karen."

I felt myself welling up and tried to stay calm enough to express my thanks, but Suzanne wasn't having any of it.

"Listen, you are one of the very few people in here that make it a pleasure to come in to work. Karen and I have both had days when we were really down and you managed to make us smile. It's our way of saying thank you."

I couldn't believe what I was hearing. It was true that Karen, Suzanne and I had spent many an hour giggling behind the curtains and gossiping in the comfort of my room. But I was shocked to realise that it was a two-way thing. I'd always assumed that they were just trying to cheer me up. I also thought of all those 'dark' days when I'd been rude and bitchy, but they'd both refused to react to my moods and even managed to turn me around.

"I don't know what to say . . ."

"There's nothing to say – just eat up, it's getting cold. Oh and Happy Birthday."

She bustled around in very 'nursey' way for a few minutes and then left my room.

* * *

Jane arrived at around seven that evening, to set up the room. We'd sorted out the 'misunderstanding' from earlier on in the week about Craig and she'd been extremely apologetic for jumping to the wrong conclusion. She admitted that she'd been a tad frightened when she arrived home from a spot of retail therapy to find Craig making the evening meal and she'd almost fainted when she saw that he was actually cooking it, rather than opening a few tins and sticking something frozen in the oven. He'd completely ignored my advice and even gone one step further and bought her some flowers. It is a well-known fact that men only buy flowers when they feel extremely guilty about something and the larger the bouquet, the more cause for guilt. The bouquet Craig had sprung for was so large that she needed two vases. This ensured that the initial discussions did not go well. She confessed that she had feared for her marriage. In the end Craig came clean, they talked all their respective fears out, harmony was once more restored to their household and, more importantly, I was removed from the doghouse and returned to Jane's inner sanctum of good friends. She even suggested I get a medal for assisting above and beyond the call of duty. Apparently Craig managed to make her believe that my real views on the baby subject were unaltered and I'd said everything just to sort him out. Which was fine by me.

I watched Jane charging around the room, putting down bowls of crisps and nibbles.

"Are you sure that's going to be enough food? People might expect to be fed."

"Don't you worry your pretty little head, my dear, it's all in hand. Can I use your trolley table?"

"What for?"

Jane grinned and tapped the side of her nose. "Wait and see." She unfolded a lacy tablecloth.

I didn't even know that she owned a tablecloth and I was about to mention as much to her when I realised that it was actually mine. Removed from the airing cupboard in my house. I was going to question her, but the whirling dervish in front of me started to mutter something else about paints. She'd managed to borrow some palettes from an arty friend of hers and set about arranging the paints that she'd brought with her. Eventually, she plonked herself down on the end of my bed and sighed.

"Done. What time is it?"

"Seven o'clock. Who's coming?" Up until this point she'd refused to tell me who'd RSVP'd.

"Never you mind. Gen said she'd be here about now and Louise might be a tad late, she's going into court on Monday. Massive case, apparently. Some bigwig's done something wrong and she's been doing the legwork. Working all hours she is." God love her, Jane was never that good at listening to Louise when she explained her work. "Oooh, music!"

She jumped up and scanned the room for the last unopened plastic bag that she'd brought with her. Finding it underneath my bed, she picked it up and extracted a smallish CD player.

"We can't play music – this is a hospital for goodness sakes."

"Of course we can. These walls are fairly thick, the sound won't carry. Craig's made some brilliant compilation CDs on the computer." Jane pointed at the volume switch. "I'm going outside. You keep turning up the volume until I knock on the door."

"OK."

Jane smiled a blinding smile and scurried out of the room.

* * *

It was around 9.30 p.m. and the party was in full swing. Whenever I thought that things were winding down, more people would arrive and stream through the door. The guys from Chicanas (Pedro, Javier and Jack) had been and gone, leaving behind bowls of guacamole, salsa and huge amounts of tortilla chips. Some of Louise's colleagues had just left after drinking too much and deciding that they fancied kebabs. Craig and Kevin were just finishing off their masterpiece on the wall to my left. Karen was in deep conversation with Louise, who'd managed to drag herself away from her briefs (lawyer stuff, not knickers, although by the way she was slurping her wine, chances are the latter would be removed at some point!). Jane was over in a corner reading Suzanne's palm – by the look on Suzanne's face, she was obviously telling her fantastic news. Gen was chatting in another corner with Daniel Holland, who was obviously on the receiving end of a 'Gen Lecture' probably about the state of the NHS or something equally as riveting. And me . . . I was alone and completely sober, but enjoying every minute.

I'd been given the choice of taking my afternoon tablets and not drinking, or forsaking them in order to get a bit squiffy. I was sorely tempted, but a twinge from my knee ensured that the tablets were taken after all. Who needs alcohol when you're high on life anyway? I know, I know: sarcasm is not big and it's not clever, but it was all I had, so give me a break, OK?

I surveyed my surroundings. The room was flooded with a riot of colour. My walls had been filled with gorgeous artistic works painted with various levels of skill by all my guests. Jane had painted a beautiful crystal ball surrounded by a rainbow of refracted light and various spiritual symbols to 'improve the karma of the room and keep me safe'. I was going to enquire what exactly I was being kept safe from, but knowing Jane it was probably more like evil spirits than evil scalpel-wielding consultants. Craig and Kevin had produced a dubious-looking self-portrait, which as far as I could tell owed more to playschool than Picasso. It resembled something that we used to see on *Vision On* when we were kids, accompanied by a caption like 'Craig and Kevin, aged three from Manchester'. Gen and Daniel had collaborated on a homage to the *Mona Lisa*, but instead of that strange-looking Italian woman, they'd done a fairly good interpretation of my good self looking like I was experiencing a jolt of pain from my pin-sites. The nurses, Karen and Suzanne, had used up most of the red paint producing a reproduction of a warm and hearty fire, complete with logs, to 'keep me warm during the cold hospital nights'. The Spanish lads had attempted to do a very patriotic copy of their national flag, but halfway through, discovered that Jane had been hoarding the remaining red paint, so I was left with a strange burnt umber and yellow interpretation of their country's pennant. And Louise? Well, Louise had declined to paint anything and stayed well away from those indulging their artistic inclinations. This was because she'd been so busy, she'd not had a chance to go to the dry cleaners and as a result would be forced to wear her suit to court the following day. And for some reason, she didn't think that splashes of paint all over it would make the right impression on the jury.

There were a couple of small cartoonish artworks as well, but I couldn't make out what they were supposed to be.

Although I'd never admit it out loud, I loved it all. It made me feel optimistic and cheery. Isn't colour a wonderful thing? For some reason, one rather large square was empty and Jane had been very protective, insisting that no one touch it.

"Are you OK?" Gen saw me gazing around the room and came over. "Can I get you anything?"

"No, I'm fine. More than fine actually. I think it's wonderful."

Just as I finished talking, the door opened and Anil came bounding through, weighed down by a large tray filled with foil containers.

"Sorry, I being late. No worry, I here now. Party can start." Anil turned and looked behind him, "You! Hurry, we waiting for you."

Behind Anil was a serious-looking man in his mid-twenties, who was also in possession of a large tray. The wafting smells told me that Anil had been cooking his little heart out. I assumed the serious guy was his no-good-lazy-nephew even though he looked nothing like Anil. Anil was short, with black hair and eyes to match whereas this man was over six foot, with green eyes and rich auburn hair. Although he had a hint of the exotic about him, he no way looked like he was descended from Thai stock. I vaguely remembered Anil mentioning that his sister had married a Scottish bloke and I realised that he must take after his father's family.

Anil put his tray down on the trolley table, then came over, gave me a big hug and pointed at the young man: "Katie, this is Steve, my nephew. Say hello, Steve."

Steve? What kind of name was that for a Thai man –

even one born in England? I obviously looked shocked because Steve walked over, stretched out his free hand and shook mine, whispering, "My mum was a big Steve McQueen fan. Happy Birthday, by the way."

"Thanks." We just looked at each other for a short time in silence. He was more interesting-looking than stunningly gorgeous. But he definitely had something. I might have lost the ability to walk, but I could still recognise a babe when I saw one. I snapped myself out of the trance and said, "Erm . . . pleased to meet you finally – I've heard a lot about you."

"All bad, I bet." He grinned.

"Actually yes, but I don't always believe what I hear."

"I bet my uncle didn't hold back though, did he?"

"Let's just say that he was eloquent on the subject."

"Actually, he's told me a lot about you too and it was definitely all good." Steve's emerald eyes twinkled and he smiled.

"I'm glad to hear it."

"I heard all about the accident, but by the looks of this party, you're obviously bearing up well."

"I'm doing OK. I have the best friends ever. By the way, this is . . ."

I motioned to his left and he turned his gaze to Gen who was looking appreciatively up at him from her four-foot-ten-and-a-half height. But before I could continue the introduction and well before Gen was able to say anything at all, Jane came dashing over.

"Steve, I'm so glad you could make it. I'm so excited to see you again. I've saved you a space over here. Here, let me take that." Jane took the tray from him and immediately handed it to a gobsmacked Gen. Taking his hand, Jane led him over to the empty square on the wall.

"What the hell was that all about?" Gen looked totally mystified at Jane's greeting of the no-good-lazy-nephew. She looked around to find somewhere suitable to deposit the tray. Making space on the trolley table, she finally got rid of it.

I shrugged. "I have no idea."

"Goodness me, Kate, I didn't know you had such famous friends." Daniel looked over at the newcomer with admiration clearly apparent in his eyes. "Do you think Jane would introduce me?"

My eminently capable consultant was obviously starstruck. Gen and I looked at each other in confusion. Louise and Karen stopped in the middle of their discussion and gawped at Steve. Suzanne stood transfixed with her mouth opened wide. Everyone crowded around the new arrival, leaving Gen and me feeling extremely left out.

"What is going on, Gen? Why is everyone acting so weird?"

"I dunno, but we're just about to find out." She marched over to Jane and dragged her back over to my bed. "Right, you. Spill. Who is that guy?"

"Don't you recognise him? It's Steve Wallace. You know, the Wallace Collection at the Rainbow Gallery in town?"

As soon as Jane mentioned the Rainbow Gallery, a tiny bulb lit up in my brain and I tried to drag the memory to the front, without much success. Jane sighed an irritated sigh and rooted around amongst old copies of *Manchester Evening News*, which were beside the armchair next to my bed. Finding the appropriate copy, she pointed at the front page story, 'Wallace Collection Arrives in Manchester'.

Gen's hand flew to her mouth, I gasped. I remembered reading the article. It enthused about the newest sensation on the art scene who had sneaked in from nowhere to win some major art prize down in London. Apparently Manchester was buzzing with the news that his collection was going to be exhibited at the Rainbow Gallery. They described his work as 'east-west Thai fusion' using the 'colours and feel of his far-eastern roots with a down-to-earth Britishness', whatever that was supposed to mean.

"That's THE Steve Wallace?" I couldn't believe that this was the no-good-lazy-nephew.

"Yep. I could hardly believe it when I found out. I told Anil that if he wanted to bring the nephew, I'd have to see him first. So he tells me that I should go to the Rainbow Gallery and ask for Steve. I'm expecting to meet a security guard or something and there he was."

"So he's not a porn star. I told you he wouldn't be," Gen blurted, having just about recovered from her shock.

"No, but he did a few good nudes in the early days. Apparently sold one of them for over thirty grand," Jane enthused.

"He could do me anytime he liked," Gen mumbled more to herself than anyone else.

"Gen!" I gaped in shock. Jane giggled and wandered back over to monopolise Steve once more.

"What?" said Gen. "Have you taken a good look at him? He's gorgeous."

"I wouldn't say gorgeous. He's nice, I suppose."

"Who's nice?" Daniel had returned to Gen's side.

"Steve McQueen over there."

"He's really nice actually. He's agreed to give us one of

his paintings to sell for our children's ward refurbishment appeal. We're having a charity auction next week – he's even agreed to be the auctioneer for it. Come over, Gen. I'll introduce you."

With that he led her over to the crowd.

I know it sounds churlish, but I was a tad miffed. It was meant to be my party after all, and yet there I was, in my bed, with no one to talk to. I found myself wishing that he had been something normal like a dentist. Everyone was swarming round this usurper, fawning all over him and acting like he was some big movie star or something. I'm not sure how I managed it, but I think I actually harrumphed. I was tired, disgruntled and my tablets were making me drowsy. I waited a while for someone to actually notice me and when nobody did, I eased myself down my bed, pulled the covers over my head and went to sleep.

I don't know what time the party ended. The next time I opened my eyes the lights were still on, but the room was empty. Extremely tidy, but empty. The only sign that there had been a party at all was a bulging binbag in the corner. I looked at my walls, where people had been painting and I had a sharp intake of breath. It was stunning. The most beautiful painting I'd ever seen. It was a tropical sunset, full of the most gorgeous purples and reds, the dark silhouettes of the clouds lending a brooding feel to the sky. I could almost feel the warmth of the tropics and the sand under my feet. In the bottom corner, in a thick black stroke, I saw the word *Wallace*.

He was talented, I gave him that, but I wasn't completely sure that I forgave him for taking over my party. There was a piece of paper on the trolley table, with *Katherine* written in the same broad hand as the signature on the wall.

155

Dear Katherine, it said, *I hope you like the sunset, and that it helps on those days when only a sunset can soothe the soul.* Pretentious git. I read on: *I'm glad we met and I hope we meet again sometime. At least to give me a chance to cancel out my uncle's comments.* It was signed, *Wallace*.

Underneath the writing was a pencil sketch. I looked closely and realised that it was me. Sleeping.

He'd drawn me sleeping.

The cheek of the guy! How dare he watch me while I was asleep. I was sure there were etiquette rules about that sort of thing.

Meet again? Not if I had anything to do with it.

Chapter Seventeen

Bared Teeth and Rabbits

February continued fairly uneventfully, small improvements in different areas all slowly adding up and pointing to the fact that I was getting better. By the end of the month, my strength increased and I had the sitting-out thing completely sussed. One morning, when the physios had been delayed, I'd even managed to get out of bed and hop the short distance to the armchair all by myself. When Chris arrived, muscles bulging and eyes wide in shock, I simply shrugged and said, "You were late."

I felt slightly more in control of my world and consequently I was feeling ridiculously happy. The vascular team had discharged me from their care, which meant two things: firstly it meant that my artery was once more considered to be in tip-top condition, although my vascular consultant did inform me that I would probably always suffer reduced circulation in my right foot, but 'considering that I could be dead, it wasn't a bad trade-off really' – he had a lovely way with words, don't you think?

The second thing was that I was now only receiving visits from the orthopods (I know it sounds like some strange alien foe in an episode of *Star Trek*, but it was much easier than saying 'orthopaedic team'). Therefore, rounds consisted of Daniel Holland saying things like 'amazing improvements' and 'remarkable recovery' to his students, whilst maintaining his professional demeanour and pretending that I hadn't seen him doing tequila slammers with my friend Gen at my party (trust me, I had!). I then heard him saying something about being 'weight-bearing' and I thought he was just having a dig at my voluptuous size.

Little did I know that these words were actually 'physio-speak' for 'you are now allowed to inflict more serious pain on your victim' because the following morning, there they were smiling their sadistic smiles and rubbing their hands together with glee.

"We'vegotasurpriseforyoutoday,Lynn'sbringingitnow." Chris's clarity of speech obviously reduced in direct proportion to the increase in his excitement.

As he finished speaking, the door opened and Lynn entered, hiding something behind her back and smiling with all her teeth showing. Now, in the animal world it's a well-known fact that bared teeth is the highest form of aggression. Trust me, I wasn't in any way reassured by this welcome. Here be monsters, as the old sailors used to say.

"Miss Townsend, I am here to officially inform you that your leg is now weight-bearing."

"Um . . . Thanks?" I felt this was the appropriate response, but she continued.

"Tada!" she exclaimed, pulling a metal frame-type thing from behind her back.

I peered at her surprise gift and the name of this new torture-implement came to my mind. "But that's a Zimmer frame."

"Yep." The grin was back and Chris was grinning right along with her.

"But, they're for old people. I'm only this side of thirty. You can't be serious."

"Now, now, Katherine," Lynn's teeth were taking on wolf-like proportions, "remember?"

"Yeah, yeah, physios never joke about such things, I know. But honestly you can't expect –" I gave up, I knew exactly what was coming.

"Rightpopyourlegsoverthesideofthebedandwe'llgetyouup." Chris reached over to assist me.

This was the easy bit. I did as I was told and found myself sitting on the edge of my bed, with my right leg sticking straight out supported by Chris.

"Right, now, I want you to hold on to Chris and stand up. Lean to the side and put all your weight on your left leg for the moment. I need to adjust the frame."

Again, I meekly followed orders and held on to Chris, who was supporting me on the right side, while Lynn adjusted the Zimmer frame to my height.

"OK. What I want you to do is put your hands here and here," she pointed to the top of the frame, "and leaning on the frame, I want you to put your right leg forward."

So far so good, this wasn't too . . . nope, I wasn't going to even think that thought, because every time I did I ended up in excruciating pain.

"Now, after three, I want you to lean on the frame and take a step forward, putting your weight through your right leg."

I can see you're thinking: why is she making such a fuss? It's only one step. But what you're probably forgetting is that I still had the metal scaffolding on my leg and I hadn't actually walked for almost two months. Think about that for a second. Add to that the fact that my leg was practically hanging off not sixty days ago and although I had the utmost faith in Daniel's ability as a great consultant orthopod, surely such damage can't heal itself so quickly? What if the knee dislocated again and I collapsed in a heap on the floor? All of these errant thoughts rushing through my brain meant that after Lynn's count, I was frozen to the spot unable to move even if I wanted to, which of course I really didn't.

"Lynnwillcountagain." Chris took control and said quite firmly, "Andthistimel'llhelpyou."

I felt my right arm being firmly gripped and a hand resting on my lower back – he was going to push me. I was certain they're not allowed to push. I was going to mention this, but Lynn began her count.

"One, two and –" she didn't say there was going to be an 'and' I mentally protested.

Chris gave me a brief shove of 'encouragement' and I took my first step since tumbling down my stairs on that fateful day.

Obviously there was pain involved, but this time I didn't feel it. I was elated. I had taken a step. OK, to be honest, it was more of a shuffle and most of the weight was taken by the Zimmer frame, but still, I WAS WALKING! And they said I'd never walk again! What did those doctors know?

I managed a few more shuffley-type steps and Lynn smiled (mouth closed – teeth covered) and announced that our session was complete for the day. Chris patted me on the back and nodded approvingly.

I floated around. OK, I didn't exactly float – I actually sat in my chair half-watching daytime TV – but mentally I was up in the clouds. I hadn't been this happy since . . . since . . . Suddenly a dark cloud appeared in the blue sky of my mind. The cloud rained down and informed me that I'd not been this happy since I'd met Matt.

Matt.

All of a sudden I was metaphorically standing in a pool of rainwater, dripping wet, starting to get a bit chilly and wondering if I'd made a huge mistake in sending him away.

I know you've probably been moaning ever since chapter seven about how I introduced and disposed of the whole 'relationship issue' without really telling you enough about him. But that was then and I didn't really know you that well and to be honest the whole thing hurt just a little too much to go into it in detail. I think I'm ready to tell you more, but please forgive me if I don't dwell too much on the fact that we used to shag like rabbits about 85 per cent of the time and believe me 'mind-blowing sex' didn't even begin to describe it. (I know, you're disappointed, but as you've probably told your boyfriend – or girlfriend – more than once: there's more to a relationship than great sex). So I'm going to focus on our day-to-day life.

Matt was lovely. He practically moved into my house after about two weeks, but the reality was that I rang him the Monday following the leg of lamb/Jane's pregnancy announcement day and offered to cook him a meal and he never really left. The eternally-unkind Jane said later that he only stayed 'cos he had a poky little flat and I had a lovely three-bedroomed house, but I was sure it was more romantic than that.

He was gorgeous.

I got into the habit of making sure that there was a home-cooked meal waiting for him when he returned home at the end of the day, and yes, I actually cooked it. In fact Delia was Yoda to my Luke and was consulted on an almost hourly basis in those days. I even managed to use up quite a few herbs from the herb garden that I'd planted outside my back door.

He was gorgeous.

Matt didn't like it when I went away. He said he missed me too much (Jane's translation: missed my cooking, more like). Therefore I made sure that I came up with enough reasons that I needed to stay in Manchester so I wouldn't have to go abroad to work. I know what you're thinking, I turned into a Stepford Wife, but I was actually happy – I think.

We spent loads of time round at Jane and Craig's, where we would be really 'couply' and have these long, grown-up discussions about the state of the world economy and European monetary policy (excruciatingly boring Matt lectures – yep, Jane again). And we used to watch interesting programmes on the Discovery Channel and discuss them afterwards (or listen to boorish commentary by idiotic . . . rhymes with banker).

Whatever Jane's opinion now, at the time it seemed idyllic and apart from a slight lack of independence – Matt didn't like me going out with the girls too often, he thought once a month was enough and we both agreed that it was best for me not to drink too much because there's nothing worse than a 'drunken shrieking woman' – I thought I was in love (for a while).

Did I mention he was gorgeous?

The gloss began to fade a couple of days before the accident, when we were out having dinner with one of Matt's colleagues and his extremely posh, stick-insect wife. We were in a fantastic restaurant in London, which was famous for it's re-working of traditional English food (toad-in-the-hole, bangers and mash etc.) with an exotic twist (i.e. venison sausages and Dijon mustard and garlic mash). With such amazingly tasty fare on offer, I was stunned when the colleague's wife ordered a green salad, no dressing and a sparkling mineral water. Obviously I went to town ordering a starter (prawn cocktail – huge bowl of tiger prawns served in a herb vinaigrette on a bed of sumptuous rocket), main course (bangers and mash – as above), a half bottle of Californian zinfandel to wash it down with and just as I was ordering dessert (sticky toffee pudding with cream and custard – yum-yum), Matt leant over and in a loudish voice said, "Should you be having a dessert? I mean, that lot will hardly get rid of the tractor-tyre you're lugging around, will it?"

With that he gave a horsey-type laugh and looked over at his colleague who was nodding in agreement. The stick-insect just sat there and smirked.

The cheek of him! It wasn't as if I'd expanded overnight. I mean, I'd actually lost weight since our initial meeting. It must have been all that cooking, cleaning and laundry that I'd been doing. Needless to say, I started to have second thoughts round about this time, but before I could really come to any 'grand decisions' I had tumbled down my staircase and had more important things to think about.

Looking back on it now, I know full well that Jane was completely right about Matt. He was boorish, selfish and not a very nice person at all. I'd been swept away by the fact that he was gorgeous, successful and fairly rich (even though he lived in a poky flat and hardly ever put his hands in his pocket to pay for a round – Jane was right about that too). The only thing I can say in my (and his) defence is that even though he may have been selfish in every other part of his life, he was extremely 'giving' in the one place that mattered: my large king-sized bed.

And that's all I have to say about that, as a famous chocolate-box-loving movie character once said.

* * *

The traffic is building up on the street in front of the café. I've been sitting here almost all day and I've not even got to the really confusing part yet. I'm nowhere nearer making any of the decisions that need to be made. The only good thing is that we're way past the halfway point and we're whizzing down the hill of the second half.

And if you think that things can only get simpler from now on, you've obviously not been paying attention and you really ought to know better.

So we continue into March . . .

Chapter Eighteen

Prognosis-Schmognosis

March went by quite quickly and my hospital life maintained the same routines, day after day, although the improvements on the mobility side were coming thick and fast. After a couple of weeks, I was whizzing around on my Zimmer frame, taking 'daily constitutionals' to build up my strength. The physios would accompany me out of the ward and down darkened corridors in order to develop my atrophying leg muscles, which in the previous two months had been forced to lie dormant. I was shuffling around with such speed and confidence that I was sure that Daniel had made an error of gigantic proportions in his doom-filled prognosis. I was certain that when I was finally discharged, I would be running marathons in no time. This confidence was further boosted by the arrival of Lynn and Chris at my doorway one morning in late March.

"Weareverypleasedwithyourprogress," Chris grinned.

"Yep, guess what we have here for you?" Lynn smiled menacingly.

"Agony? Pain? An invitation to go four rounds with Mike Tyson, which by the way, I'd actually prefer to another one of your sessions of anguish, thank you very much." As you can probably tell, I wasn't in a great mood that day.

"Look!" Chris was almost bursting with excitement.

Lynn held up a pair of crutches and Chris clapped his hands in delight.

"Crutches? For me? You shouldn't have! No, really!" I feigned boredom then allowed the sarcasm to seep out of my voice. "I can hardly contain my excitement."

"Right, Katherine, this is going to be much more difficult than the Zimmer frame. We're really going to give that knee of yours a good try-out. Up you get!"

Without the need for Chris's assistance, I lifted myself up and in no time at all I was standing unaided beside my bed, albeit a little lopsidedly (leftsidedly?).

"Tada!" I demonstrated the amazing feat with outstretched arms.

"Letsnotgettoocockyjustyet,eh?" Chris sulked.

Lynn sneered. "Yeah, there may be some pain to come. Your knee might not be ready for crutches just yet."

I looked her straight in the eyes and growled, "Bring it on."

"OK, I want you to take it really slow at first. Understood?"

I nodded and she went on to explain the correct way to hold and use the crutches and when she was absolutely certain that I'd grasped all the concepts involved (it was crutches for crying out loud and she was acting as if it were brain surgery) she handed them to me, one at a time.

"Areyouready?" I'd almost forgotten that Chris was in the room, he'd been so quiet. "DontworryI'llbebringinguptherear."

"Yeah, yeah, I bet you say that to all the girls," I joked in a brash attempt to disperse the tension which had suddenly swelled in the room. My joke went down like a lead balloon and I swear that Lynn made that same noise that Marge Simpson makes when Homer does something really, really stupid.

"OK, Katherine, moment of truth. I'd like you to take a couple of steps forward. Don't forget to let the crutches take the weight."

I closed my eyes and lifted up my right leg and placed it in front of me. I took a deep breath and leant forward . . .

I'd almost expected the world to end or at least for my reality to come crashing down around my ears like one of those cool special effects that they use in films. Instead I simply took two, not entirely pain-free, steps towards Lynn.

"Good, Katherine. For today, we'll just take a little walk up and down the room here and we'll see how your knee reacts overnight. Let's go."

I walked achingly slowly, like a very frail, infirm old woman, but inside my mind was soaring. Of course I'd be able to walk again when this was all over. I KNEW IT!

* * *

"Well . . . um . . . Kate . . . er . . . that's not strictly true." Daniel looked extremely uncomfortable and squirmed in an awkwardly-unbecoming manner for an orthopaedic consultant.

Daniel had appeared with Gen in my room the following afternoon, presumably having followed the smell of the pepperoni pizza that she had brought with her for me to eat. I'd been regaling them for around half an hour with the wondrous tales of my amazing ambulatory abilities and chastising Daniel for his premature and erroneous prognosis. Once I was in full flow, Gen surprised me by going beetroot red and getting up quite hurriedly. She left us rather mysteriously to 'chat' because as she'd put it 'we obviously had things to discuss'. Although I found her behaviour strange, I was so full of the fact that I had been able to traverse the corridor for five metres and return to my room, showing great stamina, that Gen's odd reaction didn't register. Before I knew it, she was gone, leaving Daniel to drop his bombshell.

"What d'you mean, 'not strictly true'?"

"Well, there are many many factors to consider when we think of your long-term outcome."

"What are you going on about?"

"I'm talking about future outcomes and the fact that you may not be able to sustain such improvement."

Why is it that medical people (and lawyers for that matter) feel that the best way to explain something to someone is to use groups of normal, understandable words in such combinations that collectively they are rendered meaningless? (See what I just did?) What I meant to say is why do medical people waffle on for five minutes when one simple, concise sentence would do just as well?

"Kate. How can I say this?" He ran a weary hand through his hair.

"You're the consultant, have a good crack at it, why don't you?"

"The external fixator is providing the stability for your knee, the crutches are bearing a significant amount of your not, um, inconsiderable weight and there is no evidence that this stability can be maintained without these aids."

Was that even English? I stared at him in confusion, what was he on about? "Translation please."

"Well to be completely blunt –"

"I wish you would!"

"The ex-fix is keeping your knee together and with the crutches you can walk."

"Well, Sherlock, that's what I've been telling you."

"Kate, let me ask you this. What happens when we remove the ex-fix?"

He looked at me earnestly and I gulped. There was not even a hint of a smile. He was serious. I started to get a really bad feeling in the pit of my stomach.

"The leg will feel much lighter?"

"Yes and . . ."

"I'll be able to go through that machine at the airport without it going off?"

"Not quite . . . erm –"

"Tell me already!"

"Well, it won't be as stable. Without the ex-fix, your knee is likely to be unable to support your weight."

"Are you saying that I need to lose weight?"

"Well that wouldn't be a bad idea, but in this case, it won't make much difference. It's doubtful that your knee would be secure enough to support any weight. Which is why . . ." He tailed off and had a pained look on his face.

"Which is why you told me that I may never walk again."

"That's right." His voice was so soft and tender.

I attempted to swallow, but my throat felt like a desert. "So even though I'm practically jogging around the hospital now, when this lump of scaffolding disappears, I'll probably be stuck in a wheelchair." I know, I know, it made no sense to continue repeating the news, but I was hoping that he'd laugh and say that he was joking and I'd be just fine, but he didn't. Instead he nodded, patted my hand sadly and left me in my room drowning in floods of silent tears.

* * *

Now I know that after all these instances of me bawling my eyes out, you'll not believe this next bit, but honestly, considering all that I had been through, I'd been quite perky overall. Apart from the occasional bursts of inexplicable tearfulness, my general mood was fairly upbeat. After all, I'd stared death in the face and lived to tell the tale.

I don't know what it was, maybe it was the way he patted my hand or the softness of his voice, but after Daniel left me that day I finally let myself accept my fate. Up until that day I was able to listen to all the things that the various experts had been saying and think to myself that they weren't actually talking about me or that they didn't really know what they were talking about. That day I finally had to acknowledge that I had already used up my quota of good fortune. There would be no remarkable recoveries, no miraculous healing processes, no moments of wonder as I emerged from this nightmare unscathed. I would be forever affected. Never again would I be able to describe myself as healthy. From now on I was disabled, unabled, hindered. A cripple. I looked down at the scars criss-crossing my leg. Big bloody great Frankenstein stitch-scars running up both sides of my calf. For a while I'd hoped that that would be the only lasting sign.

It was a lot to take in. Deep down I knew I could deal with it. If only . . .

I don't know how long I sat there reflecting on this turn of events, but it must have been quite a while, because the next time I looked over at the window, night had fallen and my evening pill ration had been placed in front of me. I hadn't even noticed anyone come in. I looked over to my side and I saw Sandi asleep in the armchair beside my bed. I looked over at the sunset painted on my wall and smiled – it really was very nice. The no-good-lazy-nephew was remarkably talented. I pondered this for a moment until something filtered through my brain.

Hang on a minute. I did a very obvious double take.

I looked back over to the armchair. "Sandi!"

"Wha . . . who . . . whe . . ." My exclamation had shocked her out of her slumber. She sat bolt upright in the armchair, eyes blinking. "What time is it?"

"Never mind the bloody time. What the hell are you doing here?"

"Now is that any way to talk to someone who has spent the last thirty-six hours travelling on planes, trains and automobiles? I've not had any sleep for what seems like weeks and what do I do? I come straight to the most hateful place in the world to visit my ungrateful wretch of a best mate."

I think you could say I was suitably chastised. "I'm sorry. Oh Sandi, I am so glad you're here! I've really . . . really . . . missed . . ." Predictably I was welling up once more and Sandi looked down at my tear-stained face, then leant in and gave me a huge hug. We hung there for an age, just happy to be with each other again. After I finally allowed her to move away, she sat down on the bed beside me, my hand in hers, while I told her everything that had been going on.

"So basically, Daniel thinks I may not walk again."

"Hang on. Daniel? Who's Daniel?"

"Mr Holland, my consultant."

"Your consultant? And you're calling him Daniel?"

"Sandi. That really isn't the point of the discussion at the moment."

"No, I suppose not, but it's far more interesting for me than listening to your ungrateful whining and whinging."

The shock of her statement took my breath away. "What?"

"Listen to yourself."

"I'm going to spend the rest of my life in a wheelchair."

"So?"

"So? A wheelchair, Sandi."

"Just you listen to me. You are alive. Considering where you are and the track record of this place, which frankly makes my skin crawl, that is certainly miraculous in itself. And if you are really asking for my opinion, I think you should be counting yourself damn lucky."

"I . . . I . . ." I decided that it was probably better for me not to say anything at all and simply let her carry on.

"You – you – what? Have you looked around recently? Did you see those poor women in that ward there? Most of them haven't even got legs any more. And are they complaining about being in wheelchairs?"

"No, they're too busy screaming the place down."

"Don't get smart with me. You know I'm right. You should be counting your blessings."

"What blessings?"

"Let's see. You are alive. You have both legs. You are intelligent, beautiful and otherwise healthy. You have

172

friends who love you and enough money that you won't be out on the streets when you finally leave here. Plus you are forgetting one very important thing."

"What?"

"I'm back," Sandi grinned.

Despite the tongue-lashing that I had received, I smiled. "And don't I know it."

"And I'm not going anywhere else until you are well enough to go with me."

"Really?"

"Yep."

"Even Mexico?" I grinned, knowing full well that Sandi had sworn never to again set foot in the country which had granted her divorce from her crazy ex-husband.

"Even Mexico." She grabbed my hand and squeezed. "We'll go there together and exorcise my ghosts. But in the meantime you need to pick yourself up, dust yourself off and come back fighting, OK?"

"OK. It's going to be alright, isn't it, Sandi?"

"Of course it's going to be alright! Anyway, he only said 'may' didn't he?"

"Huh?"

"Your consultant said you may never walk again. You never know, you might have a miracle in you yet."

"But what if I don't?"

"Then you just get in your wheelchair and roll away into the sunset."

"Ooh," I had an interesting thought, "I might even be able to get one of those electric wheelchairs. I'll be able to whizz around everywhere. I love those electric ones."

"See, not all clouds are rainclouds." She yawned a

massive yawn. "Alrighty, I'm going home to bed. I'll be back tomorrow."

"See you, Sandi. Welcome home, honey."

"Thanks, hon." She smiled and started to leave the room. Turning back she said, "By the way, Kate . . ."

"Yeah?"

"Daniel?"

"Oh, go to bed, you old cow. You look like crap."

Chapter Nineteen

Sleeping Beauty and April Fools

Sandi was true to her word. She visited every day and as March turned into April, she was practically my only visitor. Louise was still swamped with her big court case. Jane and Craig had gone off on a 'last-chance holiday as unencumbered people', a three-week trip around the world. Gen had a project in Sheffield that was taking up all her time and energy. She still phoned Daniel on a regular basis to check my progress and she wrote to me virtually every day complaining about Sheffield and her evil client.

Have I mentioned that Gen is an architect? My goodness, how totally remiss of me! Not only is she an architect, she is a fabulous one. Give her a barren piece of land or an old run-down house and she will turn it into a home to end all homes. She creates space where there is none and light where previously there were only shadows. Her Sheffield project was a nightmare for her as her evil client was, to quote one of her letters, 'an irritating mess who can't make up his mind'. His instructions changed on a daily basis and this was one thing that she really had difficulty dealing with. Disorder was Gen's nemesis. She liked everything to be ordered and organised and the only reason she stayed on the project was that evil client knew several influential people involved in the regeneration of the Salford Quays area. This was Gen's golden fleece, a large area of an up-and-coming part of Greater Manchester, full of old warehouses and derelict buildings surrounded by the Ship Canal and other man-made water sources. All she had to do was make evil client happy and her dream of designing an apartment complex in Salford Quays was a done deal. According to her letters, making him happy was proving to be a task of Herculean proportions. My replies took the form of reminders of the 'big picture' and pleas for her to be patient. Now, I am not ignorant of the great irony involved in this, such advice coming from someone to whom patience is as alien as a Vulcan death-grip.

Then, on the first day of April, two things happened which finally confirmed that I had indeed been transported to Planet Crazy.

The first was peculiar, but initially not that strange. It was eleven thirty in the morning. I'd only had one April Fool's Day joke played on me by Karen and Suzanne. They'd been on the night shift and had exchanged my crisp white bedclothes for black satin ones while I was asleep and had basically turned my room into a rather good approximation of a tart's boudoir. Only half an hour to go and the whole nonsense of the day would be over with – and then my door opened. In came a rather large squarish thing cradled in the arms of a seriously miffed deliveryman, who'd had to carry it all the way from the car park. It was about four foot long by three foot wide and his arms were 'bleeding killing' him. I tried to tell him that obviously he'd delivered it to the wrong room when he produced an A4 padded envelope.

"You Kate Townsend?"

"Yes, but –"

"Then it's definitely for you."

"But I –"

"Got nothing to do with me. Sign please." He stuck a piece of paper under my nose and offered me a pen.

Reluctantly I looked at the paper and confirmed that the name was mine and the address was correctly written. I had no choice but to sign.

"By the way," the deliveryman said, while readying himself to leave, "you're meant to open the big one first."

"Oh, OK. Thanks."

"Yeah, yeah." He grumbled and left.

I got up from the armchair that I had been sitting in, and grabbing my crutches, I walked over to the package. It was covered in a heavy brown wrapping paper and tied with string. Unable to undo the knots alone, I pressed the call button. In no time at all a nurse appeared.

"Hi there, can you help me with this please?"

"Sure. Let's see. Hmmm." She peered at the package as if it were a new kind of dressing-pack. "Do you want to keep the paper? I mean, it's good quality."

"No, I don't think so."

"Suit yourself, here goes." She took her scissors from her pocket and began to cut around the edge. "Ooh, it's a painting."

My heart began to speed up. "A . . . a . . . painting? Really? A painting?"

"Yep." She grinned at me. "Oh my!"

"What? Oh my, what?" A heavy weight fell into the pit of my stomach. I had a feeling I knew what she was going to say.

"It's a painting of you. At least it looks very much like you. It's jolly good."

She ripped the final bits of paper off and turned it around. It was me. Sleeping.

"Yes. It is, isn't it? Can you – can you . . ." My head began to spin and all of a sudden I felt dizzy. "I need . . . um."

Quick as a flash, the nurse was beside me, helping me onto my bed. "Are you OK? Should I get you some water? You look awfully pale."

"I'll be OK. I think."

"Well, you just sit down there and get your breath back." She looked at the painting once more and said, "That's one of those Steve Wallace paintings, isn't it?"

"Yes. How did you –?"

"I went to the Rainbow Gallery with my hubby – he's into that sort of thing. I don't know much about it myself, but they were nice pictures."

"Oh." I was having trouble speaking.

"That'll be worth a bit, won't it?"

"Huh?"

"I said, that'll be worth quite a bit, won't it?"

I shrugged, unable to use my mouth any more. She was a nurse, couldn't she see I was in shock? She should have been running for blankets and hot, sweet tea or something.

"Someone must really like you."

All I could do was nod in a daze.

"Oh well, I can't stand here chatting all day." She smiled and headed for the door. "You lucky thing!"

I continued to stare at the canvas and although it was very clearly there, I couldn't help but pinch myself periodically to make certain that I was not dreaming. I closed my eyes and leant back on the bed. Feeling the other package that the deliveryman had tossed on the bed, I brought it out from under me. It was unmistakably the no-good-lazy-nephew's writing. At least I had something other than the huge work of art to stare at now, I thought miserably. I turned the package over and over in my hands, fearful of what it might contain. It trembled in my hands and I took a deep breath and prepared to open it. But before I could rip the envelope, there was a knock on the door and it opened a crack.

"Kate, can we come in?" It was the nurse from earlier.

I nodded – my ability to speak had definitely deserted me – and motioned for her to enter. In came a crowd of people, some nurses and some doctors. They all trooped in and crowded around the painting. I heard murmurs of 'D'you think it's real?' and 'Wow', but I ignored them and continued to concentrate on the envelope in my hands.

Preparing myself for God knows what, I tore open the envelope and tipped it upside down. An A5-sized booklet dropped out along with a smallish gift-wrapped, oblong box and a letter. I went for the letter first.

Dear Kate, please accept these gifts as belated birthday presents. You were my inspiration for the painting and therefore, by rights, it belongs to you. I am truly amazed at your courage and beauty. I have been unable to stop thinking about you since that night. Look closely and maybe you will see what I saw when I watched you sleeping. See what haunts my every waking moment and fills my dreams at night. Wallace.

I laughed. OK, I admit that it was more hysteria than

mirth. I was dumbstruck, confounded, terrified and the strangest thing of all was that I had no idea why the entire episode had affected me so much. Some painter guy had painted a picture of me. What was the big deal? Why was I in such a mess? Why was my head no longer capable of rational thought?

"You're in love with him," Sandi announced authoritatively later on that day when she came to visit.

"Now that is the most ridiculous thing I've ever heard in my life."

"Why?"

"Because I hardly even know the guy. All I know is that he's the no-good-lazy-nephew."

"OK, stop right there, Missy. I think we can dispense with Anil's descriptions at this point seeing as he is, according to this booklet here, 'the most exciting artist to emerge in recent years' and by the amount of new work they're showing in the," she looked at the front cover of the booklet, "Steppmann Gallery, he's anything but lazy."

"I know nothing about the guy . . ."

"Well, apparently," she began to read from the booklet, "'he was born in Glasgow, but spent his formative years in Thailand with his mother's family, which is where he developed his eye for colour. He returned to the UK in 1997 after travelling extensively, paying his way by painting portraits and doing odd jobs. He went to live with his parents, who had by this time moved to London. Oliver Steppmann, London's leading art collector and gallery-owner, discovered him in Trafalgar Square selling his pencil and charcoal drawings. He won the Sundown Award last year and has since become one of the most collectable artists in London.' There you go, apart from his favourite colour and shoe size, all the information you could ever need." Sandi looked up from the booklet and over at me, bathed in a glow of total smugness.

"He's too young."

"He's just turned twenty-seven."

"That's too young."

"And you're over sixty, I suppose."

"You know what I mean."

"You're only twenty-nine for goodness sakes."

"Thirty-one."

"Everyone shaves off a couple of years when they hit thirty."

"He's too young."

"Bollocks. He's the same age as Randy."

"Nice one, Sandi."

"What?"

"Well, if you were hoping to convince me that true love sees no age, using the example of your crazy, cross-dressing ex-husband isn't really going to do it."

"You know what I meant."

"Yeah, but bringing into the discussion a man that you met, married and divorced within a year, is that really the best thing . . ."

"Just because we got divorced, that doesn't mean that I didn't love him. I still love him."

Her final comment was so off-hand I thought I'd misheard. I watched her idly flicking through the booklet. I was sure she didn't just tell me that she was still in love with her ex-husband. I mean, she showed no outward sign that she'd just uttered the most important sentence of her life.

Then I noticed that her normally steady hands were shaking.

"Sandi?"

"Huh?"

"Sandi, look at me." I was going to force her to speak if I had to, but we were going to have this discussion whether she liked it or not.

"Oh. My. God." Sandi's eyes went wide and her eyeballs seemed to, jump out of the sockets. "Have you looked at this?"

"No, I couldn't. Why?"

Sandi opened the centre pages and spread them out in front of me. There was my painting. It was me on my bed asleep, a faint smile on my face, like I was in the throes of a glorious dream, my hair falling over my face in such a way that I looked like the most mysterious woman in the world. I read the text below the picture and grunted.

"Is that it? A grunt? Kate, did you read it?"

"I read it."

"Did you read the bit that said that that canvas over there is worth a hundred thou?"

"Yep." I looked at my fingernails and decided I needed a manicure.

"And the bit where he said that it was a labour of love and was therefore not for sale."

"Yep." Maybe a bit of polish too.

"And the title – did you read what he'd called it?"

"Yep." I know, next time, I'll go for a French manicure.

"'Sleeping Beauty'?"

"I read it, Sandi."

"And all you can do is grunt?"

"Uh-huh."

"Well, if that's it maybe he should have called it 'Grumpy, the Ungrateful Dwarf Bitch from Hell' instead."

"Wha . . ." That shook me, but I was determined not to look at her. I continued examining my nails.

"The guy has just sent you a fantastic painting worth a fortune, proclaimed his love, sent you –" She picked up the oblong box and pointed it at me accusingly. "What's in here?"

"I dunno."

"What d'you mean you dunno?"

"I've not looked."

The sound that came out of her mouth was a curious mixture of exasperation and disgust. She ripped off the ribbon and tipped the contents of the box into my lap. The intake of breath was swift and sharp, from both of us. Gleaming in my lap was the most amazing watch. Gold, with a diamond in the twelve position.

"It's a Rolex," Sandi breathed.

"It doesn't matter. It's all going back."

"What do you mean 'going back'?"

"I'm sending everything back to him."

"No, you are not."

"Yes, I am."

"You better bloody not. If you do I will never ever speak to you again."

"But, Sandi, there is no way I can keep these."

"Give me a damn good reason why not, Missy."

"One good reason eh? How about, that bloody painting is worth more than my house. The Rolex is probably worth more than the contents of it."

"So?"

"Who gives someone presents like that? He's mad as a hatter."

"A mad hatter who sounds like he is, at the very least, seriously infatuated. It might even be love."

"I haven't got time for love. My body is using all my energy getting better. I can't go through that and be in love. I'm just not strong enough."

"You can't use your injuries as an excuse forever. One day you'll be out of here. What pretext will you use then, Kate?"

As if on cue, Daniel Holland appeared.

"Hi Kate. I can't really stop right now, but I have some good news. Good Lord!" He'd spied my rather large artistic gift. "Is that what I think it is?"

"Yep. Amazing, isn't it?" Sandi uttered.

"Incredibly beautiful. Such delicate brush strokes." Daniel mused.

"And the colours, don't forget the colours."

"Hey, guys? Hello? I hate to break up this art appreciation lesson, but you said you had some good news for me?"

"Huh? Oh yeah, we're going to be taking you to theatre tomorrow. See if we can get that ex-fix off. You know that is truly remarkable – he really is incredibly talented, don't you think?"

Actually it was a good thing that I was already laying in bed. An amazing stroke of luck, because while Daniel and Sandi were still gazing at the canvas in awe, I managed to faint clear away.

I did say it was a very bizarre day, didn't I?

Chapter Twenty

The Ex-Ex-Fix

I looked above my bed to see the small 'nil by mouth' sign and I was thirsty, really thirsty. I glanced at my watch – it was six thirty in the morning, the earliest that I'd ever woken up since I'd been in my little private room. Today was the day. On this day, April 2, I would be free of the shackle which bound my leg. I would be devoid of metalwork and I would finally discover if I was destined to walk again. A multitude of questions spun frantically around my head. Will I survive surgery? Will my knee hold up? Will there be pain? Can I handle the needles which would inevitably be involved in the whole process? Why did he send me that painting? Why was I thinking about that? How did I survive so long in hospital? How soon can I go home once it's off? Was I in love with him? Where did that come from? Will I be able to take care of myself when I'm out? Can I cope? Can I cope? Some of the questions I wanted answers to, others I'd rather not know. I simply lay in my bed trying not to feel dizzy.

It must have been around eight o'clock when Karen popped into my room to check on me.

"Oh, you're up. We thought we'd have to wake you and I drew the short straw." She smiled.

"Yes, I'm up alright. I don't think I slept much last night."

"Excited, huh?" She started to take my blood pressure, inflating the rubber balloon around my arm until it was fairly uncomfortable, then releasing it slowly and evenly.

"Terrified, more like. I can't believe I'll finally be rid of this thing . . ." I started to imagine what it would be like.

"Might," Karen murmured. "Your pressure's fine. I just have to check your temperature."

She stuck a gun-shaped contraption into my ear for a moment until it emitted a beep, then removed it. She peered at the reading, nodded with a satisfied air and returned her attention to my babbling.

"I'll never have to wake up with this scaffolding on my leg . . ." I pondered.

"Might."

"I'll be able to sleep on my front. Ahh, bliss, my front . . ."

"Might."

"I'll be able to . . . Hang on, what are you on about?"

"Well, I was just saying, you might get rid of it, you might never have to wake up with it and you might be able to sleep on your front. That's all."

"What d'you mean, might? Daniel said –"

"Daniel?"

"Mr Holland." Her eyebrows shot up. "Focus, Karen, he told me he'd be taking it off today."

"I think you'll find that he said he'll 'see if he can get rid of the ex-fix'."

"That's just semantics, isn't it?"

"Not necessarily."

"Why?"

"I think you should speak to him about it. He'll be in shortly anyway."

"Karen!"

"Speak to Mr Holland." Suddenly she looked very shifty indeed. "I'll have to get on. Good luck, Kate."

"Yeah right, thanks," I mumbled as she left the room.

* * *

Two hours I had to wait for Daniel to arrive, TWO BLEEDING HOURS! Heaven knows what sort of crap went around my head in that time. I'd worked myself up into a dignified frenzy. When he finally arrived, I was convinced that I was part of a great conspiracy to keep me in hospital forever.

"So why won't you take it off now," I attacked as soon as he entered the room.

"Good morning to you too, Kate."

"Why not?" I insisted.

"Kate –"

"Daniel!"

"I don't know if it will come off today. It all depends."

"On what?"

"On whether your body has healed."

"Explain."

"It's been ten weeks. By now it should be time to remove the external fixator, *but*, and it's a very big but, if the body has not repaired itself sufficiently for the knee to be stable, then we can't take it off."

187

"So what are you saying?"

"We'll take you in, remove the fixator, then test the stability of the knee. If it's stable enough, we'll wake you up and it'll be gone. If it's not, then we'll put it back on and try again in a couple of weeks."

"But, why can't you tell now, you know, with x-rays and stuff? Ten weeks seems a long time. Why can't you tell?"

"Because different people take different times to heal and you might be a –"

"Slow healer. I know, I get it." I was so deflated, I felt my face wrinkle up like a popped balloon.

"Have you signed the release?"

"Yep."

"You'll be going up in about an hour. Are there any other questions?"

"No questions. Just the one request."

"And that is?"

"No needles."

"Come on, Kate, that's impossible. Needles are a necessary constituent, I'm afraid. All surgery involves –"

"No, I don't mean during surgery. I mean, I want to go under with gas and once I'm under you can practice acupuncture on my arse if you like, but no needles before, OK?"

"I don't know, Kate. Going under with gas carries a higher risk and you've had rather a lot of surgery already." He shook his head. "I don't know if I can promise –"

"No deal then. Either no needles or no surgery. I'm not messing around here."

It was petty, I know, and more than a little reckless, but seeing as I'd had no control over anything at all in my life at that hospital, I decided there was no way on this earth that I was going to back down. We stared each other out for a few minutes and Daniel blinked first.

"Alright. As long as you are aware that it carries a greater risk."

"Fine with me, I'm on bonus time anyway. Deal?"

"Deal."

* * *

Have you ever wondered what it's like to have an operation? Let me tell you what it was like for me. They wheeled my bed into the theatre ante-room and the anaesthetist came up to explain that he was going to put a mask over my mouth and I was to breathe deeply. It smelt like sweaty socks in a swimming-pool changing-room. Basically yucky.

"OK, Katherine, can you count backwards from one hundred for me?"

"Of course I can."

"Go on then."

"Oh, you actually want me to do it? I thought you were just asking me . . ." The blackness descended.

"Katherine, Katherine, wake up, Katherine." The nurse's voice emerged from the darkness.

"Wha . . .? Do you want me to count now?" Each word came as if through a mouth full of toffee.

"No, Katherine, it's all finished. You're in the recovery area."

"Oh."

And that was it. The clock showed that I had lost an hour of my life. There. Whoosh! Gone. I drifted off into a light doze and pondered about the cumulative effect of all my operations. I added them all together and realised that since January I had lost around twenty-four hours of my life. An entire day, poof! Vanished.

I realise that you're not really interested in my lost days – you want to find out what had happened while I was in theatre. I know you want to know whether I was metal-free, but I just want to remind you how desperately I wanted, no, needed the ex-fix to be an ex-ex-fix. When Daniel calmly dropped his bombshell about removing my metalwork, I realised one very important fact. I had completely used up my entire internal stockpile of patience. Patience, which had always been in very short supply anyway. I wasn't sure how much longer I could survive. I'd just been hanging on waiting for the day that I could leave. The monotony of the hospital routine had been like a tiny, but utterly relentless, drop of water, slowly wearing me away. I realised that unless I was discharged soon, something really bad might happen. I'd managed, bar a few small blubber-bursts, to keep myself under control. I'd not fallen into depression, I'd not felt suicidal, I'd not even felt murderous bouts of anger. Alright, I confess, for a brief moment I did want to kill Mr No-good-lazy-painter-nephew-how-dare-he-be-cute Wallace, but apart from that . . . Face it, for such an impatient person, I'd been acting like an angel, but in reality, I was hanging by a thread. Which is why I didn't even want to check my leg after the operation. I was afraid that if the ex-fix was still there, the thin strand would snap and even I didn't know what would happen. I suspected it might have something to do with going totally and utterly insane.

Before the operation, I'd phoned Sandi, to tell her that I probably wouldn't be up to visitors. She'd argued that I might need someone for moral support, but had acquiesced in the face of my stubborn insistence. They'd brought me back to my little room so I knew that, apart from a few nurses, I would be undisturbed.

I took a deep breath. Limbered up my fingers and prepared to stretch my arm down towards my knee.

I couldn't do it.

My eyes obstinately remained closed. If only I could just prise one open, I'd be able to see the telltale rise of the bed-clothes indicating the presence of the scaffolding. Nope, they were both determined to stick like glue. I gave my hand a good talking to and finally managed to persuade it to have another reccy.

My fingertips recoiled as if burnt. They'd felt the smooth, metal pins heated to my body temperature, due to the fact that they were still firmly screwed into my thigh bone.

I did not cry. I didn't even blink. I was strangely empty, as if all my emotions had been sucked out through the pin-holes of the ex-fix. A numbness pervaded my entire being. There was nothing inside me. I saw nothing, felt nothing, there was nothing left.

Except a huge black cloud.

The bottom had fallen out of my world and, yep, I could clearly hear the ping of a thread snapping. Feeling returned to my body, I could feel every inch. Every synapse zinged like harp-strings. Then I felt the most incredible pain. At once I knew that this dull ache could not be taken away with tablets and pills.

Taking into account my state of mind at this point, you would probably agree this was probably not the best time for anyone to pay me an unannounced visit.

Would it surprise you to hear that there came a knock on the door followed swiftly by the very tall, firm, cute form of

Steve Wallace partially hidden behind a rather large bouquet of flowers?

Put yourself in my position. I didn't know what to do. This was a man who had a history of taking advantage of any of my possible reactions to create another masterpiece. All I wanted to do was go to sleep and never wake up again, but I already knew how good he was at the sleeping form. I could see it now, an entire Kate Townsend collection. If I showed the pain I was feeling inside, there'd be 'Agonising Beauty', then with all the irritation I felt at his arrival we could have 'Exasperated Beauty'. I couldn't even scream and shout because images of the new centrepiece for the collection entitled 'Beauty-in-a-bit-of-a-Tizz' kept flashing into my brain. I must admit I was flummoxed. He stared at me, I stared at him. He had the faint hint of a smile playing around his lips. Now that really pissed me off. What the hell was he doing just turning up at my bedside? Didn't he know that I was going through a crisis?

Not a word had been spoken since his arrival. And, I swore, as sure as eggs is eggs, there wasn't a damn thing he could do to make me utter even so much as a grunt in his direction. Nothing was going to make me react to him in the slightest. Nothing.

Wallace placed the flowers gently on the trolley table beside my bed, leant over and kissed me.

OK, so I was wrong.

It was the softest most delicate kiss I'd ever experienced. It filled me with a long-forgotten feeling, that started in my loins and worked its way slowly up to my brain. For a fraction of a second a 'how dare he?' flitted through my mind, but I did the only thing I could.

I let go.

Chapter Twenty-one

Devils and Serenity

Looking back now, I can see that in a way Steve Wallace saved me, but at the same time he destroyed me. Alright, that sentence may have been a tad overly dramatic. At the time, I knew only one thing: he was a very dangerous man. I admit, he wasn't dangerous in a Jeffery Dahmer kind of way, but it was more an exotically-sexy-blow-your-socks-off kind of danger, which was just as lethal but with far less call for blood, murder and life prison sentences. What I'm trying to say is that he scared the hell out of me. You want to know what happened after he kissed me. And I have only one thing to say.

It wasn't pretty.

After the initial bliss of his lips touching mine and my surrender to the kiss, I waited for my indignation to kick in. Even when he'd moved away and called the nurse to put the flowers in something for him, I waited for the anger to rise up in my belly and explode. But nothing happened.

He perched on the bed beside me stroking my hair. A part of me was willing my arm to reach up and remove his hand, but instead, I felt my lips curve into a contented smile. I was devastated and disgusted with myself. I was sure my body had been taken over by aliens. He'd been in my room for around fifteen minutes and still not a word had been spoken. I desperately wanted him to say something, for I knew that the break in silence would snap me out of this . . . this . . . trance-like thing that had come over me.

"Talk to me."

Wow, had his voice always sounded this sexy? I'm sure it wasn't that deep and husky the last time he was in the room. He was softly-spoken, but with a firm authority. It sounded like he had the slightest touch of a Scottish accent, but not enough to be definite that it was there. There was a vague American twang on certain words, but mainly it was a fairly neutral English voice.

"They didn't take it off."

My voice sounded so pathetic. If I hadn't been feeling so weak I would have thrown up with the revulsion of it all. Where was my fighting spirit? It was as if a little devil had appeared on my shoulder, determined to give me a good talking to. Get some gumption, girl! Tell this guy where to stick his flowers and his concern! Tell him to get lost and take that monstrosity of a painting with him! Sleeping Beauty, my arse – it doesn't even look like you. Go on, tell him! My mouth opened.

"I love it." The devil threw a miniature hissy-fit and exploded in a puff of fractious smoke.

Wallace's eyes followed my gaze and rested on the painting. "It's my favourite."

"I love the sunset too."

"I had views like that nearly every evening in Thailand when I was growing up."

"What was it like?"

"Thailand?"

"Yeah."

"Special."

"How special?"

"As special as you. Hot and fiery, but full of contradictions, sometimes peaceful but mostly turbulent and impatient."

His mention of patience brought me back to my little room and face-to-face with my immediate problem.

"They didn't take it off." I repeated, more to remind myself that despite the slightly raised heartbeat caused by the man in front of me, I might as well be dead because my life was over anyway.

"What?" His emerald eyes showed a faint glimmer of confusion.

"That." I pointed to my leg.

"They must have had a reason."

"I'm not healed."

"Then it was a good decision to leave it."

"I'll never be healed."

"Of course you will."

"Nope, I'll never walk again."

"I'll carry you."

If I had the energy, I would have laughed out loud. Instead I simply smiled at the picture that popped up in my head. "Thanks for the offer, but that's not really practical."

The silence descended once more between us. The only sound I could hear was the soft swishing of Wallace's hand on my hair.

"Talk to me. Tell me about your paintings."

"What do you want to hear?"

"Everything."

He smiled down at me and began to tell me the story of my painting. His words were like a balm to my spirit and I let myself be carried away in the serenity of his voice.

* * *

"I knew it!" Sandi had been standing in my room for less than two minutes the morning following my visit from Wallace.

"Knew what?" I tried to put as much angelic innocence into my voice as I possibly could.

"Let's look at the evidence: you have a smile on your face like a Cheshire cat that's been locked in a cream factory. There is a massive bunch of flowers, obviously bought by a rich man –" She could see that I was about to interrupt and she raised her hand to stop me. "Please don't insult my intelligence by denying it. Besides, there are orchids in this bouquet."

"A bunch of flowers does not a love affair make."

"Ah, so you admit that there's a love affair going on?"

"That's not what I said."

"You didn't have to say anything at all – it's written all over your wall." She pointed at the new addition to the *Wallace* signature. Beside the strong, black strokes, there were three little words written in a thick red marker.

"He must have done that while I was asleep."

"Well, at least he's not an arrogant prick like your last one."

"Matt wasn't an arrog –"

Sandi waved her palm in my face to silence me. "Spare me."

"If you disliked him so much, how come you never said anything at the time?"

"Like you would have listened. You were swooning all over the place. I almost expected you to say 'him Tarzan, me Jane' half the time."

"OK, so I wasn't really myself."

"You were a feminist's nightmare."

"He's gone, isn't he?"

"Thank God." Sandi sat down. "So, what's Steve like, then?"

"Lovely."

"Lovely and rich."

"He's sensitive."

"Sensitive and famous."

"Sandi!"

"What? He's rich and famous, anything else is just a bonus. You'll get married and, ooh, you'll probably even get into *Hello!*"

She started to babble on about A-list parties and celebrity bashes. My head started to spin and a cold finger of fear began to creep down my spine. The smile disappeared from my face. She was right. He was rich and famous. Why did he want me? He was on a totally different planet. Our worlds weren't even in the same galaxy. What was he thinking? This could never work. We were too different. What was I thinking? He was gorgeous, sexy and talented and I was . . . I looked down at the metal protruding from my leg.

"Why can't I have just broken my leg?"

"Huh? What are you on about?"

"Why did I have to have something so serious. I mean, a broken leg . . . all I'd have needed was a plaster cast. I'd have been completely fixed in six weeks." I sighed. "Six weeks, think about it."

"Maybe it's because you never do anything by halves. Remember at uni when you were doing your dissertation. You had to track down one of the guys who worked on that first computer thingy."

"The ENIAC machine. So, what's wrong with that? It's research."

"You flew to Pennsylvania to interview him."

"So? I needed a primary source. It was really cool. He had photos and everything."

"Yeah, yeah: 18,000 vacuum tubes and it filled a huge room, I know. But don't you think it was a little over the top?"

"I got a first, didn't I?"

"Yes, you did. But that's just it. You're an over-achiever. This accident was just another indication of that."

"Are you calling me a control-freak?"

"No, I'm just saying that sometimes you reach for the stars, that's all." She paused while thinking of more examples for her argument. "Take Steve. You could have stuck with boring old Matt, but no, you have to go for the hottest art property in London. Not that there's anything wrong with it – I'd go there myself given half the chance . . ."

"Sandi, stop. It's not going to happen."

"What?"

"Me and Steve. I've decided not to."

"Since when?"

"Since then."

"But you were happy when I came in. Me and my big mouth. Just ignore everything I said. Remember how happy you were before I arrived."

"I won't ignore what you said. You were right."

"I'm never right. Jane's the one who is right. Wait until she gets back. Don't make any hasty decisions."

"I'm not making hasty decisions. I realised a truth."

"What sort of truth?"

"It'll never work."

"Why not?"

"Because."

"Because you're a big fat wuss."

"Because, he is the hottest property in London and what hot property would want to go to celebrity parties with a big fat wuss in a wheelchair?"

"Steve Wallace isn't like that. He likes you as you are."

"Steve Wallace doesn't matter. He doesn't really know me anyway. This is about me. I can't take the risk. My life's a mess as it is. I'm going to need all my energy for me. I'm not going to start a relationship. I won't. I can't."

"Alright, I see that this is not the best time to discuss it. You're obviously a bit emotional. We'll talk about it another day."

"We're not going to talk about it. You think this is easy for me? I've been stuck here for months. Every time I have a ray of hope that things are getting better, something else happens to bring me down. I can't handle it any more. I can't face it. Sure these things are great at first, but every relationship turns to crap eventually. Look at Matt. It was wonderful in the beginning, but then look what happened – apparently I was going out with the merchant banker from hell – yes, I was talking in rhyming slang – and I find out my friends were too chicken to tell me. I've had enough. I'll need all my strength for when I get out of here. I'll be perfectly fine by myself, in fact better than fine. It'll be great."

Sandi shook her head slightly, but wisely decided not to contradict me. I could tell she was taken aback by my outburst, but had realised that discretion was the better part of valour. She picked up her handbag and said, "I'll come back later this evening with some Chinese. Have a good day."

"I will."

As soon as Sandi had left, I pressed my call button. While I was waiting, I rummaged around in the bag full of documents that Craig had dropped off before he'd gone on holiday. It had to be in there somewhere. My fingers closed around something that felt like the item I was searching for. A few minutes later, Suzanne's head peered round the door.

"What can I do for you?"

"Suzanne, can you do me a favour?"

"Of course."

I opened up the chequebook that I'd found and began writing out a cheque. "Could you get hold of a courier company and ask them to deliver that painting back to the Steppmann Gallery in London." I tossed the little *Wallace Collection* booklet to her. "The address is in there. I've signed this cheque. You'll have to fill out the rest once you've found out how much it costs."

"But, Kate –"

"Could you do it for me?"

"Of course I can, but –"

"Thank you." My voice brooked no argument and Suzanne knew that I had made up my mind.

"I'm going to need some help carrying that. I'll be right back." She disappeared, returning moments later with another nurse.

Just as they were leaving, I had another thought. "And Suzanne, I'd rather that Mr Wallace not visit me anymore."

Suzanne frowned and I could tell she was just itching to say something, but instead she just uttered, "Whatever you say."

So there I was, alone in my room. I'd done the right thing. Of course I'd done the right thing. As if in confirmation, the little devil hopped back onto my shoulder, executed a celebratory pirouette as though accepting applause and began to take a succession of triumphant bows.

Chapter Twenty-Two

Bride of Dracula

"Are you sure you're alright, love?" The waitress peers anxiously over the table at me. "You're looking right peaky. Shall I get you a cup of tea?"

I shake myself out of the half-trance that I found myself in and smile sadly. "You sound like one of the nurses."

"Nurses, eh? You been in hospital then?"

"Yes, I was in Manchester General."

"Then you're lucky to have got out of that place alive. I hate hospitals me, but that one, well, it's the kiss of death, if you get my meaning."

"What d'you mean?"

"I mean, loads of people go in, but very few come back out again."

"That's hardly the fault of the hospital though."

"Oh I know, but Irene only went in for her gall bladder and turned out she had . . ." The waitress lowered her voice to barely a whisper, paused dramatically and breathed, "cancer."

"Again you can hardly blame the –"

"Same thing happened to Dorothy from the newsagents – went in for an in-growing toenail and found out she had lung cancer. But then again, she did smoke nearly a hundred a day, God rest her soul." She hastily crossed herself and continued. "Too many coincidences for my liking. Me, I go up the Royal Infirmary if anything's bothering me."

"Well, I found it perfectly fine. In fact the nursing staff were excellent as far as I'm concerned."

"Aah, but what about the night staff?" She taps the side of her nose a couple of times and wanders off winking at me.

I begin to wonder if she isn't just that teensy-weensy bit barmy. Then I remember: the night staff.

I called them the 'people of the night' 'cos they all seemed to be really really creepy. Most of them were agency staff and not my normal nurses. The majority of them were pallid in their complexions; their skin had that faint yellow tinge like vampires who didn't ever emerge into the daylight. There was one nurse, who I called the 'Bride of Dracula' because it seemed to fit her perfectly. She was tall and very skinny with a v-shaped hairline. She rarely spoke, but when she did it was in a deep, hoarse whisper. She immediately took an intense disliking to me; I was never sure why. The only thing I could come up with was that she resented the fact that I had a room all to myself, which my friends had filled with all my cool stuff from home. Whatever the reason for her dislike, she made sure that I knew of its existence. Especially in the early days, when I couldn't move out of my bed and had to rely on the bedpans and was forced to call for assistance in the middle of the night. I can still clearly remember my first encounter with the Bride of Dracula.

"Yessss." She hissed menacingly at me through a small crack in my door.

"I . . . um . . . could I . . . have a bedpan, please?"

"If you must," she whispered and disappeared.

I waited and waited. About fifteen minutes and an awful lot of pained 'holding-in' later I was forced to ring for assistance once more.

"Yesss." The hiss was definitely more irritated this time.

"Um . . . I'm really sorry, but I . . . need it quite . . . er . . . desperately now."

"We do have other patients. We can't all be running around after people like you, you know."

Now, normally I would have queried the 'people like you' comment quite forcefully, but I was fully aware that further delays in the fetching of the bedpan would result in a rather nasty 'accident' so I simply whimpered, "Please, it is pretty urgent now."

The BoD sighed loudly muttering that 'some people need to learn patience' and closed the door.

Just when I was about to lose the small amount of control that I had over my bladder, she returned.

"Can you lift yourself up?" she murmured.

"Yes." This was only a very small white lie, because I really didn't want to tell her that I'd never in fact attempted it before. But I was certain that I could do it, so it came out a bit more forcefully than it should have.

"Go, on then."

I tried to remember what the physios had taught me about using the handle above my bed – should I sit up and lift or lift myself into a sitting position? I was frantically trying to remember.

"Will you get a move on. I do have others to take care of, you know."

I grunted in a weird sort of amusement at the idea of her actually taking care of anyone, but decided it was time for me to grasp the nettle (or the handle, if we're being 100 per cent accurate) and with a huge burst of effort I raised myself just high enough for her to thrust the bedpan underneath. And thrust she did, so hard and so awkwardly that she managed to wedge one of the sides between my buttocks, so that instead of sitting on top of the pan, it was sideways on and cutting painfully into me. There she left it and disappeared, presumably to 'take care of' other patients. And that's when I realised that she meant 'take care of' in the mafia sense, obviously.

After a very difficult period of trying to manoeuvre the cardboard pan into the correct position, I did my business. I hoped that she would remember to come and retrieve the bedpan, knowing full well that it was a vain hope. Another twenty minutes I waited and finally, unwilling to press the bell again, I decided that I would try and remove the pan myself. It was a delicate operation, but I eventually managed it. With a triumphant flourish I placed it on the trolley table beside my bed, covered it with a couple of large paper towels, pushed the table away from me as far as I could and went back to sleep.

When I awoke the following morning, I saw that the bedpan was still there and wasn't quite sure what to think. On the one hand, I was horrified that she hadn't returned to dispose of the contents of the bedpan, but on the other, I was pleased that she hadn't been roaming around in my room while I was asleep. I checked my neck for puncture

marks, just to be on the safe side, and then made a decision.
I would never again allow myself to be at the mercy of the
'people of the night'. From that point on, until I was able to
make my own way to the toilet and unless one of my nurses
were on night duty, I would refuse to drink anything after
six o'clock at night, take a rather large sleeping tablet and
sleep right through until morning.

Thinking about it now I realise that this incident was
pretty horrific, and was shocked that I'd almost forgotten all
about it. I wonder what other experiences I've managed to
sublimate . . . but I suppose I should really get on with the
story.

Chapter Twenty-three

Passing Out Parade

In the two weeks that followed the banning of Steve Wallace from my thoughts and my mind, I had what I delicately refer to now as a relapse. Both Sandi and Daniel carried an almost constant look of concern. In the face of my wildly swinging moods, they must have been anxious because they called in the 'big guns'. Daniel began prescribing Valium and before I knew it, more little pills appeared in my four-hourly medication cup. And one unusually sunny day for that time of year, out of nowhere, Gen appeared. In my tranquillised state, it seemed that she must have been on 24-hour suicide watch or something, because every waking moment, her face swam before me. Her hands stroked my hair and her soothing voice was like a soundtrack to my endless days. She muttered something about it being nearly Easter and her needing a break from evil client and it took me a few days to realise that she'd taken time off work to look after me.

Then one day, without ceremony, I was wheeled out of my room and into theatre. In my heavily sedated state, I didn't really register what was going on. I didn't even mind about the time that was stolen from me during the operation.

I was vaguely aware of shushing noises and I felt the presence of many people. There was a hazy hum in the air as if a group of people were trying to be extremely quiet. I was still groggy from the operation and the medication, so it took some time to force my eyes open.

"She's waking up," I heard Sandi whisper.

The silence was immediate. I ventured a quick peek, opening just one eye. As soon as my vision cleared I saw a huge banner. 'Congratulations' it shouted in its huge red lettering.

"Surprise!" A multitude of voices bellowed.

"What's going on?"

Sandi was in front of me, pointedly staring at my knee. I looked down and realised that I was without metal and all that was left were dressings where the pins had been.

I looked around the packed room. I saw Gen and Daniel, standing off to the side, looking nervous as if they weren't sure that this party was a good idea. Jane and Craig were back from their holiday. Jane, apart from looking like she'd swallowed a basketball, was deeply tanned and radiant – they'd obviously had a great time. Louise looked very tired and she'd visibly lost weight; her blouse was very loose. She'd not been eating properly – I reminded myself to have a word with her about that later on. The guys from Chicanas were there, clapping their hands in glee. There was Anil, smiling his normal happy smile, and my eyes scanned the rest of the room, hoping to see . . . I was looking for . . . I closed my eyes . . . of course he wasn't . . .

"Here you go!" Sandi passed me a cup of what looked and smelt like sparkling apple juice. "You're not allowed alcohol, so we're saving you some of the champers for when you can. Congratulations!"

I looked at the bottles of champagne that she'd pointed at. They looked strange. They had my name on the labels. I pointed at one and Jane hurriedly passed it to me.

Kate Townsend Vintage
Congratulations on being Metal-Free
Getting Better all the Time!

"Aren't they fantastic? I didn't even know you could get personalised champagne. There's another case at your house." Jane was animated. "I haven't had any myself, so make sure you save some for when I can drink again."

"Yeah, he sent two," Sandi said excitedly.

"Who?" Of course, I knew the answer.

"He wanted to come, but they wouldn't let him in. Something about express wishes of the patient," Gen muttered disapprovingly.

"Hey, guys, this is meant to be a party!" Sandi shouted, "Someone turn up the music!"

Sandi grabbed Daniel and started dancing. Gen and Anil joined them and, before we knew it, the party was in full swing.

Jane came and perched beside me on the bed and began telling me all about their holiday, but I must admit, I wasn't listening that hard. My attention was focused on the champagne bottle, which was still in front of me. In the small print, beside the details of the vineyard, were the words *To my Sleeping Beauty ~ Love Always*.

No, I said to myself, don't even think it.

* * *

In the days after the party, my mood improved and Daniel agreed that I no longer required the Valium. My world became clearer once more. I was allowed three days in which to recover from the effects of the operation and then it was business as usual. Lynn and Chris appeared in my room, immediately after rounds, which led me to believe that they had been lying in wait like a couple of vultures.

"Morning, Katherine. How are you today?" Lynn chirped.

"I'm fine, thanks. I can see that you're in a good mood. And you, Chris, how's your day shaping up?"

"Getting better all the time, Katherine." His words were as clear as day and he had a wicked glint in his eye.

"So what are we going to do today?"

Lynn left the room and returned with the familiar metal cage of the Zimmer frame. "Today, we're going to start learning to walk."

"Walk? I can already do that. I graduated on to crutches remember?"

"Ah, yes, but that was before." Lynn quite rightly pointed out, "You'll have to learn –"

"Towalkwithouttheexfix." Chris completed her sentence. I swear he was starting to get far too excited and I wasn't certain that it was altogether proper. I glanced down at his nether regions, just to make sure. Nope, maybe it was just his voice after all.

"That won't be too difficult surely?" My words held a confidence that my mind wasn't really feeling.

"Letsseeshallwe?" Chris offered me his arm.

"I'll be fine." I brushed him away.

"Before you do, just remember that you're not to weight-bear until I say so."

Why didn't she just say, don't put your leg down getting out of bed? I tutted – medical people! I swung my legs around, planted my left on the floor, leaned over until my weight was over it and lifted myself off the bed. "See. Easy."

Two pairs of eyebrows raised in an inscrutable fashion. Lynn moved forward and placed the Zimmer in front of me. Chris moved round behind me.

"You ready, Chris?" Lynn addressed a space just over my right shoulder. She never usually did that.

"Yes ready." Why were they making such a fuss? It wasn't as if I'd never used a Zimmer frame before.

"OK, Katherine. Take a step forward. Just the one, OK?"

"Righty-ho! Here I go!"

A flash went through my brain. My knee felt as if it were being crushed and it began to crumple like a piece of aluminium foil.

So that was why Lynn made sure that he was prepared, I thought, as I passed out into the safe strong arms of Chris.

Lynn roused me a little while later. Why were they still here? Couldn't they tell that my knee wasn't strong enough to support my weight? They should just leave me to sleep. Go away, I thought irritably.

"Go away," I repeated out loud with a pout. "It's not going to work. My knee won't work."

"Now, now, Katherine, where's your spirit?"

"You saw what happened. It won't hold up."

"Katherine, it's perfectly normal. Even a totally healthy knee would buckle if it hadn't been used for three months."

Three months? I counted back. Twelve weeks, yep, that was definitely three months. I tried to get my breath back.

"You mean, I've been here for three months?" That was a gas bill. A quarter of a year.

"Yep, and we've been here with you for most of it."

"Aren'twelucky?" Chris muttered.

"Right now, chit chat over. Let's get going again."

"I'm not sure I'm up to it right now. Can we have another go in the – OW!" I screeched as Chris yanked me upright and placed me in front of the Zimmer frame.

"Onthree."

"One, two, three!"

I took a step forward. The pain was still pretty bad, but I leant over onto my left leg and forward so that the Zimmer could take the strain.

"ThatsgreatKatherinekeepgoing."

With Chris encouraging from the back and Lynn bullying me at the front, I managed to complete another couple of steps before they announced our session was over for the day.

I walked! I really did it. Without the ex-fix. Maybe I was due for a small amount of good news. God knows I'd earned it, hadn't I?

Daniel arrived later on that afternoon, for another one of his 'chats' about my progress.

I didn't even wait for him to get settled. "Don't tell me – you're going to have to take me back in to whip it off for good this time?"

"No, actually, Kate, I have good news for you."

"Oh, yeah?" You can't blame me for being suspicious, can you?

"Yes. When we went in this time, we noticed a great improvement in the stability and I've just read your physiotherapist's report and apparently you took some steps today."

"OK, but what does that mean?"

"It means it's looking more and more likely that I was overcautious with my prognosis."

"Hang on a minute. Let me translate. What you are actually saying is that you were wrong."

"Well I wouldn't go that far, I –"

"You told me I was going to spend the rest of my life in a wheelchair."

"I may have suggested that –"

"So now you're saying I might not have to."

"Well, yes."

"So you were wrong."

"I may have been slightly erroneous, yes."

"You were wrong. Say it."

"OK, Katherine. I was wrong, but –"

"No, buts. You were wrong. Be wrong. Stay wrong. Let me gloat." I smiled broadly and, to his credit, Daniel had the decency to look sheepish.

After a few minutes of silence, I felt I'd basked in his wrongness for long enough so I said, "OK, you can carry on now."

"You'll be able to walk, but –"

"How did I know that there was going to be a 'but'?"

Daniel ignored me and continued. "But, it'll be a long

road. A long, long road to recovery and it's unlikely you'll ever be how you were before."

"How I was before?"

"You'll never have full range of movement. There was just too much damage. As it is you don't have any cruciate ligaments . . ."

I dared not ask what cruciate ligaments were – I didn't care. Apparently I could have a full active life without them or so he was telling me. He began a long list of things that I wouldn't be able to do: sports, running, exercising, trampolining. I wasn't too concerned. Who'd want to do any of that anyhow? I would be able to walk. I had a question, but I wasn't sure if I wanted to hear the answer.

"When?"

"Huh?"

"When will I be able to walk?"

"Kate." He looked disapproving.

"What? I want to know."

"How long's a piece of string?"

"Yours or mine?"

"Excuse me?"

"Your string or mine?"

"Kate, that was a rhetorical question. You are the only person on the planet who could answer a rhetorical question with a completely serious question of their own." He shook his head in disbelief. "What difference does it make whose string it is?"

"Well, your string would probably be much longer than mine for one thing. Mine would definitely be very short."

"That's what I mean, Kate."

"What?"

"Be patient."

That was the full sum of his medical advice. Be patient. I began to seethe, then I realised that there was no point. Daniel got up to leave.

"How can I be patient? Is there something I'm missing? Tell me how."

"There's an art to being patient, Kate."

"Go on then, Yoda, hit me with it!"

"Stop pushing. Just let go." He turned and went towards the door.

I understood what he meant, honest I did, but the devil inside of me refused to let him have the last word.

"Let go of what?" I shouted at the door.

Chapter Twenty-four

Crotchless Knickers and Doughnuts

The rest of April was like a long rollercoaster. My efforts to walk were stuttering at best. Each time I thought I was improving, I had another setback, which threatened to suck me into another 'relapse'. This was prevented by a constant stream of visiting friends keeping my spirits up. They'd obviously agreed that I wasn't to be left alone for any longer than a few hours at a time.

Sandi had obviously done her duty for the time being and had disappeared off for a week to 'sort out some paperwork', but I suspected that she'd hooked up with a sexy bod and was sorting out a completely different need altogether.

Gen had returned to work, but was commuting to Sheffield so that she could still keep an eye on me. She usually popped in really early in the morning on her way to Yorkshire with coffee and sweet things. Together we read the papers and discussed the weighty issues of the day, like which actress had had her boobs done and did we think that the latest celebrity marriage was going to last longer than a bout of flu?

Jane came in mid-morning and stayed the day. She helped me with the exercises that the physios had given me. We watched daytime TV – actually we spent most of our time discussing daytime TV so there wasn't much watching going on at all. We ate junk food, entirely guilt-free – we both had concrete excuses: she was pregnant and I was poorly, such great luck. We munched and talked through soaps and cookery programmes until it was time for her to get going.

Louise's case had finished and so finally she was able to spend time with me. She'd usually appear at around seven in the evening and stay until the nurses kicked her out. My visits with Louise were more restful than with any of the others. She wasn't as butch as Gen, as boisterous as Sandi or as erratic as Jane. Louise was a good influence.

"Kate, d'you think this guy's got a big dick?"

Alright, maybe she wasn't such a good influence after all. She was pointing to a GQ model, one of those gorgeous, brooding men who was modelling for an Italian designer. I'd noticed that she'd been more and more sex-obsessed lately and this was very unlike Louise 'frozen-knickers' Carter.

"Why should this be our concern?"

"I was just thinking. He obviously works out, so we have no idea what he looked like before he got all buffed up. He was probably really small and skinny. He's built up his body by exercising, but you can't work out your dick, can you?"

"Speak for yourself. I work mine out every day."

"You've not got one." Ever the serious lawyer, Louise had

never been good at spotting a joke. "What I'm saying is: say you're a nine-stone weakling –"

"Chance would be a fine thing."

"Kate. Listen to me and stop cracking jokes. I'm serious."

"You always are."

"What's that supposed to mean?" Louise shook her head and pointed a finger at me. "Nope, I'm not going to let you force me off track. You always do that. I'm going to finish my thought and we'll get back to this."

"Be my guest." I smirked – that lawyer's brain of hers was never easy to deflect.

"My point was –"

I interrupted, "Long and going nowhere."

Louise threw the magazine at me. "I give up! I really hate you sometimes."

"Now, now, Miss Carter, you know you love me, I know you love me. Don't try and fight it."

All Louise could do was laugh. I loved to hear her laugh, mainly because she did it so rarely. It was a perfect woman's laugh, like the tinkling of a crystal bell. I'd always imagined that it was what Victorian women sounded like, but there was something different in her laugh that evening, a brittleness.

"Tell me about it, Louise."

"About what?"

"You're obsessing about magazine mens' dicks. What's going on?"

"I'm not obsessing. I was pondering."

"Semantics. Spill."

"He left me."

"Who? Taxi driver?"

"Yep."

218

"But I thought you were ready to get married and everything."

"So did I." A solitary tear ran down her cheek.

I was shocked. This was a woman who only ever showed emotion when she'd imbibed a pint of tequila. Now, she was sitting in my armchair, completely sober, crying her eyes out. Call me selfish, but I didn't like it at all. Louise didn't cry; the world was no longer a safe place.

"What happened?"

She sniffed. "I got a pay rise."

"Huh?" I admit I was confused. I really wasn't expecting that one.

"I did a great job on the Sullivan case and they gave me a pay rise," she sniffed once more, "and a bonus."

"But that's good, surely?"

"I thought so, but Terry wasn't particularly happy about it. He said that we could never work, we were from different worlds and where he came from, men should do the breadwinning."

"But that's ridiculous! Why should it matter? Who thinks like that these days anyhow? It's not the 1950s!"

"It doesn't matter to me. But he said I was taking away – his – his – manhood." She managed to squeeze the final words out before she broke down again.

"How?"

"I don't know!" she wailed. "Sometimes, I'd come home with little things for him. You know, gifts. I was working so hard, I suppose I felt guilty that I'd not seen him much, you know. I got little things: clothes, aftershave, a cordless drill, that sort of thing."

I let the cordless drill thing go past – this wasn't the time. "So, that's not too bad, is it?"

"No, but then he bought me a pair of diamond earrings."

"Diamond? Real diamond?"

"Yep."

"But how could he afford that?"

"Exactly!" She sounded triumphant. "That's exactly what I said and he went loopy. He started ranting about why I won't let him buy me stuff – I'm always buying him stuff, why can't he do the same?"

"Diamond earrings are not the same as a cordless drill." I knew I just couldn't let it lie. Fortunately, Louise continued.

"I know! But he just couldn't understand that I was concerned that he was spending money that he hadn't got. I didn't need diamond earrings. Anyway, I felt really, really guilty and when they gave me the bonus, I wanted to get him something in return – something, you know, special."

"Oh no." It was more of a groan – I could guess what was coming.

"So, then Sandi was telling me about Steve Wallace giving you a Rolex and I thought, everyone needs a watch –"

"You didn't!"

"I did. It was beautiful. But when I gave it to him he freaked. He accused me of trying to control him, control everything. He said I kept trying to outdo him to prove that I earned more than him. To make him feel like he was nothing. I just kept telling him that I loved him, but he wouldn't listen. He threw the watch on the table and said that he couldn't take it any more. He even said that he hated George, and that the only snake I should have in the bedroom should be the one in his trousers. Then he packed up and left."

"When was this?"

"'Bout two weeks ago"

Two weeks? He'd only been gone for two weeks and already she was in the throes of dick obsession. God, he must have been fabulous in bed. Focus Kate, tell her something comforting.

I cleared my throat. "I'm not that partial to George either. Especially when he sheds his skin. Yeuch!"

She burst into tears, just more vocally this time. Good one, Kate. What on earth do I say now?

"Louise, it'll be fine. He'll come back." She howled like I'd just slapped her in the face with a halibut. I needed to take control of the situation. "Listen to me. I want you to answer this honestly. Do you want him back?"

"Uh-huh." She sniffed.

"Then go get him."

She stopped dead in the middle of a sniff. "How?"

"You're an intelligent girl. You'll figure something out. I'm sure you can convince him that he can't do without you. It can't be that difficult – you argue complicated points of law on a daily basis."

"I do, don't I?"

"Yep."

"You're right. I can fight for him, can't I?"

"Of course you can. Just go about it the same way you would one of your cases." I contemplated this for a moment and added, "But with a lot less clothing. Don't forget men are controlled by their downstairs brain."

"Gotcha." Louise got out her notebook and started writing. "You are a genius."

"All in a night's work, Ma'am." I tipped my imaginary hat.

I watched her scribbling away in her pad. Every now and then, she'd look up and say things like, 'crotchless knickers?' and 'edible bras?', stuff I really didn't want to know about. I was just glad to see her looking more like her normal self.

"Look, I'd better be off. I've got a few things to plan." She started packing things away in her handbag and putting on her coat.

"Get some sleep first, and Louise –"

"Yeah."

"Eat something, won't you?"

"OK, I will. Good night, Kate."

Damn, I was good.

* * *

By the end of the month, I had graduated onto crutches once more and I was feeling much, much better about my recovery. Lynn and Chris were almost beside themselves with pleasure at how far I'd come.

Daniel had been right. I'd stopped trying to force the improvements and had started to simply 'go with the flow'. I just took each day as it came. Soon, I was wandering around the corridors on my own, building up the strength in my knee, hoping against hope that the more I walked, the more likely I'd eventually be able to lose the crutches and walk unaided.

"We're not trying to fix you up like new, you know, Kate," Daniel explained when he returned after rounds to snack on the doughnuts that Gen had dropped off with coffee earlier that morning.

"What are you doing then, Danny-Boy?"

"I'll let that one go, but only because you've been doing

so well these past few weeks, Kate, my old girl." He jabbed me in the ribs. "What I'm trying to do is give you a knee, which allows a workable range of movement so you can walk pain-free."

"Workable range of movement?"

"Yeah, workable: enough movement for you to be able to carry out everyday tasks. Your knee will probably never fully bend. Think about it: it's been kept straight for twelve weeks – it's stiffened up. You're going to need plenty of physio when you finally leave."

I'd given up asking him when that might be. Instead, I simply dreamt of the day that I would finally go back to my house. I tried to remember what it looked like. It was another lifetime, the days of a completely different person. I'd long ago realised that my life was irreversibly altered, but I still couldn't imagine what my new one would be like. I'd been in hospital so long, I almost believed that I belonged there. Having my private room didn't help matters either.

One major thought spun around and around in my head. Would I be able to cope? Then there were the minor thoughts: could I cope without nurses on the end of a call button? Without the physios forcing me out of bed each day? I'd got into a routine. As much as I poked fun at hospital monotony, I'd been sucked into its comforting rhythm. Suddenly I realised that I didn't actually want to leave. I was safe here. Would I be able to look at my home in the same way? After all, that's where I had the accident? Every time I went down those stairs, I would be reminded of it. How would that affect me?

I was so deep in thought that I really didn't catch Daniel's question when uttered.

"What do you think?" he repeated.

"About what?" I said distractedly.

"Have you been listening to a word I've said?"

"Yeah, sort of. You were going on about needing physio when I get out."

"Kate. That was about ten minutes and three doughnuts ago."

"Three doughnuts? Do you not know how to feed yourself? How come you're always eating all my food?"

"Your stuff is so much more interesting than what I have in my fridge."

"What do you have in your fridge?"

"Right now?"

"Right now."

"Um . . . two lemons, half an onion, a tube of squeezy cheese and some leftover Thai food."

"I think you'll find the Thai food was mine to start with."

"You're right, forget the Thai food."

"Here, take the rest of these. It looks like you need them." I passed him the remaining doughnuts and rooted around in my locker for additional supplies. "There you go, take these as well."

"Gee, thanks." He looked at the tube of Pringles, then at me with a shocked expression. "I don't believe it."

"What?"

"Gen warned me about you and your ability to send people whizzing off on a tangent before they've had time to catch their breath."

"Huh?"

"We were talking about you going home and all of a sudden we're talking about food. How did you do that?"

"Lots of practice, I guess." I smiled: at least I was good at something.

Then Daniel's words began to sink through into my consciousness.

"Me going . . . home?" My throat constricted. Was I hearing things? "Did you say I was going home?"

"Yep."

"When?"

"When do you want to go?"

I stared at him, expecting him to laugh and say that it was all just a joke, but he was completely serious.

"I can just say a day?"

"Yep, within reason. You'll still have to stay in a couple of days because you have to be assessed by the occupational therapist. Your physios say that you can do stairs with no problem, they think you'll be fine. You'll have a home visit and then you can go. So what day do you want to leave?"

It was a Thursday, so I said, "Next Thursday?"

"Next Thursday it is then." Daniel slapped his thigh and stood up. "I'll be back later. I hear its chilli for dinner tonight. Have a good day, Kate."

"You bet your little consultant booties I will, Mister," I smirked.

I sat in silence for approximately thirty seconds, before pressing the call button. In next to no time, Suzanne appeared.

"Get me the phone, Suzy-baby. Katie has plans to make."

"Huh?" She looked at me as if I'd gone mad.

"I'M GOING HOME!" I shrieked.

Chapter Twenty-five

Dip into the Postbag (Interlude)

You may recall that I mentioned a bag of stuff that Craig had dropped by before going on his holiday with Jane. Well, seeing as I was preparing to pack up and leave, I decided to actually examine its contents. The bag contained the various bits of mail that I had received. The official ones had been opened by Craig, so that he could maintain an overview of my affairs. The personal ones he had left sealed, obviously unwilling to pry more than absolutely necessary. There were quite a few surprises in store for me as I read the letters.

The first one was a letter from The Balacci Corporation. It had been opened, so I knew that whatever they'd wanted had already been dealt with by the efficient Craig. I decided to read it anyway, just to get up to speed. The letter was dated February 28.

Dear Katherine, it read, *We have recently been informed by Mr Craig Fuller, who is acting on your behalf, that you are unlikely to be discharged from hospital for at least five months.*

We would hate to be the cause of any additional strain during this trying time. Therefore, after consultation with Pirkka, we have decided to continue paying you in full until such time as we are able to discuss further action after your discharge from hospital. Do not concern yourself with your clients. Claudia Hermann from the German office has temporarily transferred to the UK to take control of your accounts. Please do take care of yourself and simply concentrate on getting better. We would hate to lose a consultant of your skill and ability. We look forward to hearing from you after your release from hospital to discuss the way forward. Please do not hesitate to contact us if we can be of assistance before then. Best wishes, Marco Balacci.

I stared at the letter in shock. Marco being nice? I must have read it wrong. I re-read the text and tried to take it all in. Marco and Pirkka, Miss Scandinavian Bitch from the depths of Hell, had agreed to pay me in full. No wonder there had been no problems from the money side of the entire episode. Maybe they both didn't hate me as much as I thought.

Then it hit me.

I had been paid my full salary, but I had been in hospital and therefore unable to spend any money. I was loaded! I scrabbled around in the carrier bag, to find some bank statements. Yippee! The statements confirmed my thoughts, Loadsamoney! If I were able to I would have danced a happy jig.

Grinning from ear-to-ear, I picked up an envelope that was unopened, obviously a personal one. I turned it around and the smile disappeared from my face. It was addressed to me care of Jane. The writing was strong, firm and undoubtedly by Steve Wallace. Below the address was a handwritten note from Jane which read, *'You better read this or I'll put a curse on you. How you could let a man this fine get away I'll never know'.* Obviously at this point Craig had stopped her because the next sentence was unmistakably in his hand: *'Just ignore her, read it only if you want to.'*

With trembling hands, I ripped the letter open. It was dated April 4, two days after I decided not to see him again. I really didn't want to read any further, but something in my gut forced me to continue.

Dear Katherine, so far so good, *Today, a package arrived at the gallery in London. I was informed that it was the painting I'd sent you. I cannot accept it back, it belongs to you. I have therefore sent it to your friend Jane for safe-keeping in the hope that eventually you will accept it in the spirit in which it was given. I tried to see you at the hospital and I was turned away. But I understand.* I was confused – how on earth could he understand? I barely understood myself. This simply served to confirm all previous thoughts I'd had about our Mr Wallace: he was as crazy as a blue-striped loon. For Goodness sakes, we hardly knew each other! I carried on reading. *You can say we hardly know each other.* OK, so a point for Mr Wallace for a lucky guess. It's not as if it was a difficult one to predict, I muttered grumpily and continued. *You can make all the excuses you want, but you and I both know that there is something special between us. I realise that the timing is not perfect. You need to concentrate on getting well. I do not want to be a distraction from this important task. Do what you need to do, but remember this: I care for you too much to lose you from my life. Wallace.*

Now, what the hell was I supposed to do with that? I pondered my predicament for a while and did the only thing

I could at this point. I hid the letter under the junk mail in the 'destroy immediately' pile and pretended that I hadn't seen it.

I opened various letters from colleagues and acquaintances all wishing me a speedy recovery and asking that I get in touch as soon as I was able. These I put in a 'to write back' pile. Just as I thought I'd dealt with everything, I found a small envelope in the bottom of the carrier bag. I didn't recognise the writing and even though I'd almost had enough of reading letters, I didn't want to leave the job unfinished. So I tore it open. It was short, to the point and managed to clear up a long-standing mystery.

Dear Kate, I was wrong. I need you. I want you back. Love Matt. PS, I hope you liked the flowers. So Matt was my valentine. That made sense in a messed-up, screwball, wrong-time-wrong-guy kind of way. There was no date on the note, so I had no way of knowing if this was a recent change of heart. It could have been written any time after Valentine's Day, but I decided it must have been fairly recent or Jane would have brought it to me earlier.

I started a new pile and named it 'cold day in hell'.

I picked up the 'to write back' pile, took out some of the fancy writing paper that Gen had had made for me and started writing. After a couple of hours, I'd managed to catch up with all the personal correspondence. It was strangely soothing and for a moment I was sad that all the new forms of electronic communication had somehow displaced letter-writing. I mean, as great as email is, nothing can really compare with opening a thick letter and settling back to read news from friends and colleagues. For example, Claudia Hermann, the German consultant who'd generously taken over my clients in the UK, had brought me up to speed on Farmer and Sons, one of my Manchester clients. Jack Farmer was notoriously finicky and more than a little prissy. Apparently he didn't appreciate having to change consultants. Upon hearing the news that I'd had an accident and was likely to be in hospital for quite a considerable time, he'd announced that it was 'exceedingly inconsiderate of me to have become incapacitated at such a delicate stage of the project'. Claudia had assured him that it was definitely not personal and although she hadn't had a chance to speak to me, she was certain that I wouldn't be making a habit of it. In my reply I told her that as distressing as my foray into disability was, it was infinitely preferable to half an hour of Mr Farmer's company and I wished her the best of luck sorting out his warped internal systems.

By the time I'd finished and apart from the writer's cramp, I felt refreshed, relaxed and ready to take on the world. At which point, Lynn and Chris appeared in my room with the intention of making me knackered and irritable again.

Chapter Twenty-six

Tears Before Bedtime

I was on the home-straight and streaking towards the finishing post. OK, maybe not streaking, more like limping along dragging crutches, but you know what I mean. My final week in hospital went by in a blur of frantic activity.

As soon as I realised that I had rather a lot of dosh in my account and that I was out of practice on the retail-therapy front, I immediately rang Jane with instructions on how she could help me remedy both situations.

"OK, Kate, I have here catalogues for all occasions," Jane said as she began throwing them on my bed one by one. "Clothing, electrical goods, computer stuff, food, shoes, lingerie, books and music. Oh and Truly Scrummy have got a new one out, it looks fab."

"Truly Scrummy? What the . . .?"

"They make bath potions, creams and you know, stuff that smells so good you want to eat it, and even though you know it'll probably kill you, you still can't stop yourself from having a little taste. Have a look, the catalogue is gorgeous. There's 'scratch and sniff' bits too!"

She exhaled loudly and plonked herself down in the armchair. She picked up a shoe catalogue and began flicking through it.

"You've forgotten something, haven't you?"

"No, they're all there. I swear. I double-checked before I left the house."

"No, Jane, think! What did I ask you to pick up from my house?"

"Silly me, you're right! I tell you this pregnancy thing is a nightmare. I have no short-term memory at all. I'm sorry." She rooted around in her handbag and withdrew my small mobile phone. "I brought the hands-free, just in case you want to be even more discreet. Plus, while I was in your house, I thought I'd bring you some stuff to wear. Get you out of those nighties finally. You have to get used to putting clothes on again."

"Thanks." I surveyed the catalogues in front of me. "Where should I start?"

"Get dressed first." She looked pointedly at my saggy boobs. "At least pop a bra on, eh?"

"Good idea."

It wasn't as easy as I thought it would be and at first I wanted to give up. But with Jane's encouragement, I finally managed to imprison my breasts in a smart Marks & Sparks number. Pulling on the rest of my outfit, I was astonished to find that despite the luxurious food that I'd been enjoying, I'd still managed to lose some weight and my clothes were baggy all over.

"Looks like I should go for the clothing first, what d'you

reckon?" I turned to Jane, pulling out the waistband of the skirt to show just how big it was on me.

Jane emptied a carrier bag containing a huge array of chocolate products onto the bottom of my bed. She grabbed a huge bag of M&Ms, I settled for the large bag of Revels, then we each picked up a clothing catalogue and started shopping. After a good hour's perusal, and after consuming half my body-weight in chocolate, I'd come up with a long list of things to order.

"Alrighty, can you order these while I check out the shoe booklet? That way, if they catch you using the phone, you can always say it's yours."

I passed Jane my list and she began phoning through my order.

Shoes were a completely different prospect altogether. Due to my injuries, my leg still had a lot of oedema – that's swelling to you and me – and I doubted if I would be able to find anything that would fit my huge right foot. This wasn't as much fun as I thought it would be. Usually shoe shopping was my passion, but flicking past page after page of slinky little pumps and strappy sandals, I realised that I'd have to find a new passion. In the end I gave up on the shoes altogether and ordered a couple of pairs of Reeboks from the Littlewoods catalogue. It was only when I started browsing through the Truly Scrummy brochure that I found my new passion.

Smellies!

They had an amazing array of gorgeous bath bombs and shower gels, soaps and moisturisers. I was in heaven and what with the 'scratch and sniff' bits I could really smell the wonderful fragrances. I devoured every page like a junkie who'd missed too many fixes.

"Jane, this is fantastic!"

"What? Oh that, yeah it's brilliant, I love the blue lagoon range. Louise gave me some soaks when I'd been driving her mad moaning about all my aches and pains. I chucked one in the bath and I've not looked back. They're all made from natural ingredients and they've got such brilliant names – squishy-wishy, that's a lavender and jasmine bath soak with glittery bits, then there's hyper hippy, orange and sandalwood rejuvenating shower foam . . ."

"Amandarama, superfolium, loopy-doopy," I continued, "I love it. You finished with the phone? I wanna give them a call."

Jane passed the mobile and I dialled the number.

"Truly Scrummy, Julie speaking. How may I help you?"

"Good morning, Julie." I couldn't believe it, a new voice! I'd not really thought much about it, but it is surprising how many people you speak to in the course of even one week. Think about it – people who deliver your milk, your post, people at the corner shop and your local chippy, your hairdresser, the people you see everyday on the bus to work, till operators at the supermarket, the weird guy that sells the evening paper in town, who instead of shouting "Manchester Evening News Final Edition" shouts something like "Manroos-fial" – the list is endless. After four months of the same people – even though they were my favourite people – I was speaking to someone new and completely different and I was determined to enjoy this conversation. "My name is Katherine Townsend and I would like to make an order. But first, do you deliver to hospitals? Well not, like, every hospital, just the one I'm in."

"Good morning to you, Katherine. I don't see why not. Did you say you were in hospital?"

"Yeah. I've been in for ages, but I'm coming out next week."

"How long have you been in?"

"Nearly four months."

"Oh my goodness, that sounds awful."

"Actually, it wasn't too bad." I couldn't believe I'd just said that.

"But you're feeling better now, I hope?"

"Yes, but I've really missed not being able to go shopping. My friend's just given me your brochure and I must say everything looks wonderful."

"Thank you. It's always nice to get feedback from our customers, especially new ones."

"Oh, I'm definitely one of those and I hope soon to be a little bit poorer as well."

"I can certainly help you there," Julie chuckled. "What would you like?"

"I'd like pages two, three, four, five and seven please."

Jane choked on her M&Ms and there was silence at the other end of the line.

Julie coughed. "I'm sorry, Katherine – I don't understand."

"No need to apologise. I would like everything on pages two, three, four, five and seven please."

"Every . . . thing?"

"Yep, every single item on each of those pages."

"Are you . . . um . . . sure?"

"Hmmm, let's see?" I pondered for a second then reconsidered. "You're right – I'd like two of everything on page nine as well please. Those bath bombs look brilliant and so nicely packaged – they'll make great presents for the nurses."

"Well, Katherine, let me see if I got this right. Pages two, three, four, five and seven and two of everything on page nine?"

"That's right." I read out my credit-card number very slowly because I could tell that she was still a little dazed. After many, many assurances that I wasn't in a psychiatric ward, Julie told me that with their priority post, I should get everything within two days.

"Would you like to hang on while I add it all up?"

"No, just charge it. You have an honest voice. I trust you. Thank you so much, Julie."

"No, Katherine, thank you."

I pressed the end-call button, looked over at Jane who was still choking on a M&M and I smirked. Julie had been so lovely. Thank goodness I hadn't been stuck on one of those automated order-lines. I felt elated, euphoric, it was better than any drug you could buy: shopping. I screamed with pleasure. I was a bit out of practice, so I couldn't remember 100 per cent, but in that moment I was positive that it was better than sex.

I raised my hands above my head like a boxer who'd just won the heavyweight championship of the world and bellowed: "KATE TOWNSEND IS BACK!"

* * *

My final day in the hospital whizzed by and before I knew it I was alone in my room on Thursday afternoon waiting for Jane and Craig to come and pick me up.

That morning, I'd had a surprisingly emotional visit from Lynn and Chris. I'd been told that I would be having physio three times a week as an outpatient and I'd assumed that I'd be seeing them for quite a while to come, so Lynn's words came as a big shock.

"So, Katherine. This is it. It's been fun."

"Yeahseeya." Chris waved and headed back out the door.

"OI! Just you stay where you are, Mister. What d'you mean 'see ya'? I'll be seeing you next week, won't I? In outpatients?"

"Nope." Lynn shrugged. "We only work the wards. You'll be assigned another physio over there."

"Another physio? But I don't want another physio!" I pouted like a little child.

"Ohstopwhiningyouwuss."

"So I won't be seeing you again?"

"Nope." Lynn patted me on the shoulder. "At least I bloody well hope not."

"What?" I can't explain it, but this comment hurt. I thought they at least liked me a little bit.

"Ifweseeyouagainitmeansthatyouareinhere." Chris attempted to look sympathetic. "Thatiswhatshemeant."

"Yeah, yeah, that's what I meant," Lynn agreed unconvincingly. "Oh well, we're pretty busy so we'd best be off. Just wanted to say bye."

"Yeahbye." They both turned around and started to leave the room.

"Hang on. I have something to say." I started to well up.

"Make it snappy then, we've got people to torture."

"I just wanted to say that although it hasn't always been a pleasure, I'm glad that I had you both as my physios. You bullied me and sometimes dragged me out of bed when I didn't want to." Tears were streaming down my face because I suddenly realised that I was really going to miss them.

237

Lynn feigned a yawn and looked at her watch, but I could see the telltale glistening of a tear in the corner of her eye. "I'm losing the will to live here, Katherine. Is there a point to any of this?"

I sniffed. "Of course there's a bleeding point. You gave me back my legs. You made me walk. And all I can say is – is – thank – you – and – I'll – I'll – miss –"

I couldn't go on any longer. I was choked up and all I could do was look from Lynn to Chris and back again. We stood in silence for what seemed like an age, but was probably closer to about a minute. I went towards the bedside cabinet in search of tissues. Out of nowhere, I heard a wail and turned to see the huge muscled bulk of Chris coming towards me in tears.

He bundled me up into his huge arms and yowled, "I'llmissyoutooKatherinetakecareofyourself!"

Chris finally let me go and Lynn snorted in disgust. "For goodness sakes, Chris, do you have to do that every time? I'm just about sick of you snivelling whenever a patient leaves. Come on, Mrs Finch needs our help."

She grabbed Chris by the shoulder and dragged him towards the door. Just before she exited, I was convinced that I saw her wiping her eyes, but that was probably just a mirage of some kind.

* * *

So there I was. Dressed in my new 'going home' outfit, sitting in the armchair surveying my now empty room. The drawings on the wall had all been painted over. All except one. In the middle of the largest wall, the sunset was still there bathing the room in its splendour and at the bottom there remained the strong, firm word: *Wallace*. Of course they hadn't wanted to get rid of a potentially priceless mural. The only thing I insisted was that Jane removed the words that had been added in red marker.

My gifts of bath bombs and other gorgeous smelly stuff for the nurses had been distributed. I said a very tearful goodbye to Karen and Suzanne, but having consulted with the girls, I invited them to be honorary members of our coven and so ensured that I'd be seeing them whenever their shifts allowed a Friday night out.

I was all set. I looked at my watch. They were late, but hey, after nearly four months in the place I was hardly going to get upset over a few minutes. The door opened and Daniel entered.

"Good, you're still here."

"Yep. So it appears."

"You've got your medication?"

"Yep, seven days' worth."

"And your clinic appointment for two weeks' time?"

"Yep."

"Well, Kate. Take care of that knee, it's my best work yet."

"I will."

Daniel put his hand out for me to shake, but I ignored it – instead I flung my arms around his shoulders and hugged him fiercely.

Before I pulled away, I put my mouth to his ear and whispered, "Thanks."

"Sorry we're late. My forgetful wife forgot where she put the car keys. Whoops, sorry, are we disturbing something?" Craig and Jane had walked in on the two of us still locked in an embrace.

Daniel extricated himself from my grasp, looking slightly flushed.

"Actually, yes. I was just about to rip his clothes off and ravish him," I leered.

"Well, you can now, can't you? After all, you're not his patient any more, are you?" Jane smiled and gave a thumbs-up.

"Well, technically, she still is. She's not been discharged from my care, she's simply been discharged from hospital." Daniel pointed out with his customary attention to detail.

"Talking of which, shouldn't we get going?" Craig looked at me for agreement.

"Yep," I nodded. Craig led the way, carrying my remaining belongings. Jane and Daniel followed him out the door.

I picked up my crutches and started to leave. Remember what they always say: don't look back? Well, of course I couldn't resist a slight glance.

"Bye, room." I said and allowed the door to click back into place behind me.

Chapter Twenty-seven

Self-Pity and Grapes

So I was home. My home, which had miraculously survived occupation by my younger brother, Benny. He'd been summoned back to the maternal breast as soon as my discharge was announced. Although he had put up a bit of a fight initially by insisting that he wanted to stay and take care of his poorly sister, the thrill of living alone for all that time had worn off, probably due to the fact that he had to do his own cooking and mother wouldn't wash his clothes or do his ironing while he was not living under her roof.

Going home on crutches seemed like a wonderful idea, seeing as I'd almost resigned myself to never walking again. Unfortunately, the reality was somewhat more time-consuming than I'd ever imagined. Going up the stairs with crutches took on 'Everest expedition' proportions. On occasions it took so long, I wished I'd packed some Kendal's mint cake for the journey. I had to set off up the stairs whenever I had the slightest hint that I might require the toilet within the next half hour. I'd wet myself on numerous occasions in the early days before I figured that one out.

Actually, while I'm on the subject of my little bouts of incontinence, can I just have a word or two about catheters? Since I had mine removed my bladder control has never been the same. I used to be the sort of person who had superb bladder muscles. I had on many many occasions 'held it in' throughout an entire transatlantic flight AND customs. In fact if 'holding it in' was an Olympic sport not only would I have won the gold medal, but I would have been a sure-fire bet for the record. My nether regions were like a vacuum-seal: nothing was getting through until I was good and ready. Now I can barely make it through an advert. Not only that, but any sudden coughs and it's like Niagara Falls in my pants.

They say a sneeze comes out at 100 m.p.h – at least that's what Andy in *Gregory's Girl* said, and seeing as he couldn't even spell, he's hardly a reliable source. But it sounds impressive, so I still like to think that it's true. Anyway, imagine that sort of force at both ends simultaneously. One day I sneezed and I swear the force of the resulting gush nearly took my knickers off. It's so awful – I'm barely looking at thirty over my shoulder and already I'm thinking about eyeing up incontinence pants at Boots (from a discreet distance, of course). As far as I can tell, they're like those pull-up things that you give to potty-training infants. You know the ones – 'Look I'm a big girl now!' – but in this case they're more like, 'Look, I'm a big girl's blouse!' with rather less call for cute teddy bear pictures. Of course the manufacturers try to pretend that they're not just overgrown nappies by giving them sophisticated adult names, but we know don't we?

Sorry about that, where was I? Oh yes, the early days at home. I took to moving around my house with a backpack, making checklists of everything I might require when I got to my destination and putting them inside one by one. There's nothing worse than finally making it up the stairs to go to bed and realising that you've left the recently purchased toothpaste downstairs. My teeth went three days without brushing before I'd come up with the list system.

Answering the phone became a chore – even though I had a cordless phone, I would be forever leaving it someplace. Then when it rang, it took me so long to locate it that the person would inevitably give up and put the phone down just as I was pressing the talk button.

Mornings were the worst though. Sometimes in that couple of seconds between sleep and full wakefulness, just before the dull ache seeped into my brain, I'd open my eyes and see the familiar sights of my bedroom: the Monet print on the wall opposite my bed, the wardrobe full to bursting, the iron bedstead with the wobbly bedknob on the bottom left corner. I'd lie there and one thought would whizz through my mind: 'Thank God, the accident was just a dream.' Then I'd look over and see the crutches leaning against my dressing-table, the pain would hit, I'd lean my head back into the pillow and sigh. It was supposed to be better than this.

I know it sounds like I was being really, really ungrateful and everything, but it wasn't how I thought it would be. Every day I looked out of my living-room window and saw my lovely nearly-new car sitting out in the driveway. A gorgeous car that I could no longer drive, due to the nerve damage in my right foot. I was virtually housebound. I loved my friends dearly and although they were always eager to help me get out and about I was unwilling to let them. After all, I was out of hospital, I should no longer be so dependent. I wanted things to get back to normal. I was home and I wanted my life back. Surely that wasn't too much to ask, was it?

I relayed as much to Sandi when she stopped by to take me shopping one day, about three frustrating weeks after leaving hospital.

Sandi started waving her hand in front of her face like she was clearing the air of a thick smoke.

"I'm sorry, Kate, are you there?"

"Of course I'm here. What the hell are you doing?"

"Oh, I'm sorry, I lost sight of you. I couldn't see you for the fog of self-pity that engulfed the room."

"Ha-bloody-ha."

"Well, one day you should try listening to yourself. You escaped that hospital, with life, limb and everything intact. You're galloping around on crutches, when by rights and according to all the medical professionals, you should be in a wheelchair. What more do you need to be happy? A frigging lottery win? Get your arse in gear and let's go shopping."

In the face of such unflinching support, what more could I do? I got my arse in gear and I went shopping. I spent far too much money and had a fantastic time.

* * *

The first two months were all about establishing routines and living through the ups, which sent me soaring to the heavens, and the downs that cut me to the core. Three times a week, a hospital ambulance arrived at my doorstep to take me to physio. My physio was much gentler than Lynn and Chris and although she did a fantastic job, I couldn't help but miss that wry, sarcastic hint of pure evil that Lynn used to exude. Her name was Lisa and she was small and slight, but stronger than a carthorse on steroids. It was Lisa's job to get my knee to bend once more. How does one unbend a stiffened knee, I hear you ask? Answer, you push it and push it until it bends. Yes, it was that simple and yes, it did hurt. It hurt like hell.

I sat on a bed, my leg outstretched, my heart full of doom. Lisa grabbed hold of my ankle, leant her entire weight on it and pushed with all her considerable might. My only job was to scream blue murder until she let go briefly, said 'You OK?' and then started all over again until our session was over. In those months, I was constantly hoarse from all the screaming involved in my physio sessions. Slowly but surely, my knee started to bend. At the end of each session, Lisa would whip out a huge protractor-like contraption that she called a goniometer and set about measuring our progress in terms of 'angle of bend'. Our goal was ninety degrees, which is the minimum that one needs for normal function. Whenever we achieved a five-degree improvement in a session, Lisa would give me a high five and we'd sit in the little cubicle basking in the glow of our success. Can you imagine? I felt more of a sense of achievement from a five-degree knee-bend than anything else I'd done in my whole life. On the days when the pain was just too much to bear and we achieved a piddling two-degree improvement, Lisa would sit next to me on the bed with such a sad expression on her face that you would think her dog had just died. As I said, ups and downs – in fact it was more like being on an Alton Towers ride.

All in all, I gradually began to enjoy my sessions with her. It was like having a little adventure three times a week. I never knew what lay in store for me in those little cubicles in Physiotherapy B. Little did I know that before the month of June had passed, I would be returning to the hospital wards.

* * *

I remember the day clearly. I was in my kitchen making a fruit salad for breakfast, when the phone rang. After checking in my ever-present backpack, I realised that I'd left the phone in the other room. Deciding to kill two birds with one stone, I picked up the fruit peelings to toss into the bin on my way past. I was so anxious to get to the phone before the person gave up that I didn't notice that some of the fruit peelings had missed the bin and were on the floor. I struggled to the phone.

"Hello," I said breathlessly – walking with crutches really takes it out of you, you know. Especially when you're trying to hurry.

"Kate?" The voice was thin, watery and totally pathetic.

"Matt?"

"Yeah."

"What's wrong?"

"Kate, I need you."

"What d'you mean you need me? Matt, we're not together any more."

"I know, but –"

"But nothing. You can't keep ringing me. It's over." Did I mention that he'd been visiting me off and on ever since I'd been discharged? He'd even taken to ringing me late at night and I was getting more than a little brassed off with him. He seemed to think that I'd made a huge mistake breaking up with him.

"Kate, I'm in the hospital."

"Hospital? Why? How?"

"I had a car accident."

I gasped in shock. As much as I was unhappy with him, I wouldn't wish such a thing on my worst enemy.

"Kate! Please come!" He croaked out his ward number and left me with a single word, "Hurry."

As soon as he hung up, I dialled Jane's number.

"Hello."

"Jane, we have to get to the hospital."

I must have sounded shaken as Jane's response held a healthy dose of panic. "What's happened? Are you OK?"

"I'm fine, it's Matt."

"Oh." Her voice sounded deflated and more than a tad disinterested. "Why? What's he done now?"

"He's been in a car accident. Can you take me to the hospital?"

"I suppose, but . . . ." She hesitated as if unwilling to voice her thoughts, "how do we know this isn't just some elaborate trick to get you back?"

"Jane!" I was really shocked. "How could you think such a thing? He could be dying or something."

"If he was dying, he'd hardly be using the telephone, now would he?"

"Please, Jane!"

"OK, but I still don't trust him. He's egotistical and manipulative, don't forget that." She sighed with a distasteful air. "I'll be there in about fifteen minutes."

"Thanks, Jane."

"Yeah, yeah." She hung up.

I feel that I should explain her distaste. Jane was aware that Matt had been trying to get back together with me and she felt it was her duty to save me from myself. She was concerned that I would somehow fall for his new 'I've changed' tack and she'd been trying to ensure that I kept a strong measure of perspective. Not only that, but she'd also done a precautionary three-card-spread, which confirmed her fears that any further coming-togethers on the part of Matt and myself would 'not only end in heartbreak, but would also change the course of my life forever'. Although at the time I'd tried to ask her what that actually meant, she refused to be drawn further and simply muttered that 'the cards had spoken and I should stay well away from him'.

With fifteen minutes to wait, I decided to have my breakfast. I heaved myself onto my crutches and headed back into the kitchen. I was still preoccupied and not paying too much attention to where I was putting my crutches and somehow, the left crutch managed to land itself on some of the stuff that had missed the rubbish-bin earlier. Before I knew it, it had slipped away from me. As an automatic response to my left side being taken away, my body flung itself over to the right and I landed heavily on my bad leg. I felt a sharp pain and I was falling – falling hard. With a heavy thump, I landed on my arse and not for the first time I was more than glad that it was 'ample' enough to cushion the blow.

After the initial shock had subsided, I lay there on the floor for a couple of minutes before I began an inventory on the possible injuries. I flexed my left leg. That was fine. No problems with the arms, so far so good. I took a deep breath and flexed my right knee as far as it would go. Pain shot up my body. I'd done something, I wasn't sure what and to be perfectly honest, I wasn't inclined to actually take a look. I reached down with my hand and ran it over the joint, hoping against hope that I hadn't dislocated it again. Nope, it seemed to be still intact.

Lisa had helped me distinguish between 'good pain' and 'bad pain'. When she pushed my knee, it hurt, but it stopped when she released the pressure that was 'good pain'. If the pain continued when there was no pressure: then that meant that something was wrong: that's 'bad pain'. I comforted myself that I wasn't actually in pain all the time – it was only when I flexed the knee. Maybe I hadn't done too much damage after all. I looked around to see what had caused the fall. I knew what it was going to be, even before I actually spied the offending item. There was only one thing that Kate Townsend could possibly slip on. Wrapped around the bottom of the left crutch was the bright yellow of a banana skin. I groaned. This was like a bad version of one of those silent comedies with Buster Keaton. How on earth was I ever going to live this one down? Jane was going to be here any minute. The best thing to do would be to get rid of the evidence, get up and pretend that it had never happened.

Have you ever tried to get up off the floor when your right knee doesn't bend? Try it. Go on, have a go. Lie down on the floor, wrap something tightly around your knee so that it won't bend and try to get up. See? It's not easy is it?

I rolled around for about five minutes feeling like a beached whale (I probably looked remarkably like one as well). I was too far away from the kitchen cabinets to use them to help me lift myself up. I was immovable. In the end, I gave up and accepted that I'd be stuck there until Jane arrived.

Not long after, I heard a key in my front door.

"You ready?" Jane shouted as she entered my living-room.

"Not quite. I'm in here," I called to her from my prone position.

"What are you doing in there . . . Oh my God! What's happened? Are you OK?" She rushed towards me, panic once more evident in her voice and eyes.

"I'm fine. I just slipped on something and I couldn't get up. Can you help me?"

"Hang on. Before I start moving you, are you sure you're OK? Maybe I should call an ambulance?"

"No. I'm fine. Honest."

"I dunno." She wavered, her hand over the phone ready to dial at a second's notice.

"Look, no blood, my knee's still attached. I'm fine. Just give me a hand up. Please."

"OK." She held out her hand then changed her mind.

She left the kitchen. I was just about to get really annoyed when I realised what she was doing. She returned to the kitchen with a chair. She was seven months pregnant. It probably wasn't the best thing in the world, to start trying to lift heavy weights such as myself.

"Good thinking, Batman. Thanks." With a little bit of effort and Jane sitting on the chair to give it stability, I managed to haul myself upright.

"Right, let's get going." I hobbled into the other room to get my coat, Jane ambling behind me.

In the car on the way to the hospital, Jane was trying to get me to explain how the fall had happened. There was no way I was going to admit that I'd slipped on a banana skin, but we all know how persuasive Jane can be. I could feel my resistance fading fast. In desperation I stared out of the car window, pretending that I couldn't hear her.

The car drew to a halt. I looked around. We were nowhere near the hospital.

"What?"

"Aren't you going to get him something?"

"No."

"Chocolate? Sweeties?"

"Nope."

"Not even some grapes?"

"Definitely no grapes."

Jane shrugged and drove on to the hospital.

* * *

Matt lay in his bed looking pathetic, covered from head to toe in big black/blue bruises. He had a massive pot on his right leg and his right arm was in a sling. Jane had left us alone after reminding me that he was an arrogant prick and the cards were against us both so I shouldn't listen to a word he said.

"I broke my leg," he simpered

No shit, Sherlock, I thought, but I managed to summon up a sympathetic, "You poor lamb".

"Kate, I'm so glad you're here. I've really missed you."

What? Since you visited me two days ago? I snorted inwardly, but said, "you poor lamb".

"It was strange. I saw the lorry coming towards me and my whole life flashed before my eyes and I realised what my life was missing."

"Purpose? Values? Morals?" I muttered under my breath.

"Huh? No, Kate, what I'm trying to say is that I stared death in the face and all I wanted in that moment was you."

"Who?"

"You."

"Me?"

"Yep."

I looked at his bruised face, hoping to see artifice or suspect motives, but honestly all I could see was sincerity. For the first time since I'd known him he was 100 per cent genuine. He loved me. He reached out for my hand and started talking to me, but I was still struck by what I'd seen in his eyes. I missed the beginning of the sentence, but the last two words gave me a good indication of what it was.

". . . marry me?"

"Huh?" I gulped then started to hyperventilate.

"I said: Kate will you marry me?"

Before I could control my breathing enough to utter a response, I felt a strong arm grab me.

"Hell no!" a voice boomed over my left shoulder. "Over my dead body!"

I think you could say that Jane had strong feelings on the subject and before I knew it, she pulled me onto my feet and began dragging me down the ward shouting stuff like, 'I can't leave you alone for five minutes', 'Have you no respect for the cards at all?' and 'What were you thinking?' My normally placid, serene and 'new age' friend had exploded like a Roman candle and for no real cause.

I wasn't going to say yes.

Honest I wasn't.

Chapter Twenty-eight

Sound and Fury

I've heard that when life-changing events occur, people go through phases, much like alcoholics. I'm not sure what the actual phases were or which order they should come, but looking back now I can identify clearly the phases that I went through. Firstly came denial – that was when I thought that everything would get back to normal. Then I accepted that things would never be the same. I oscillated between these two for a long while in hospital. Then upon my release I went through a long, long self-pity stage. The entire time, I felt that I had missed something out, that there was a phase that I should have been going through, but hadn't quite got there. July was when the phase hit the fan, so to speak. Let me explain . . . .

* * *

July came and my life consisted of physio, physio and more physio. My sessions with Lisa left me so tired that the girls were concerned that I might fall again. I didn't have the energy to argue with them, so I let them take charge. Before I knew it, Gen was installed in my house. They said it was for her work, but secretly I believed it was to stop me from saying yes to Matt. He'd been informed that I needed time to think and should therefore not call me until I had come to a decision. Gen was like a guard-dog, getting to the phone before I could reach it, practically screening my calls. Unsurprisingly, I didn't get to speak to Matt at all.

Gen's Sheffield project was complete and evil client had turned into happy client and had recommended her services to a company who was developing a warehouse in Salford Quays into studio apartments. As I lived near enough to the Quays it simply made sense for her to stay over at my house.

When I was not at physiotherapy, I spent most of my days convalescing in my garden. I'd assumed that convalescing was much like pottering, but with much less wandering around, and it sounded a lot better than 'lolling about on a lawn chair', which is what I was actually doing. For the first time in years, the summer was hot and glorious, so Gen and I spent a lot of time in my garden. She was working on her plans and I was working on my tan. Strangely, I enjoyed it. It was relaxing. Apart from the marriage proposal hanging over my head, the ghost of a sexy artist haunting my thoughts when I wasn't concentrating and trying to decide what to do about work, oh, and the sudden disappearance of Louise, my life was very simple. Or so I thought. In actual fact my head must have been like a pressure cooker, slowly building up steam. I was so busy thinking that life was great, I didn't realise that the next phase was anger. Sure, I'd had snatches of it in the hospital, but I hadn't had a truly impressive blow out.

Now bearing in mind that this is me we are talking about, can you guess the moment that my head decided to explode? How about if I started the next sentence with the phrase, 'On July 22, Steve Wallace came to visit . . .' See, you're getting the hang of my life now. So here goes.

On July 22, Steve Wallace came to visit. Actually, first Anil came by the day before to check the lie of the land, hinting every so often that his nephew was in Manchester, until finally I told him that I would be happy to see Steve. The girls (apart from the vanished Louise) all came round the night before with pizza and vids and ended up staying the night. All morning on the 22nd, I was a nervous wreck, I'd snapped at Gen so much that she'd stormed off in a huff. Jane tried waving at me with a crystal to cleanse my 'nasty little, ungrateful aura' before announcing that 'it was truly impossible to cleanse something that black' so she left in despair. Sandi announced that if I was going to be in such a mood, she'd rather have her legs waxed than speak to me again in a hurry and had therefore taken herself off to the beauty salon.

I found myself completely alone and pacing my living room waiting for him to arrive. Pacing on crutches is a matter of pure will; it's not that easy and you really have to want to pace. I'd managed to work myself into a bundle of raw nerves and just when I wanted to tear something limb from limb, the doorbell rang. I wrenched it open to see the gorgeous form of Steve Wallace in front of me.

"Steve," I squeaked, still hiding behind the door, "come in."

He smiled that sexy smile of his and brushed gently past my arm on his way to the living room.

255

I watched him get settled on my sofa and cleared my throat. "So . . ." I stared intently at my feet.

"Why don't you sit down?"

"Coffee." I focused on his hands, marvelling at their beauty.

"I'm sorry? Coffee?"

"Would you like one?"

"No, I'm fine." He patted the cushion beside him and beckoned me.

I dragged my eyes away from his strong hands and focused on his hair. How had I never noticed how unusual the colour was? "Cake?"

"Cake?"

"Yes, Jane made me a cake. Would you like some?"

"Not just yet."

Don't look at his eyes, Kate, just don't look at his eyes.

"Katherine, look at me."

It was the way he said my name that did it. If he'd said it any other way, everything would have been different, but he didn't, so it wasn't. I glanced up and like a spaceship caught in a tractor-beam, I was captured. "I . . . I . . ."

"Come sit by me, Kate."

There it was again. Short form, long form, it didn't seem to matter. I was done for. "I . . . I . . ."

It was the deep emerald mothership calling me back. I was drawn towards him and before I knew it, I was sat on the sofa beside him, my hands in his, gazing into his eyes.

"I couldn't stay away any longer." There was an ache in his voice.

I dragged my gaze away from his eyes and was drawn inexorably to his mouth. I saw it move, but was unable to hear what was said. I was mesmerised, imagining only the feel of his lips on mine, our breath mingling, the feel of his hands on my back.

"Kate."

His head leaned towards me and finally his lips touched mine. My head imploded and my body was one huge bundle of lust. The only thing I wanted was him to be inside me. In no time at all our clothing was in a messy pile on the floor and I was admiring his body. His skin was golden brown and so soft it made my hands tingle with delight. I wanted to taste him, smell him, drink of him until he was part of me . . .

I suppose you want to hear the details, the way his lips caressed my entire body, the way his breath felt on my neck, but I'm not telling. Suffice it to say the fireworks were out that day and they exploded many, many times.

Afterwards we lay on the sofa, sweating, breathless and spent. I still maintain now that everything would have been fine if only he'd not uttered his next words.

"To think, we might never have met."

"What?" I muttered, unwilling to let his words force me out of my dream state.

"My uncle had been trying for months to get us together, but if it hadn't been for your party, I'd never have come."

"My party?" Seeing as he was determined to have a chat, I decided to start putting my clothes back on.

"Yes, your friend Jane told me all about how depressed you were. She begged me to come and cheer you up."

I pulled my T-shirt over my head. "Begged?"

"Yes, begged. She's very determined."

"I suppose she is." I couldn't help it, but I didn't like where this was going. I searched around for my underwear, hoping that he'd give up trying to talk to me and help me look, but he was too wrapped up in his thoughts.

"They say everything happens for a reason, don't they?"

"Do they?" Giving up on my knickers, I put on my skirt instead.

"Yes, and now for the first time I believe it. Your accident brought us together."

I was rankled, but I tried to keep calm, knowing that I would fail miserably. "So what you're saying is that I had my accident so that we could meet." I sat down in the armchair.

"Something like that, yes."

He smiled over at me and that's when it hit me: he was actually glad that I'd had the accident. A fury welled up inside me. I would like to say that my emotions were in turmoil, but that wouldn't be telling the whole story. My mind, body and soul were a seething mass of havoc. I was inert, but at the same time electrified. I know now that I was being unreasonable, but at that moment I truly felt that he was happy that my former life had been taken away from me, pleased that I would never again be able to jog for a bus or play sports. The steam that had been building up in my head began to rise and I felt it pressing against my temples, throbbing around my head. I got up and walked towards him. Before I could stop myself, my hand rose to his face and slapped him hard.

"How dare you!"

He stared at me in shock, unable to utter a single word.

"How dare you come in here, take advantage of me and then tell me you're glad I nearly died."

"Take advantage? Katherine, you ripped my shirt off!" He held up his shirt – it was in a sorry state.

But I was on a roll and nothing was going to stop me. "It was a flimsy shirt." OK, so maybe there was hope. If he could just find the right words, he might be able to salvage something.

"Look, Kate, I know that you're a bit emotional, but –"

Those were very definitely the wrong words. "Emotional? I'd like to see you go through what I've been through these past months and not be emotional! I've got every right to be bloody emotional. You swan in and out of my life being all I'm-such-a-cool-dude-and-I'm-so-bloody-calm-even-I-don't-know-how-I-do-it. We can't all be androids like you, all strong and silent! I'm weak and I'll shout my fucking head off if I have to. I think I've earned the right."

"OK, maybe now's not the time. You've obviously misunderstood what I meant, I –"

"Oh, I misunderstood, did I? OK then, Mister, explain to me in small words so that my tiny brain can understand what you meant."

"Kate, I don't think –"

"I know you don't think – maybe you should think once in a while."

"You are overreacting, Kate – I was only trying to say that I'm glad that the circumstances allowed us to meet."

"By circumstances, I assume you mean the accident. Well, that accident destroyed my life and you're happy about it. Well, how dare you take pleasure in the destruction of my life. You think I deserved this misfortune?"

"No, Kate, I –"

"You were just looking at the bright side, eh? Well, let me tell you: there *is* no bloody bright side!" I was shouting now, reaching a noise level that even I had never before experienced.

"But Kate. . . ."

"I didn't deserve this. No one deserves what I've been through. I take so many damn pills that I rattle and when I don't take them, I'm in so much pain I want to die. Hang on, maybe I should have died. Maybe I deserved to die as well, eh? What d'you think Stevie-boy?"

"Kate, that's not what I meant . . ."

"GET OUT!" I screamed the words at him, my face no doubt contorted into an evil caricature. "GET OUT OF MY HOUSE!"

I grabbed my crutches and lumbered into my kitchen. Unlocking the back door, I stumbled into my garden to catch deep lungfuls of fresh air.

I sat down on my lawn chair, hugged myself and cried as if my life depended on it. "I didn't deserve this!" I repeated the words over and over, breathing deeply.

I vaguely registered my front door closing, but I didn't move. I remained in that position until Gen arrived back and helped me gently to bed.

* * *

A week afterwards, I read in the paper that the renowned artist Steve Wallace had headed off to New York to introduce the Americans to his remarkable work.

This news sent me spiralling into another depression, but this time I was determined to get through it by myself. Against the wishes of my wonderful friends, I insisted that I wanted to be on my own and sent them all packing. I assured them that when I was once more up to having visitors I'd let them know.

I needed time to sort myself out and I needed to do it alone.

Chapter Twenty-nine

Hatches, Matches and Dispatches

Think you're confused? Imagine how I felt.

I sat around my house day in, day out, thinking. Leaving my home only to see Lisa for our sessions.

By the beginning of August, we'd finally achieved the hallowed ninety-degree bend in my knee and, with the overall improvement in my walking, I'd managed to graduate from crutches to a walking stick. My balance had improved and I walked with only a slight limp.

Once I was back in my home, I thought about my life, about what had happened to me and how I really felt about it. And I read. I took a taxi to the bookshop and bought over a £100 worth of books. I took them all home and proceeded to read my way through them. There were self-help books, fiction, non-fiction, biographies – in fact if it had a cover, I read it. Some of the books made me think, some of them made me forget, but all of them helped bring me back my equilibrium.

My mind started to drift to thoughts of death. I think the psychobabble people like to call it something fancy like, 'realising your own mortality'. But Jane, during one of our rare phone calls, said that she likes to think of it as simply 'embracing the future'. Then again, she also likes to say that 'maybe not all alien sightings are hoaxes', so of course she'd see it like that.

However, as with everything else in my life, my contemplations of mortality were not so straight forward. When I think of my demise, I in fact had to look not to the future, but to the past. I didn't tell you this before, mainly because it was too soon and I didn't want you to worry about me. But here I am out of hospital and you know that I'm OK, so I can let you in on the secret. I actually died once, don't you know? Yep, I essentially ceased to be for a minute. The details are a bit sketchy – I was busy dying at the time, don't forget – but apparently for a brief while, during that first massive operation, I was an ex-Kate Townsend. Luckily, the fabulously talented Mr Holland managed to get my old heart beating again.

And now we come to the real crux of my thinking. I was really pissed off about it! No, silly, I wasn't pissed off about the fact that he stuck those two electric-shocky-iron-shaped-bits on my chest. No, not at all. I was pissed off that I didn't have one of those near-death experience thingys. I mean, I departed this plane of existence for a couple of minutes and did I see any bright white lights? Did I fuck! Lovely gentle winged-angels guiding me through a door into a romantic, swirling, white mist? Nope, not a single condensed droplet of water in sight. The word beautiful never popped into my head for a second. No placid, soothing music, no calm relaxation, no sudden understandings of the meaning of life. NOTHING. I didn't even have the fun of having one of those floaty, bugger-me-I'm-leaving-my-body-behind-and-I'm-looking-down-at-myself moments. All I got was a blank space where time should have been. And to be perfectly honest with you, I felt cheated.

Everyone has them – at least if you read all those articles in women's magazines you would think that that's the case. Every Theresa, Diane and Hermione has had one. Every time there's a miraculous recovery from a serious injury, they can't stop themselves from telling everyone within a fifty-mile radius about the white light and floaty feelings. And the one time I have something really exciting happen to me, I don't even get enough of a story to tell my postman, let alone *Take a Break* magazine, which is, by the way, a magazine for busy, fulfilled people with busy, fulfilled lives and definitely NOT a boring magazine for saddos.

So after contemplating death I realised something, and forgive me for sounding ever so slightly bitter and twisted for just one moment. But it occurred to me that death wasn't something I should fear and, more importantly, it's not all it's cracked up to be.

It took a while, but after all the thinking and moping around my house, one day I woke up and for the first time in my life, I was at peace. With the world, my life, and finally with myself.

Just after 10.00 p.m. on August 18 I was preparing for bed when my phone rang.

"Kate? Jane. Hospital. Baby." Sandi sounded breathless as if she was running. "Be at yours in five."

"OK."

And she was gone. I shrugged and continued getting ready for bed. Then the meaning of the phone call sunk in. Jane was having the baby, Jane was having the baby! I swear I started running around in circles, although that might have had more to do with the fact that I was using my walking stick like a maypole. At last, the time had come and, I looked down, I was dressed in flannelette pyjamas. I limped around my bedroom as quick as I could, trying to find a suitable outfit for the birth of a friend's baby.

Just as I finished dressing, I heard a key turning in my front door and Sandi's voice shouting, "Hurry up, we'll miss it!"

"What d'you mean 'miss it'? Oh no, no, no, I hope that doesn't mean what I think it means. Friendship can only go so far and in this instance there are definite limits to my friendship. There is no way I'm actually going to be in that room with her," I said, making my way carefully down the stairs.

"Of course you are, she wants us all there." She motioned me to go out the door first and closed it behind me.

"All of us? There?"

"Yep."

"So Louise is back then?"

"Oh yes, she got back from her honeymoon yesterday." Sandi hurriedly unlocked her car doors.

"Honeymoon? What honeymoon? She's had a honeymoon?"

"Yeah. She said it was all your idea."

"Was it?"

"Apparently."

"I'm almost 100 per cent certain I never mentioned honeymoons."

"So? As of today it's old news, anyway." Sandi revved her engine, put it in gear and sped off.

"Oh." I let thoughts of Louise mull over in my head. Then a different one intruded. "She doesn't really want us all in the room with her, does she? You were only joking, right?"

"No, she said Craig would drive her mad, so he's not allowed in. She wants us."

My stomach felt all queasy. "I'm not sure I want to –"

"Oh stop being a wuss. Our best friend is having a baby and she wants us there. It's an honour."

"It's disgusting." I shivered.

"Oh for goodness sake," Sandi muttered.

"Alright, but I'm not going anywhere near the 'business' end."

"She doesn't want you anywhere near the 'business' end anyway." Sandi laughed. "She said that you're such a wimp, you'd probably faint at the first sight of blood and end up dislocating your knee again."

She cackled and screeched around the final corner, coming to an abrupt halt in the hospital carpark.

* * *

Approximately fourteen hours later, which apparently was a short time on *First-time Pregnancy World*, Jane gave birth to a baby girl. Now I know you won't believe this, but even I thought she was gorgeous. The following day, we returned to the ward to find a still exhausted, but completely ecstatic Jane. After a brief scuffle with Gen, who was heard to utter the words, 'I refuse to allow you to saddle the poor child with that name,' Jane made her announcement. With a glass of champagne provided by Sandi, we toasted the arrival of Katherine Sandra Louise Fuller (Katie for short).

Unwilling to end the celebration just because the nurses threw us out of the ward, the four remaining coven members retired to the local pub, where we heard the story of Louise's marriage.

After the little pep-talk in my hospital room, Louise had started her charm offensive with very few results at first. But with her trademark single-mindedness, she persevered. After all her small victories (it seems that the crotchless knickers did the trick), it always came back to the same problem. She was too successful. Just when she was about to give up, Terry arrived at her doorstep with a plane ticket and a proposal. Without telling her, he'd been going to college in the evenings and learning about website design. In July, he'd started his own business with his younger brother, got a couple of good clients and even though he wasn't raking in the money, he was happier about himself. Which in turn led to the realisation that he needed Louise. Seeing as she'd not had a day off in yonks, Louise took advantage of the many days owed to her. Leaving his brother in charge of the business, they flew off almost immediately and got married on a beach in the Caribbean.

"Well, I'll never forgive you," Sandi complained.

"Huh?" Louise looked up in confusion.

"How could you get married without us?" Sandi pouted.

"It's not as if it was planned, as such," Louise reasoned, "It was sort of spur of the moment."

"You could at least have told us you were going. You scared us half to death just disappearing like that," Gen began lecturing.

"But, I thought you'd be —" Louise looked as if she were about to cry.

"Happy for you. Of course we're all happy for you," I soothed. "Sulky and Grumpy over there are just sad they weren't part of it, that's all."

"I know — why don't you have a blessing ceremony?" said Sandi. "Then we can all get nice new dresses and have a real party."

"Life's not all about parties, you know, Sandi," Gen sighed, "and anyway, you're one to talk. You sodded off to the States and came back with a husband, remember?"

"Yeah, that's right, see," said Louise, happy that the heat had been deflected from her.

"Just 'cos we're talking about Sandi at the moment, it certainly doesn't mean that you're off the hook yet, Mrs." Gen glared at Louise, who sank sheepishly back into her chair.

"You are such a bully." Sandi prodded Gen in the shoulder with a beautifully manicured, index fingernail.

I thought it was time to step in to stop this turning into an all-out scrap. "Ladies, ladies, please. I would like to make a toast."

Three surprised faces turned to me.

I raised my glass. "To new lives!"

Three large smiles appeared and they raised their glasses and tapped them against mine.

"To new lives!" they chorused.

* * *

September began with fantastic news. At the end of a Friday session, Lisa announced that I was being discharged. I'd made as much progress as was possible and there was nothing more she could do for me. She warned me that I should still continue with my exercises, but apart from that I should get back on track with my life.

The first thing I did upon my return home was pack up all my shoes – my prize collection of shoes that I could no longer and would never again fit into – and dispatched them via a reputable courier service to the person who was destined to received them in my will anyway.

The following day, I spring-cleaned my entire house with the help of my new cleaner – did I mention that I'd got a cleaner? – Suki, and disposed of everything that smacked of my old life. This was an extraordinarily easy task seeing as Suki was remarkably proficient at hiding stuff anyway. After her first visit, I noticed that everything had been ever-so-slightly moved. It was as if my entire house had been shifted about a fraction of a degree so that it looked pretty much the same, but wasn't. The tea towels in the kitchen had been moved a few centimetres to the left which meant that when I was in front of the oven with the door open, I could no longer grab one to take the dish out of the oven without moving. The cutlery was put back in different trays, so when I went to get a spoon I ended up with a knife, and so on. In my bathroom, I was unable to locate anything at all. What's more, she insisted on hiding my tampons. Usually I had them beside the toilet bowl on the floor in an innocuous floral box, but after a visit from Suki, I found them behind the four-pack of toilet roll underneath a bottle of bleach. OK, I understand that some women feel that tampons can be construed as offensive in mixed company, but for goodness sakes: I LIVE ALONE! And the only people that really visit are my friends (who happen to be female). I tried explaining to Suki that neither I nor my friends would faint with horror if we were to catch a glimpse of a stray tampon, but she simply looked appalled and coughed uncomfortably. When I think of Suki and her hiding habits, what I find most interesting are the things that she chooses not to hide. She's forever forgetting to put the cover back on my dirty clothes basket. And she insists on displaying my secret stash of *Take a Break* magazine on my coffee table, when everyone knows that you hide it under the bed where no one can ever find out that you actually read it. Don't ask me why I read it, I just do. But of course I read it in a post-modern ironic sort of way. And to cap it all, in the bathroom, where she likes to hide everything, guess what item sits on the Suki-cleared shelf, all alone and therefore so obvious that she might as well put massive red arrows around it for a slightly subtler effect? My multi-coloured collection of condoms. Despite her faults, she's very good and worth her weight in gold, so there was no way I'd let her go.

So there we were, creating my new life. I cleared a large space on the main wall in my bedroom, relegating the Monet print to the spare room.

I got on the phone to Marco and had a long heartfelt discussion with him. I told him that I was officially fit enough to work and thanked him profusely for all the help that the company had given me while I was sick and I realised that he was a really nice guy. I had decided that I no longer wanted to work full-time and having gone over my finances with Craig, with a few adjustments in my spending habits, I didn't need a full-time job. Marco and I agreed on a freelance contract, which he arranged to send over as soon as possible. The work situation settled, I crossed that off my mental to do list. The other items on the list were more complicated and therefore I decided I needed assistance coming up with a solution. I wasn't sure I could face the entire coven, so I chose two of the girls, made the phone calls and waited for my guests to arrive.

Gen was first, letting herself into my house and surprising me as I exited my kitchen.

"So, what's up?"

"Nothing."

"It's just that you sounded so worried on the phone. Are you OK?"

"I'm fine, a bit confused that's all."

"Confused? Is that one of the side effects of your medication. You should tell Daniel."

"Not that sort of confused, Gen, for goodness sakes. You really need to loosen up."

"I'm loose. I have fun. It might not be your idea of fun, but I have fun."

"When was the last time you went out?"

"We were out just after the baby was born, remember?"

"Not with us, Gen. When was the last time you went out on a date?"

"I went out for lunch with happy client, the day before yesterday. And we didn't talk business all the time."

"Ooh, Gen, you are such a tart!" I dripped with sarcasm.

She made to slap me and I was saved by the sound of someone opening my front door.

"Helloooo," Jane called, "it's only us."

"Come on in, we're in here."

Jane entered the room with Katie in a carry-cot/car-seat

combo, followed by Craig carrying a large rectangular object.

"Very expensive delivery for Miss Townsend," he called as he came in.

He leant the painting against the coffee table and went in search of power tools to help him attach it to my bedroom wall.

The doorbell rang and I was baffled. Everyone I'd called was already there. I wasn't expecting anyone else. I opened the door and saw a slightly miffed Sandi.

"What are you doing here?"

"A-ha, so you were planning on leaving me out?"

"Leaving you out of what?"

"Whatever you've got going on over here."

"There's nothing going on here."

"So why is Jane here? She told me she was coming over. And why is Gen not at home? I bet she's here too."

"She is, but –"

"I knew it. What's going on and why wasn't I invited?"

"Honestly, Sandi, nothing's going on."

"Well, then you won't mind that I told Louise to get her bum round here too."

"Why?"

"'Cos something's going on. Can I come in?" She pushed past me and waltzed into the living room.

I followed after her insisting, "There's nothing going on."

"What's going on?"

Jane and Gen looked at me as I arrived trailing behind Sandi.

"For the last bleeding time, there's nothing going on!" I shouted.

The doorbell rang again and Craig called, "I'll get it."

Seconds later, Louise bounced into the room. Seeing everyone gathered, she looked at me and said, "What's going on here then?"

The three others looked over at me and in unison they burst out laughing. Unable to do anything else, I joined them. Not knowing what it was all about, Louise's gaze moved from one woman to the other before whining "What? What have I missed?"

As Sandi was filling her in on what had been said, Craig popped his head round the door and said, "What on earth is going on in here?"

As one all five of us turned and said, "Nothing!" And fell about laughing.

"You bloody women are mad. Katie and I will be going upstairs now. I don't want her catching whatever you lot have. Can I watch telly up there, Kate?"

"Yeah," I chuckled, "of course you can."

Gen went off with Jane to make refreshments and Sandi took charge of finding the perfect musical accompaniment to a serious chat.

Louise turned to me and asked, "By the way, Kate, why on earth did you send me your shoes?"

"A thank you would be too much to ask, I suppose."

"Thank you, but why have I got your entire collection of shoes?"

"Because I can't use them any more and I'm sick to death of you walking around in pig-ugly shoes."

"Pig-ugly?" She could hardly say the words. She looked down at her feet.

"Yep, it's time you glammed up and there's no better place to start than by slipping into a pair of Jimmy Choos."

"Did someone say Jimmy Choos?" Sandi stopped her perusal of the CD collection and came over to us. "What about them? They're sooo nice!"

"Kate sent me her entire collection of shoes."

"Her entire . . ." Sandi was at once both shocked and seriously pissed off. She turned on me and demanded, "Why does she get the shoes?"

"Well, for starters, she's got the same size feet as me."

"I can fit into a size six."

"In your dreams, girl. Not in a million years."

"What's this?" Jane and Gen had returned with a tray of steaming mugs.

I smiled, "Sandi reckons she can fit into a size six shoe."

We all focused on her less-than-delicate, size eights and burst out laughing.

* * *

Two hours of intense discussion later, I summed up. "So basically, Gen, you think I should go with option one."

"Yes."

"Jane, you think I should go with option two."

"Very definitely, it's in your cards."

"Louise, you think both options are a bad idea and I should take longer to think about other options."

"Neither of them sound 100 per cent to me," Louise said resolutely.

"And finally, Sandi, you wouldn't even let me explain either option because you'd already decided on an option three that involves parties, shopping and Mexico."

"Too bloody right. Let's take your leg out for a dance!" she grinned.

"Well . . ." I sighed the deep sigh of a person in utter bewilderment.

"Well?" the girls echoed.

"Fat lot of good you lot are. I'm back at the beginning again. Cheers, you've really helped!"

"Charming," Jane said. "Are you sure you don't want me to do a five-card spread? It might help."

"No, Jane. I think she should do this one without any supernatural help, don't you?" said Gen.

"Yeah." Sandi smiled.

"Yeah." Louise patted my arm.

"I suppose," Jane said, uncertainly at first, but then nodded and squeezed my hand. Before I knew it we were in the middle of a huge group hug. All five of us suddenly tearful.

Before it all got out of hand, Sandi, as usual, saved the day.

"So when's the party?"

Chapter Thirty

Full Circle

So here I am in this café. It's October again, a year after my story began. And what a year, I think you'll agree.

There are a couple of things that I still have to explain before I tell you about my options. Firstly we'll talk about my car.

Although my gorgeous nearly-new car was completely useless to me now, being a manual and all, I was loathe to get rid of it. I knew that I would never again have the physical capability in my right foot to use a manual car, but in spite of everything, I'd been clinging on to the faint hope that miracles do happen. I still believe that miracles happen, but I have reluctantly come to the conclusion that I have already had more than my fair share of them. So, with Gen holding my hand, I sold my car and watched the new owner drive it away. Then Gen and I went shopping for a new one. My knee, although bending to a full ninety-degrees, prevented me from easily getting into and out of most cars, so my choice was fairly limited. In the end, I settled on a Toyota Yaris, a gorgeous car with more buttons and gizmos than the Starship Enterprise. It was slightly higher than normal cars, which meant that getting in and out was easy as pie. I was in love. It was a deal. I counted out the cash and bought me a car! Now 'Harris the Yaris' belongs to me. We sent him off to have the adaptations made and this morning at six thirty, Harris was delivered to my doorstep, complete with hand-controls.

* * *

Then there was Matt. My Adonis. I know you want to know what happened, so I'll tell it quickly, OK?

He visited me just before Katie was born. He came to my home to have one last-ditch attempt to convince me to marry him. At least that's what I prepared myself for, but instead, he just wanted to chat. I was fully equipped to deal with everything except what actually happened. I know you're going to groan when I say this next bit – Jane and Sandi nearly threw up when I told them – but Matt really has changed. He handed in his notice at the bank. He moved down to London, bought a gorgeous house and is now the Financial Director for a children's charity. He earns a lot less money, but as he told me 'money isn't everything'. His accident made him turn his entire life around. He realised that his old life had no substance and that he had treated people abominably. Like an alcoholic on a twelve-step programme, he decided to make amends with all the people that he felt he'd wronged. So he stood in front of me and apologised for the way that he'd treated me. It was the sweetest, most heartfelt apology that I ever had the pleasure of receiving and I kissed him. One thing led to another and we ended up in bed.

I know it was stupid and I know that it was definitely the wrong thing to do, but damn we were still good together and did I mention that he was still gorgeous. The morning after, he proposed again and when I refused to give him an immediate answer, he took his leave telling me that I knew where to find him and he was willing to wait for me.

* * *

This morning, I woke up ridiculously early to accept delivery of Harris and had my first drive – to the hospital. I had, as I later found out, my last visit to the outpatients clinic with Daniel Holland. But before I tell you about this morning, let me fill you in on my previous clinic visits. Initially, I saw Daniel every two weeks. Each visit saw me stronger and more confident. In June, Daniel told me that he no longer needed to see me on a fortnightly basis, and I was doing so well that every two months would be sufficient. At the end of August, I appeared in his clinic.

"Hi Kate, you're looking a bit peaky."

"Hey, Danny-boy, so're you." I smiled and gave him a jokey punch in the arm.

"No, really, Kate, I don't like it. I think I should do some tests."

"Oh, do you have to? I'm fine, honest. No needles, please."

"Are you eating properly?"

"Define properly?"

"You know what I mean."

"So I've been having a few more take-outs. Have you ever tried cooking on crutches?"

"You're not on crutches any more."

"I know, but I was."

"Kate," he sounded exasperated, "you have to take care of yourself. Your body needs vitamins, minerals, it needs the fuel to sustain the improvement. Do you want to be back in hospital? I can make you come back, you know."

"Oh, Danny-boy, lighten up. I promise that I'll eat more veggies. I'll even eat spinach if I have to."

"Promise?"

"I promise."

"OK, but I'm still going to have to take your blood."

"Vampire."

"Arm out."

"No."

"Kate, I'm not joking. Watch." He picked up a pad and started filling out a form.

"Whatcha doing, Danny-boy?"

"I'm filling out a hospital admission form. What's your date of birth again?"

"OK, OK, here!" I stretched out my left arm "Suck me dry, why don't you?"

"Thank you, Miss Townsend."

He put the rubber tourniquet on my left arm and hunted around for a vein.

"Looks like my veins are all on holiday. Such a shame you'll have to do it another ti . . . OW!" I glared at his smiling face. "You did that on purpose."

"I did no such thing. Stop being a baby."

I watched as he went ahead with filling a second vial and began to get a little concerned when he started preparing a third.

"Erm . . . that's a lot of blood, Mr Holland."

"There's a lot of tests, Miss Townsend."

The more I stared at the third vial the larger it appeared and before I knew it, it was the size of one of those massive test tubes that I used to do weird experiments with in chemistry class.

"No, really, Daniel. Are you sure you need all that? I mean that's a Hancock, that is."

"A what?"

"A Tony Hancock – you remember that famous blood donor sketch?"

"Oh yeah, nearly a whatsit."

"For an orthopaedic consultant, you're not that great with your anatomy are you? I think you'll find it's 'nearly an armful'."

"Lucky for you I know where the knee is though, eh?"

"Daniel, can you stop now, I'm feeling a bit –"

"All done," he said with a flourish. "I dunno Kate, why do you have to be so difficult?"

"Admit it, you like playing butch!" I batted my eyelashes at him and, despite himself, he grinned.

"Just to be on the safe side maybe you should . . ." Daniel trailed off, turned and rooted around on a side table looking for something.

"What? I should what?" He turned back to face me and held out a little plastic vial. I looked at him as if he were mad. "What am I supposed to be doing with that?"

"I want to do the full gamut of tests, so I'll need a urine sample as well."

"There's no way I'm peeing into that. Besides, it's physically impossible – we women don't have a pointing device like you blokes, you know."

"You're a smart girl. I'm sure you can figure something out."

"Well, what if I don't want to?" I jutted my chin out and gave a stubborn grunt.

Daniel gave me a stern look, picked up the admission form and started filling it out once more. "What's the name of your GP again?"

"Alright, alright, but I'm peeing under protest." I sniffed indignantly. "Do I have to do it now?"

"No, just drop it off next time you come in for physio."

I reluctantly took the vial and muttered, "You're a big bully-boy."

"Yeah, but I'm cute with it, right?" he grinned.

He told me to make an appointment for the beginning of October and if there was anything serious in the tests, he'd be in touch. He hadn't been in touch, so I knew everything was fine. Just to be on the safe side, the whole week before this morning's visit, I ate three meals a day and loaded up on spinach. There was no way he was sticking any more needles in me.

So this morning, full of the joys of autumn, I drove to the clinic.

"Good morning, Kate."

"Morning, Danny-Boy."

"Kate, please, it's our last meeting. Can you for once show me even a tiny bit of the respect that I deserve after all my years of medical training?"

"Huh?" What was he on about? Why was he so grumpy?

"Can we at least pretend that I'm your consultant?"

"Oh. I'm sorry. Good morning, Mr Holland." It took a while, but eventually his words sunk in. "Last meeting?"

"Yes. I'm going to discharge you." Daniel gave me a brilliant-white smile.

"Really?" I grinned back, but not fully believing what I'd heard.

"Yes, really. Of course it doesn't mean that we'll never see each other again. I'll want to see you in about a year or so. We need to talk about cruciate reconstruction, but apart from that . . ."

"It's over?"

"Yes, Kate, it's over."

I couldn't contain my joy. I jumped up, screamed and grabbed him in an enthusiastic hug. "Daniel, please don't take this the wrong way, but I really love you, you know!"

"I know. I'm going to miss you." He paused and looked like he was about to say something, but decided against it at the last second.

"What?"

"What, what?"

"What were you going to say?"

"Nothing."

"Daniel?"

"It's just . . ."

"Just what?"

"When were you going to tell me?"

That stopped me in my tracks. What the hell was he talking about? How could he know? I'd made a decision this morning and the only one who could possibly have guessed was Gen. I couldn't talk to Jane, she hated Matt. I could never have told her that I was thinking of accepting his proposal. Gen wouldn't have told Daniel. I knew that they still talked – by the way, I thought there was something pretty fishy going on there, but this really wasn't the time to be thinking about that, where was I? No, she definitely would not have told him about Matt and me. But, I looked over at Daniel and he definitely knew something.

"Kate?" he prompted.

"Tell you what?" I bluffed, extremely badly because I could tell that I was blushing all the way to the tips of my ears.

"Tell me that congratulations are in order."

Damn, I'll kill that Gen! Why couldn't she keep her bloody mouth shut. There must be something going on between them though, 'cos it really wasn't like her to blab stuff.

"Congratulations?" I croaked. "How did you know? Did Gen tell you?"

"Gen? No, Gen didn't have to. I got the test results back."

The blood which had been very recently coursing through my facial capillaries suddenly stopped and rushed back towards my heart. I felt dizzy. I collapsed onto the examination table. I felt like I'd been punched in the gut by Mike Tyson.

"Test results?" I gasped finally.

"Oh my!" Daniel looked shocked. "You don't know, do you?"

I shook my head. Daniel cursed under his breath.

"I'm sorry, Kate. I thought you knew." He took a deep breath. "You're pregnant."

* * *

A killer blow, don't you think? I'd slept with both Matt and Steve – either of them could be the father. Daniel organised an appointment to have a scan, to find out when I was due, which would tell me how far gone I was and therefore who the father was. My initial reaction was to go home and call the girls together for a very important coven meeting, but the more I thought about it, the more I realised that this was my decision. Mine alone. So I drove, and drove, and ended up here in this café.

To be honest with you, even after re-hashing my past year, I still don't know what to think. Maybe I thought that by the time I got back to the present day, the present would have changed and I wouldn't be pregnant, but I am. I'm pregnant. I'M BLOODY PREGNANT! As if I wasn't confused enough before. Suddenly my discussion with the girls about my options seemed like a million years ago. Aah, it was so simple back then. I had two options.

Option one: Marry Matt. A nice safe option. He's sexy, smart and a 'new man'. Both of us have changed since we split up; I really think that we stand a good chance of making it now. Despite what Jane thinks, Matt would be very good for me. He really loves me.

Option two: Go to Steve. This is the risky option. I have treated him badly. There is something between us, something special, but we live in different worlds. Only yesterday, Gen showed me an article about him and how the Americans love his work. He's a star and I'm just some woman who slept with him and threw him out of her house. If I choose this one, I'll be burning my bridges. What if I get to New York and he doesn't want me . . .

So now I had more information and a possible third option: Tell neither of them about the baby, go home and prepare to bring it up as a single mother. I have enough in my savings to do this. I have plenty of friends who will unquestionably help me. Hell, Katie is a ready-made playmate for him or her. But the more I think about it, the more I want to just go home, hide under my quilt and pretend none of this is happening to me. What am I going to do?

I must have said that last bit out loud because the waitress comes bounding over to me.

"About what?"

"I'm pregnant." I suppose it won't do any harm, I mean maybe she can help. The girls were no real use and she does have quite a few years of living under her belt.

"Oh, is that all?"

"What do you mean, is that all?"

"Well, you're not the first girl to get pregnant, you know." She wipes the table dismissvely and starts to move away.

"Now hang on just one minute, you know nothing about me. You have no idea how complicated it all is."

"Are you married?"

"No."

"Do you know who the father is?"

"Possibly"

"Is he married?"

"No."

"Is he in prison?"

"No."

"Dying?"

"No."

"You dying?"

"Well, we're all —" The waitress just rolls her eyes, so I decided that this isn't the time to be smart-mouthed. "No."

"So stop your moping and get on with it."

"It's not as easy as that?"

"Sure it is." She moves over to the door of the café and turns the sign to 'closed'. Then picking up a couple of Cokes from the counter, she returns to my table and stretches out her hand.

"My name is Margaret, pleased to meet you."

"Kate." We shake hands and she sits down.

"Tell me all about it, Kate."

"Well it's a long story and I wouldn't want you losing custom." I look pointedly at the 'closed' sign. "Are you sure the owner won't mind?"

Margaret does this kind of weird thing and starts having a discussion with herself. I start to wonder whether it was a good thing to be locked in with a mad woman and just as I'm ready to bolt, Margaret stops.

"She reckons it'll be OK."

"This place is yours?"

"Yep, all mine." She smiles, pats my hand and says, "Go ahead, dear."

So out it all comes, my life before, Matt, the accident, the painting, the artist, the relapses, Matt, the options, the baby, everything.

"OK." Margaret leans back and takes a deep breath. "First things first. Do you want to keep the baby?"

"Yes." I say this without hesitation. I know what you're thinking: first she tells us that she hates babies, then she wants to keep it? What's wrong with this woman? But don't worry, I've not changed my mind. I probably do still hate babies, but it's mine and it's here, so at least I'll find out one way or the other soon enough.

"Alrighty, you're having a baby, let's drink to that." She picks up the Coke can and taps it against the side of mine. "Cheers."

I join her in the toast, but without much enthusiasm.

"So, how does this fact change your options?"

I think for a brief while and realise that it doesn't, not much anyway. Although deep down, I suppose I did know who the father is, it is irrelevant because now it's a case of 'love me, love my baby'.

"Next question. What do you want out of life?"

"Honestly?"

"Honestly."

"I need to have a holiday, just like Jane and Craig. I want to see the world and have a bit of a blow out before it's too late. Who knows when I'll get the chance again?" I get really excited just thinking about it and start to babble: "I've always wanted to see the Pyramids, have a take-out in China, swim with dolphins in the Caribbean sea, have tea in the Kremlin, see that really big, red rock in Australia – oh, and I definitely want to see the Hollywood sign. I could start out in Los Angeles, fly to the Caribbean, Australia, China then on to Russia and back to the UK."

"That sounds good, but isn't that a little bit like running away?" She puts her head to one side and smiles sympathetically. "It's always good to get away, but when it comes down to it, in your situation, it's just postponing a decision. It won't go away, you know. At some point you'll have to . . . you know."

"Decide where I want to be?"

"Exactly." She takes my hand again and squeezes. "So what's it going to be? Matthew in London, Steve in New

York, or see the world and hope you can decide when you get back?"

I think for a while and my mind goes blank. "Well, Margaret, I still don't know. The only thing I do know is that my first course of action is fairly simple. All three options require a plane ticket."

"You don't need a plane ticket to go to London."

"If I choose Matt, I definitely want to see him today, but there's no way I'm driving down to London, so I'll fly down. I need to speak to a travel agent."

"You still have to say where you want to go to."

"It'll come to me."

"I hope you're right."

I close my eyes and refocus on the options. Then with shaking hands, I pick up the phone and dial the number of the travel agent that I used to use for work.

"Golden Travel, Sharon speaking."

"Sharon, it's Kate Townsend."

"Hi Kate, long time no hear."

"Yep, it's been ages. I've had a bit of a hectic time of things lately. But I need you to make a booking."

"Is this going on the account or is it private?"

"It's private."

"OK, where to?"

I make a decision and take a deep breath.

Wish me luck. I'll let you know how it goes – don't worry.

Chapter Thirty-one

Wait, There's More

"Ladies and gentlemen, welcome to Los Angeles, where the local time is 3.30 p.m. and the temperature is a sultry twenty-eight degrees. We hope you have enjoyed the flight. The captain and his crew would like to thank you for flying with us and look forward to having you travel with us again soon."

I listened to the announcement with a smile; I was actually in Los Angeles. I could hardly believe it. It had been two weeks since I left the café and I had spun through it in a whirl of packing and organising.

I told you that I'd let you know, didn't I, how it worked out? So here goes: I chose the world. I figured that everything else could wait a while.

The girls and I had one last 'big night out' before I zipped off on my great adventure. We were going to go to the Thai Palace, but I couldn't face Anil. His nephew had told him that things didn't work out between us and instead of blaming me, as he quite rightly should have done, he laid all the blame at Steve's door. Anil's repeated apologies at having let his famous-but-still-ungrateful nephew loose on my feelings simply made me feel more guilty. So instead we went to Chicanas and there were so many bombshells dropped that I'm surprised the place was still standing at the end of the night.

It all started quite gently – well as gently as it could possibly be with seven raucous women together. The coven had been expanded to include Suzanne and Karen, my lovely nurses. I remember tapping a fork against my glass for a little bit of hush.

"Ladies and . . . er . . . well . . . Sandi."

"What's that supposed to mean?" Sandi glared at me.

"Since when have you been a lady, Sandi?" Gen giggled.

"Look who's talking. I haven't seen you wear a skirt in yonks, Miss Imogen," Louise chuckled.

"Oi, watch your language, Mrs still-so-much-a-newly-wed-that-she-hardly-ever-gets-out-of-bed-these-days. Anyway, is it my fault that the only skirts that fit at the moment all have Barbie motifs?"

"Girls, girls, please. You can argue later. I have things to say."

"Get on with it then!" Six voices heckled.

"I just wanted to thank you all for being such constants in my life. Whenever I needed you, you were all there. There is no way that I could have got through the past year without you all. And that goes to the new witches as well as the old ones."

"Hey, not so much of the old," Jane piped up, acutely aware that she was the oldest in the group and only a couple of years short of her thirty-fifth birthday – a fact that we'd all been ribbing her about since she turned thirty-three a week before.

"Sorry, Methuselah. I'll be more diplomatic in the future."

"Lend her your walking stick, Kate, I think she's gonna need it."

This was followed by more heckling and more laughter. But I had news and I wasn't going to be side-tracked.

"Hey, let me finish. It's important stuff I'm saying here." I coughed and continued, "As you know, today I went for my first scan and the dates confirmed what I thought all along. The father –"

"Hang on. You went for a scan today?" Jane queried.

"Yeah."

"I thought you wanted me to go with you?" Jane seemed a bit put out.

"I did, but I thought I'd do it alone. You don't mind do you?"

"I suppose, but it's been ages since I saw Daniel. I was going to bake him a cake and everything."

"I didn't even see Daniel." I shook my head in despair, "Why would I be seeing an orthopaedic consultant for a scan? Silly."

Jane blushed, but seemed to recover quite well. "Yeah, but I bet you went to say hello, didn't you?"

"I did, but he wasn't around." Then I remembered, "Ooh, Karen, you'll never guess who I did see, tho?"

Even though I'd addressed Karen, the other five girls all leant forward in anticipation and joined in with the question. "Who?"

"Do you remember that cute A&E doc who was really

good at getting blood out of me that time. I have no idea what his name was, but he was brilliant, remember?"

"Peter."

"Huh?"

"His name's Peter and he's now a Registrar. At least he will be, when he starts his new job." Karen said authoritatively.

"How do you know all this?" Suzanne looked confused. "I'd not heard anything about him moving on."

All of a sudden Karen looked like the cat that was too busy supping champagne to bother with boring old cream.

"She's been keeping secrets. Look at that face." Jane was the queen of the secret-sniffer-outers, don't forget!

"SPILL! SPILL! SPILL! SPILL!" We all chanted so loudly that Pedro looked like he was wondering whether he'd have to throw us all out.

"Well, he popped up to the ward, just after the blood incident, to see how you were and we got talking."

"And one thing lead to another, I suppose," Suzanne offered.

"Why do people always say, 'one thing lead to another?' That's such a lazy way of telling a story." Louise piped up. "I was listening to a woman on the tram telling this other woman a story and I swear she said something like, 'Judy and me went out shopping on Saturday. We popped into BHS to get a dress and the sale was on. Somehow I lost track of Judy in the rush. Anyway, one thing led to another and she woke up drunk in Piccadilly Gardens with two black eyes and a dolphin tattoo on her arse.' How does that work? We missed the whole story there."

"You're making that up." Gen was forever the sceptic.

"No I'm not. I'm sure it went something like that, anyhow."

"Yeah, right," we all said in unison, while chuckling our heads off.

"Hey, stop interrupting, you guys. Karen, you were saying . . .?" Suzanne was determined to hear the whole story.

"Well, we got chatting and –"

"You're shagging him!" As usual Sandi got straight to the point.

"I've been seeing him, yes," Karen conceded.

There were shocked exclamations of 'no!' and 'I don't believe it!' And lots of surprised head shaking and smiles.

"But you're married?" Louise sounded stunned. Having only been married for a short while, she found the whole thing very distasteful.

"Unhappily married, yes, Louise."

"But –" Louise spluttered. But before she could go any further, I interrupted.

"So . . ."

"Well, it was all going so well. It's not as if I even tried to hide it from Will, my husband. I kept expecting him to confront me so that we could have it out, but to be honest, I don't think he even noticed. Then Peter got offered a job at Bristol Royal Infirmary and he asked me to go with him."

"And are you going to?" Suzanne, who was the most shocked to hear the story, seeing as she'd known Karen a lot longer than the rest of us, asked the question that we all wanted to know.

"Well, I've thought long and hard, and yes, I'm going with him. I love him and we're good together. I only made the decision this morning. I think I'm going to ask for a divorce. So . . . anyhow, he doesn't know it yet, but I think it's going to be a tough weekend for Will . . . well . . . for both of us, I suppose."

There was a shocked silence. No one really knew what to say. What can you say in such circumstances? It's not often you got to see a marriage breaking up right in front of your eyes, especially when one of the affected parties hadn't a clue it was happening. It was like a motorway pile-up, ghastly, but fascinating. We didn't want to, but all we could do was stare at Karen. This wasn't how I wanted things to be. I had to think of something. I could see that Karen was about to cry with all the tension that was floating around the room, so I picked up my glass and stood, calling the girls to attention.

"Come on, girls. A toast. To Karen and new beginnings!"

One by one they all stood with me – even Louise, who was trying not to take it all personally. Together they raised their glasses and chorused: "To Karen and new beginnings!"

Then in a brief lull between the nachos and the arrival of the chilli, I was telling Gen about my last visit with Daniel and how I'd cursed her big mouth, before I'd found out that it was my own body fluids that had given the game away.

"I was so stupid."

"You usually are."

"No, really, I'm so sorry for even thinking . . . I mean I know that you'd never betray a confidence."

"No, I wouldn't."

"I even thought that you'd been having an affair with Daniel."

"Really?"

I vaguely noticed Gen squirming slightly, but I was still wrapped up in regaling her with my stupidity.

"Yeah, how ridiculous is that! You and Daniel!" I started to cackle.

"Yeah, really funny. Hahaha!" Gen laughed unconvincingly and excused herself to go to the loo.

As I watched her leave, I had a brief flash of intuition, but dismissed it. What a ridiculous thought. A few minutes later, Gen's mobile started ringing in her handbag. I fished it out, just as it had rung off. On the screen was the message 'missed call' and underneath as plain as day it displayed the caller's number below the words 'Danny mobile'. It couldn't be, could it? I didn't mention it to the others. If there is something to be said, I'm sure we'll hear it from the woman herself someday.

The other revelation was from Louise, who made an announcement of her own. Halfway through the chilli course, she stood up.

"Guys. I too have something to tell you all."

"Don't tell us – you're emigrating to Australia? Or doing a survival course in Outer Mongolia, perhaps?" I think all the revelations were getting the better of Sandi.

"No, I'm having a baby, too."

"Really? What the hell's going on with you lot? Have you all been drinking sprogging water?"

"Well, I'm sorry Sandi, but if everyone else is getting pregnant, there was no way I'm going to be left behind. I'm due on the first of May."

"That's great, Lou. Congratulations." I went up to her and gave her a big hug.

"So when are you going on tour?" Gen wanted to know.

"Huh?"

"Well, it seems it's the thing *du jour*. You know, have an extended holiday before the birth."

"I don't think so, I'm planning on working right up to the end."

"And what does your esteemed husband have to say about that?" Again, it was a question that we all wanted to ask, but only Gen was brave enough to venture it.

"Nothing. He can't stop me. Just because we're married it doesn't mean he can tell me what to do. I'm my own woman you know." I swear she stamped her feet when she came out with that last sentence.

"OK there, Mrs Pankhurst. Don't bite my head off!"

"Sorry. I just get so used to having to defend myself . . ." Her voice trailed off and we all nodded sympathetically.

"And what happens afterwards?" Gen really was fearless.

Louise looked a bit sheepish and muttered something like, "Well, we're still in negotiations on that one. Terry, as usual, is adamant that I give up work, but I can't see that happening, so I suppose we'll have to cross that bridge when we come to it." She shrugged her shoulders and smiled a weak, hopeful smile. As for the rest of us, I'm certain we all had the same thought in our heads. As the song goes, 'There may be trouble ahead . . .'

All in all, it was a fabulous night.

So there you go, all the ends tied up.

OK, OK, I know, that's not quite accurate. There's still one huge question to be answered. Who is the father of my child? In order to answer you I'll tell you what happened on the morning of my flight.

Jane, Craig and Katie waved me off at the airport. Just as I was leaving Jane handed me an envelope and whispered the words, "He deserves to know."

In the departure lounge, I opened it up to find an article from the previous day's newspaper. In reality, I didn't need to read the whole article, the headline was enough: 'The Wallace Collection Goes Hollywood!'

Beneath the text of the article, Jane had written one word, 'Fate?'

Yes, the baby is Steve's and as Jane said, it must have been fate, because even though I'd been determined to go it alone, I still ended up in the same place as him. I decided to give up, stop pushing and let fate decide what was to happen to me. The whole journey, one thought kept moving through my head. 'I won't go looking for him. If I see him, I see him. If I don't, I don't.'

* * *

"Miss, do you need some help?" The steward looked pointedly at my walking stick.

"No, I'm fine." I got up, grabbed my handbag and made my way slowly to the plane door.

The plane had parked in a gate that was well away from the terminal building, so we had to descend some stairs and get on a coach. As I left the plane, I looked up at the clear, blue Californian sky, closed my eyes and let the heat of the sun wash over me.

"Are you sure I can't help you down the stairs, Miss?" The steward looked even more pointedly at my scarred leg and stick.

"OK, then. Can you hold my bag while I hold onto the railing?"

Even though I found it fine going up and down stairs with my walking stick, most people insisted that I needed help and I found it far easier to let them assist me than dissuade them. That's not to say that I never needed help. Although well healed, I had finally come to terms with my success and most of all, my limitations. I could walk, but not far. For long distances I will always need a wheelchair, but I found that even in the largest shopping centres, there were plenty of seats where I could rest and recharge my batteries. The leg still swelled up if I spent too long on my feet, but it looked far worse than it felt. I will never run a marathon, but I can easily buy my bodyweight in clothing in the town centre. I can never go to the gym, nor will I ever be able to participate in an aerobics class, but as Sandi quite rightly points out, the only purpose a gymnasium serves is to exercise our guilt muscles. I have accepted that I'll never be perfect, and best of all, unlike so many women who spend their whole lives striving for perfection, all I have to do is look down at my scars and relax. Who needs perfection? I'm just happy to be alive and have all my limbs intact – and I can win every single 'compare the scars' contest hands down!

The steward insisted on accompanying me all the way through immigration and to the baggage hall. At which point I managed to lose him by hiding in the loos.

Of course, my bags were the last to come through, but I didn't mind. At least they hadn't got lost. I picked them up, loaded them on the cart, fending off all offers of assistance from various other passengers, who rushed to my aid as soon as they saw my limp. I had to physically stop myself from batting them all away like annoying flies with my stick. It was and still is a difficult thing, because on the one hand, I was lucky that people even cared, but on the other, even crippled people like me want a veneer of independence, however flimsy it may be. And believe me, if ever I needed help, I certainly wasn't shy in coming forward.

Leaning heavily on the trolley, I pushed it through the customs channel. Surprisingly I wasn't stopped and interrogated. I put that down to the fact that no one wants to be the one to interrogate a disabled person and smiled. See there were definite advantages! Once outside in the arrivals hall, I realised that I had a nagging pain in my leg and went to find a bench or something that I could sit down on. A rather kind man offered me his seat immediately, again a perk of having a walking stick. Once seated, I took out my little pillbox and a bottle of water. I wasn't in a rush, in fact I had all the time in the world, so I just sat and people-watched while I waited for the painkillers to kick in. The place was heaving with people. Every one of them seemed happy. At airport arrivals, all sins are forgiven. Couples who argued non-stop before they parted, at arrivals, they are always pleased to see each other – bickering can wait until the drive home. Families waiting for other family members. Lovers waiting for their other halves. I watched a couple come through the doors with a very sulky gothic teenager – all black eyeliner and spiky-black spider-hair – in tow. I guessed that they were visiting parents. Sure enough, the wife waves at an elderly couple who make their way carefully through the crowd. The wife hugs the elderly woman so affectionately it has to be her mother. The elderly man, shakes the husband's hand heartily and with great warmth. They obviously like each other tremendously. But that isn't what made me smile. That handshake wasn't what defined an arrivals hall. I looked at the sulky teenager, who was trying to act very cool and moody, but when faced with her Grandma and Granddad, a huge grin spread across her face and she held her arms wide to receive a group hug. For a second I caught a glimpse of the happy carefree child inside all that gothic doom. And that is what it was all about. If I had to describe an arrivals area to a blind person, I would say, excitement and joy – you could feel both in equal measure.

I had no idea how long I'd been sitting there, but I thought it was time for me to get going. I stood up and started to push my trolley. Then a thought occurred to me. I couldn't remember the name of the hotel or the address, so I was rooting through my bag for the reservation form and guess what, I walked straight into someone. I looked up and . . .

"Kate?"

He looked, well, how could I describe him? He looked yummy, like a giant chocolate cake with real chocolate icing and covered in hundreds and thousands. Very, very tasty. His eyes showed a hint of fear or it could have been concern and the closer I looked the more I saw that he seemed tired. He had grey pouches under his eyes, not quite bags, but very nearly. He looked slightly different. Leaner? Browner? His hair was lighter and more dishevelled. His voice even sounded faintly altered, more American. But despite all these differences, it was very definitely Steve Wallace.

"Steve? How did you –?" Of course I knew.

"Your friend Jane is a bit of a bully, isn't she?"

"Er . . ." A loud whooshing sound went rushing through my mind like the wind in a hurricane, blowing away my entire stockpile of thoughts, words, sentences, just as easily as a rickety, old, wooden house.

Steve ran a shaking hand through his hair. "Are you OK? Do you need to sit down?"

"Fine . . . I'm . . . fine . . ." I had to make sure that my mind wasn't playing tricks. I shook my head in an effort to gain some clarity. Get a grip, Kate. This isn't a dream. You are in California and that really is Steve Wallace. Say something! "Steve?"

"Yes, it's me, Katherine." He smiled, "Kate."

Even though he appeared in my dreams most nights, I'd forgotten so many things about him. I'd forgotten how his eyes shone like emeralds lit from the inside, how his nose crinkled when he smiled, and most of all I'd forgotten how much I loved hearing his voice say my name.

"Jane?" I croaked, finally.

"Jane?" He looked bewildered for a split second then said, "Oh, she rang me this morning. She said she'd forgotten to give you a very important message, so she insisted I meet you at the airport and pass it on for her."

"Message? What message?"

"I don't really understand it myself, but she assured me you would."

"OK, what is it?"

"It was in your cards."

I suppose even fate needs a helping hand sometimes. I

smiled, Steve held out his hand and with an internal nod of thanks to Jane, I grabbed it with pleasure.

"Steve, we have to talk."

"Yes, we do. But not now." He leant down and kissed me gently on the forehead. "Come on."

He took hold of the trolley with his free hand and together we walked towards the exit doors.

"How about your leg?"

"It's a bit creaky, but it's fine. I'm fine."

"Are you sure?"

"I'm sure." I looked down at my hand clasped in his and smiled, "Better than fine. I feel great."

Then I remembered. Should I tell him?

Steve started talking about all the plans he'd made for us. There was so much to do and so little time.

"There's a reception at the Gallery tonight. I have to make an appearance, but I can probably get away quite quickly. Then we can have a meal at this brilliant Indonesian restaurant that I found – not quite Thai, but I won't tell my uncle if you don't."

Should I tell him?

"Then tomorrow, I'll take you sightseeing. There's so much to show you. The Hollywood sign, the walk of fame, Mann's Chinese Theatre, where all the hand and foot prints are. Then there's Hollywood Boulevard and Rodeo Drive. We can even go to the studios if you like. I've made a few contacts; we could even get in on a film set if you're up to it. Oh, Kate, I can't believe you're really here." He stopped, leant down and kissed me enthusiastically on the lips.

Should I tell him? I began an internal dialogue which

seemed to match Steve with its babbling. I'd never heard him so animated. Boy, he could really talk when he wanted to. When did that happen? *He's nervous, Kate.* So, Mr Wallace wasn't as cool and calm as he always seemed. *Focus Kate. Tell him.* Oh yeah, 'cos that'll really calm him down, won't it? I'll tell him later. Or should I tell him now? How will he react? Do I have to tell him at all? Not a bad idea. What he doesn't know . . . *He's got a right to know.* Well, I've got a right to be left alone in my own head. *Concentrate, Kate. Tell him.* No. *Tell him.* NO! *Later?* Yes, later.

There, decision made. I tuned Steve back in.

". . . I can't believe it's just us two. No uncle, no friends. I mean I like your friends and everything, but I'm so glad that it's just us. You and me. We'll be like two musketeers, OK, there are meant to be three, but we can write our own version, what do you say? The Two Musketeers, eh? Kate?" Steve finally paused for breath. "Well, Kate, what d'you think?"

Tell him now, Kate. Shut up, we agreed, I'll tell him later. *Listen to what he's saying, tell him now.* "No! SHUT UP!"

"Kate?" He stopped in his tracks and looked at me. I might as well have stabbed him in the heart he looked so destroyed.

Well at least I knew how to get his attention. I stored the info away for future use. "I'm sorry, Steve. It's not you, it's . . . I've got a lot on my . . . ."

We were close to the exit doors and standing beside one of those Italian café concessions. For some strange reason I didn't want to leave the airport building. If I was indeed going to tell him, I felt I needed all the good karma that the arrivals hall provided.

"Can we go in here? I need to sit down for a while."

Steve looked relieved. "Of course. I'm sorry, I should have . . ."

"I'm fine, just a bit tired."

He pulled out a chair for me to sit on and sat opposite me.

"You, OK?"

"Steve?"

"Yes."

"I have something to tell you."

"Can't it wait?"

"No."

"Listen, Kate. I know we have things to discuss and we should discuss them, we really should, but do we have to do it now? It's just so wonderful to see you and I only wanted us to have some happy time before you got all annoyed with me and dumped me yet again. We could be so happy together if only you'd let us. We do belong together, whatever you want to say, we do. I promise you we do. Give us a chance. I swear you won't be sorry."

A calmness descended over me. I immediately understood that it didn't really matter how he reacted. I would survive whatever happened. If he didn't want the baby, then fine. I'd already decided to go it alone in any case. It was just important that he knew. I smiled. What's the worst that could happen? I closed my eyes and said the words: "Steve. I'm pregnant."

There was total silence.

I opened my eyes. So that's what an over-six-foot-half-Scottish-half-Thai-goldfish-out-of-water looks like. I'd always wondered. It wasn't the worst response in the world,

I suppose. He'd opened and closed his mouth so often I was wondering if I should have some target practice using the olives that the waiter had discreetly placed on the table just before my big revelation. Obviously he made a run for it after he heard the words that came out of my mouth. I didn't expect him back any time soon, but I did expect Steve to actually say something. I peered at my watch. Thirty-five seconds and still no sound. Should I worry now or see what the olives taste like? I'd never had a taste for olives. People were forever telling me that it was something you acquired. Maybe now I was pregnant . . . forty-five seconds. You know the olives weren't that bad. Not sure about the green ones though. This was getting ridiculous – nearly a minute and he was still doing his fish impression. I wonder if I should throw some water over him? No, hang on, give the guy a chance. It wasn't as if I took the news that well myself. I remembered Daniel telling me that I was silently horrified for at least two minutes. One minute forty seconds. That's it, I'm going in.

"Steve?"

"Hmmmnn?" Alright, so it was nearly a word.

"Shall I get you something to drink?"

Steve came up for air. Good, he was breathing again. Good sign.

"July?"

"Yes, Steve. July." I swallowed hard. Can you be arrested for putting someone into a catatonic state?

"I'm going . . ."

"Where?"

"I'm going to . . ."

"Where are you going, Steve? Tell me. Talk to me."

"I'm going to be . . ."

"Sick? Oh God. I'll get a bucket. Waiter!"

The waiter eyed me warily and refused to come anywhere near the table, which in the circumstances was a good move because the next thing that happened was an eruption.

Steve stood up and roared, "I'M GOING TO BE A DADDY!" Then he rushed around the table and in one swift movement picked me up as if I weighed less than a feather – which we all know is a practically impossible feat in itself. It must have been the same adrenaline-rush thingy that allows people to lift up articulated lorries when their children are stuck underneath.

After five minutes of jiggling me around in his arms shrieking like a mad thing, Steve finally put me down.

"God!" He exhaled and grinned. "I'm hungry. Food. Not eaten. Days. Get food. You hungry?"

Great. My sensitive artist-type had turned into Neanderthal man in less time than it takes to boil a hard-boiled egg.

"I could probably eat something." I mean, one of us had to speak in full sentences.

"Waiter!"

"Yes, sir." The waiter appeared at the side of the table as if by magic. "Congratulations, by the way, sir," he nodded in my direction, "Ma'am."

"Thank you," Steve answered for both of us – what did I tell you? Caveman! I crossed my fingers and hoped this was merely a temporary transformation brought on by a sudden rush of 'baby news' testosterone. Steve puffed out his chest a little and spoke in a very butch, manly voice. "What are the specials today?"

"All the specials are on the blackboard, sir."

I looked at the blackboard menu.

Soup of the Day, it said.

"And the soup is?"

"Minestrone, ma'am."

Just at that precise moment, another waiter appeared with a bowl of minestrone for a lady on her own at another table. I sniffed the air and smiled.

You know, as I always say: It's funny how little things come back to you suddenly. One whiff of a certain smell and you're whisked off . . .

Well, you know the rest.

The End

AUTHOR'S NOTE

Although I spent a length of time in North Manchester General Hospital, this novel is neither a reflection of that time, nor is it a reflection of that hospital. It is important to remember that this is a fictitious account of a hospital stay. The similarities between Kate Townsend's hospital sojourn and my own are very few. The only common elements are the injuries, the infection and the length of time spent in hospital. Any other similarities exist merely in your imaginations and are therefore purely coincidental.

There are a few things to say about my time in hospital. For the first time, I had experience of the National Health Service and I was both uplifted and immensely relieved. The NHS is a beautiful thing, and everyone in the UK should be proud of it. Not only was the medical care free, but it was consistently of a very high quality. In any other country, my accident would have crippled me financially as well as physically.

My family were brilliant throughout this very difficult time and nothing at all like Kate's. My accident was worse for them than for me. While I was enjoying my drug haze, they had to live through all the shocking, scary and sometimes downright terrifying medical revelations as they happened.

Kate's friends were not half as gallant as my own. Melissa Hind visited me so regularly I'm sure that some of the nurses thought that she was a patient sometimes. Carl, Sue and Eliah, Angela, Sarah and Lise did many things above and beyond the call of any friendly duty. And they still continue to talk to me, despite knowing that anything they say is likely to appear in one of my books somewhere.

The nurses, although nice to Kate Townsend, were eminently more caring, smart and generally wonderful to me. Michelle, Jackie, Kay, Damon, Eileen, Suzanne, Gill – you know I could never thank you enough. I will never forget Ward 15 as long as I live.

The physios in the novel were made just a little bit sadistic for storytelling purposes and, in real life, they were not like that – they were much, much worse.

No, I'm kidding! They are a bunch of talented and dedicated individuals who restore people's lives on a daily basis. Steff and Chris forced me to get out of bed and started me on the road to recovery. Lyndsay Bamber was a good friend, who allowed me to live vicariously through her fabulous tales of her nights out on the town – and she even helped me relearn how to walk in between stories. Louise helped me build up my strength physically and, although I'm not sure she knew much about it, she helped me sort myself out mentally so I could come to terms with what had happened to me. Graham joked and cajoled my knee into bending once more. I actually enjoyed my physio sessions with Graham, who inflicted such pain but always apologised for it. And then on to Chris Orr, who was my last but one of my faves. He helped to improve my balance so much that I was able to dance again.

My consultants at the hospital were miracle-workers and still keep a close eye on my knee. Kudos to Mr TH Meadows, for your incredible skill and kindness and Mr Rae, for being tough but honest.

Heroes and Saints all. Thank you so much for giving me back my life.

This novel was written while I was recuperating from my own ordeal. Unlike Kate, who had to make do with her back garden in Manchester, I had a more beautiful setting for my recuperation: the glorious windward island of St Lucia. My St Lucian family welcomed me with open arms and hearts and I would like to thank them all for making me feel joy once more and for providing all the distractions I needed when I was trying to avoid writing (as well as getting me hideously drunk on rum). So *Irie* to the St Lucia Crew, especially my cousin, Gena Rawlins, Curtis Auguste and all the lads at Speedway.

While I'm going on thanking everyone I would like to thank Gaye Shortland, who is definitely the brightest star in my heavens. Like anyone who has had the absolute pleasure of working with her, I am honoured to have her as my editor.

This book was written to a soundtrack of Morcheeba, Eddi Reader, Eminem, Pink and the ever-present George Michael. So in the words of a certain Swedish band, 'Thank you for the music'.

To the members of the South Manchester Writers'

Circle, especially Terie Garrison and Anne-Marie Biggs, who made sure that the continuity and style of the book was right. Thank you so much for all your help, comments and encouragement.

A quick mention to my brother, David Murphy, who wasn't happy that the main character of 'Luggage' only had a sister. This time, the main character has a brother. Are you happy now, Dave?

To James Dowdall, whose unexpected friendship has meant so much, far too much to express in words. Sometimes, Mr Scally, I wish your discipline was even half as great as your talent.

And finally, the deepest thanks and love go to my mother, Josephine Clairmont, who, even though she's had a bad enough year of her own, has had to put up with a lot of crap from me and had her holiday interrupted on a daily basis to listen to each chapter as I wrote it. She listened and encouraged effusively even when she would rather have been at the beach.